THE BRAT

Anthony Milligan

Disclaimer

This book is a work of fiction. Any resemblance to any persons, living or deceased or any business defunct or current or any actual event is coincidental.

Cover picture:

taylor-hernandez-DLKR_x3_7 unsplash.jpg

Copyright © J A Milligan 2020

The moral right of Anthony Milligan to be identified as the author of this work has been asserted in accordance with the copyright, design and patents act of 1988.

All rights reserved. No part of this work shall be used, copied or stored in a retrieval system, transmitted by any means or photocopied in any form without the written permission of the author or his agents.

Blocat Publications Oldham UK

Contents

Chapter 1 1

Chapter 2 23

Chapter 3 36

Chapter 4 45

Chapter 5 53

Chapter 6 61

Chapter 7 65

Chapter 8 74

Chapter 9 100

Chapter 10 109

Chapter 11 123

Chapter 12 128

Chapter 13 143

Chapter 14 153

Chapter 15 164

Chapter 16 171

Chapter 17 193

Chapter 18	199
Chapter 19	215
Chapter 20	222
Chapter 21	235
Chapter 22	257
Chapter 23	292
Chapter 24	299
Chapter 25	323
Chapter 26	330
Chapter 27	335
About the author	362

THE BRAT

Chapter 1

As his Mercedes ate up the miles, Dawson Jukes took yet another deep breath, releasing it slowly. Another fifteen minutes and he'd be home. Be calm, he told himself it's over and there's an old single malt waiting.

He switched on cruise control now that he was on the straight empty stretch of moorland road and hit the Jazz FM button. The car filled with soft notes as a decadent saxophone wailed and a muted trumpet wept softly in the background. A woman with a velvet voice started a Blues-in-the-night number. He felt the tension of the last fourteen hours begin to ease.

Dawson was watchful for the PTSD symptoms, that always lurked, awaiting their chance to attack.

The woman he had been protecting had whined his whole shift long, her every pronouncement beginning with 'hey, I want…' or 'hey, I need…' or 'hey, go get me...' with never a please or a thank you. *Sod her, listen to the music* his inner voice said.

A momentary flash of white on the furthest reach of his headlights brought him to full alertness. So fleeting was the movement that, at first, Dawson doubted himself. A bare leg? Surely not. There was a foot, though, a small white foot rolling into the ditch, wasn't there?

He braked hard, switching his headlights to main beam, craning forward to the windscreen. Nothing.

Dawson dismissed it as a trick of his exhausted brain. A rabbit, man, you're too damn tired. He was pressing the accelerator when from behind a tuft half of a small pale face appeared then ducked instantly. In that split-second he recognised terror.

He stopped ten metres short of where he believed he'd seen the apparition. Leaving the headlights on, Dawson walked slowly along the edge of the road. 'Hey,' he called down into the ditch 'whoever you are come out. I won't harm you.' There was no response.

Returning to his car, he retrieved a torch from the glove box. Walking slowly back Dawson illuminated the deep ditch with the bright, narrow beam. He heard a frightened yelp and a young girl scurried up onto the road and turned to face him. She was stark naked.

'Please mister, please' she pleaded, her eyes wide and her voice trembling 'please... don't let them get

The Brat

me. They're going to kill me. I'll…I'll do anything if you help me to get away.'

Dawson's face tightened. Shock, pity and horror surged through him, each fighting for precedence. He switched off the torch not wanting to see the naked child before him smeared with filth from head to toe. He wanted to lower his gaze, to turn away, as a sick feeling kicked into his guts. He resisted, forcing himself to see the pitiful sight she presented. The girl's age he could only guess was somewhere between twelve and fourteen. She attempted to cover her nakedness as she trembled before him. Crossing one arm over her breasts, she placed the other between her legs. Her chest heaved as she gasped in the cold night air, her large tear-brimmed eyes pleading with him.

His hand went to his head as he rubbed his crewcut in bafflement. It was a moment before he could gather his wits, Dawson's mind was reeling, struggling to comprehend what he was seeing. He looked around, mystified, there was no sign of anyone else.

'What the hell?' he managed at last 'Jesus, girl, what's happened to you?' She didn't answer as she stood before him, shivering uncontrollably.

Dawson's head began to clear. First things first he thought, he went to his car and collected his Puffa jacket 'here, kid, put this on.'

The girl took the coat hesitantly, her shaking hand brushed his, it was icily cold. She held the coat beneath her chin seeming uncertain as to what she should do with it.

'Here, let me help' she whimpered and stepped back.

'I'm not going to hurt you, girl, I promise.'

She seemed to sag then looking utterly forlorn as tears came gushing in silent rivulets, clearing twin paths down her grimy cheeks. He took the coat, draped it around her shoulders and zipped it up before placing his arm around her and guiding her gently to his car.

She hesitated as he opened the rear passenger door. 'Please mister…'

He tried to smile 'It's OK, I'm a bodyguard. I look after people.' It was the only thing he could think of and he felt stupid saying it.

She slid in reluctantly and across the seat to cower on the far side sobbing quietly.

Climbing behind the wheel, Dawson killed the music, turned up the heating then took out his phone.

'Please mister, please, don't ring the cops, they'll just put me back into the care home then they'll get me again, *please,*'

Her accent was broad and local, Bury, Rochdale or Oldham he guessed but what was she doing out here?

The Brat

The A635, known locally as the Isle of Skye road, crosses bleak high moorland between the towns of Oldham and Holmfirth in the North West of England. A rush-hour rat run, it's a lonely place at 4 a.m. Often lashed by wind and rain or shrouded with fog, on this early March morning it was cold, clear and still. The stars looked huge and bright away from the light pollution of the big towns.

Christ, I don't need this he thought, but he kept his frustration under control. 'Isn't care the safest place for you, kid?' The stricken face in the rear-view mirror told him it wasn't. He rubbed his chin uncertainly. What the hell was he to do for the best?

Headlights behind him illuminated the car's interior, throwing javelins of light off the mirrors. The girl flung herself on the floor between the seats whimpering in terror.

The lights slowed as they approached, the black Toyota four by four drew alongside and stopped. The window went down, and a swarthy face leaned out. He was in his mid-forties, unshaven with dark narrow eyes under black, unkempt hair. Dawson lowered his window 'Can I help you?'

The accent was Eastern European. 'You broke down?'

'Nope, just stopped for a piss, waiting for you to pass, mate, I hate headlights in my mirror.'

The guy seemed to consider this for a second then nodded. 'You see anybody walking up here?'

Dawson feigned surprise 'Walking? At this hour?'

The man hesitated. 'It's embarrassing' he said. 'My niece, she runs away, no clothes, she not good up here.' He tapped his temple then pushed his hand upward and outward through the window. 'We look for her, she needs her medicine, urgent.'

Dawson didn't like the man's exaggerated hand movements or his glib explanation. Lying bastard, he thought.

'Sorry, can't help you, mate.'

He put his seatbelt on and put the Merc in gear to pull away. The guy spoke to his driver and the Toyota pulled sharply forward blocking his way. The man jumped out.

Dawson released his seat belt; his hand going to the door catch. The bloke was big and burly but fat around his middle. He swaggered up to Dawson's window, chest out, his jaw jutting aggressively.

'We check your car, mister. So many perverts about.'

Dawson flung the car door open with lightning speed hitting the man even as he tried to leap back. Then he was out of the car his fists clenched, his anger cold. The guy gave a growl and launched himself, swinging a wild punch. Dawson sidestepped with the agility of a fox. He grabbed the back of man's neck, and, using his momentum, slammed his head into the edge of the car roof. The guy dropped to his knees with a groan and Dawson brought his

The Brat

huge right fist crashing into his temple with a force that felled him.

The beeping of a headlight warning behind him told him the Toyota's door had opened. The driver was out and holding a baseball bat. He looked nervously from Dawson to his felled comrade then he slowly advanced raising the bat.

Faced with this new threat, Dawson's anger changed instantly into focused calm. His voice was quiet and emotionless. 'You come at me with that, pal, and I'll break your legs with it.' It was more a statement of fact than a threat. He stepped back, away from the fallen man, his hands clasped lightly over his crotch, eyes of steel, shoulders relaxed.

The driver had seen how easily his comrade had been dealt with and hesitated, then he lowered the bat. He was in his mid-fifties with a deeply lined angular face and the same narrow eyes as the first man.

He pointed at his companion 'I just take my friend' he said, his voice uncertain 'we go, we leave you alone, OK?'

Dawson nodded 'drop the tool and take him' he retreated a further pace allowing the man to help his groaning friend stagger back to their vehicle. Once aboard, they drove rapidly off until they disappeared over the horizon towards Holmfirth.

Back in his car, the girl was now weeping with relief.

'Oh, thank you, mister, thanks, you've saved my life.'

Dawson grunted and drove off. Whatever her problem was it wouldn't be resolved sitting at the roadside asking questions and the men might return with reinforcements. But what the hell was he to do with her?

Turning right, up the rough track onto the moors, the car bounced over the ruts for half a mile to the house he rented in the pine plantation. Once a barn for storing snow drift fencing, it had been turned into a weekend retreat until the elderly owner had lost interest and now rented it out as a holiday let. It was cheap in the winter season and it came furnished which suited Dawson. He liked it because was away from people. People who asked questions, nice people who wanted to socialise and, importantly, people who may be looking for him. It was hard to find and easily defended. On the downside, the phone signal was patchy at best. He parked and walked to the house, the girl following, looking around her with fearful eyes.

'What's your name? How old are you?'

'Charlene, she said, 'Charlene Keenan, I'm fourteen. Please mister….' he cut her off.

'I'm Dawson Jukes, Charlene, you're safe now, OK? I'm going to help you.' He pointed to the bathroom, 'you go and run a hot bath; you hungry?' she nodded. 'While you are getting cleaned up, I'll

The Brat

make you some grub and see if I can find you something to wear.' She gave a shy half smile as he handed her his bathrobe, her eyes downcast. 'Fresh towels are in the cupboard.'

It was now 4:35 a.m. and the adrenaline from the fight had worn off leaving him beyond exhausted. He tried to think of solutions but all he had was questions. Did Charlene have relatives who could take her in? One thing was certain, he couldn't keep this young girl here for long. Christ, he thought, I don't need this. He poured himself a large scotch, downed it, then poured another, then he went to the kitchen to find eggs, bacon, beans, and bread.

She sat at the kitchen table bundled in his ten-times-too-big bathrobe wolfing down the food like a hungry Labrador pup. She mopped the plate with a slice of bread and washed it down with strong coffee. He watched her over the rim of his glass wondering if one was supposed to give kids coffee. He almost smiled at the absurdity of the thought, realising he didn't know a damn thing about kids.

Digging out his old sleeping bag, Dawson gave it the sniff test. It barely passed. He spread it on the couch in the living room and brought an extra pillow. 'Get your head down here, Charlene. I've found some old swimming shorts with a drawstring waist and a T-shirt. They'll swamp you but at least you'll be covered.'

She smiled weakly, he could see her eyes drooping with fatigue now that she was clothed, warm and fed.

Dawson left her to it and took a shower. He opened his laptop and checked his security cameras whilst sipping yet another scotch. Just two foxes and a stray sheep. It was unlikely that they'd be found tonight. He reset the alarm system then loaded his shotgun, laying it in bed before stretching himself between the sheets. Despite the shower, he felt dirty somehow, like he'd touched a turd. He downed his drink in one gulp and dowsed the light. Sleep came almost immediately, so did his nightmares.

*

Dawson awoke in full sunlight it was eleven-thirty a.m. She was standing in the doorway, the huge T-shirt hung off her skinny shoulders like a windless flag around its pole. Her expression was questioning though she remained silent, watching him. He sat up, rubbed his eyes, and looked her up and down. She was around 1.6 metres tall with shoulder-length blonde hair. She had expressive dark green eyes and a button nose splashed across with freckles. A huge pink bow-lipped mouth hung over a pixie chin.

'You have bad dreams too, mister. I have them a lot. Sometimes I wake up screaming.'

'Oh, god, did I scare you?'

'Yeah, a bit at first, then I understood.'

The Brat

Dawson looked down, he covered his eyes with one hand, rubbing his brow 'sorry, kid, it was that fight, it brought back some bad memories.'

'You were shouting about bombs n' shit. I dream about men chasing me with their cocks out. That's when I wake up screaming.'

He took a sharp breath. Just what the hell kind of life did this kid lead? Feeling embarrassed, he didn't press the matter.

'Want some breakfast? '

'Yeah, thanks.'

Dawson usually slept naked but last night it didn't feel right, somehow, so he'd donned a pair of boxer shorts. He got up making sure the shotgun stayed covered and took a pair of jeans from the wardrobe. He held them up 'do you mind? I'd like to get dressed.'

She gave him a cheeky grin 'you've got nowt I ain't seen before, mate' she quipped then turned towards the kitchen.

It had been a facetious remark by her, but it hit him hard. He remembered the child abuse cases he'd read about a few years previously. He recalled the waifs and strays he'd seen in Iraq. Orphans begging, their hands outstretched in supplication, desperation in their luminous brown eyes. Poor little bugger he thought, suddenly panged with guilt at his earlier selfish thoughts of just how quick he could be rid of her.

There had been little he could do for those Iraqi kids other than toss a few coins, but maybe he could help this one.

He thought about the men he had rescued her from. People like them had only one use for girls of her age. He gritted his teeth, his mind made up, his guilty feelings trans-mutated to anger in that moment. But exactly what he could do he didn't know.

In the kitchen, she lolled against the breakfast bar whilst he busied himself at the stove. He turned to the table, plates in hand, and looked at her more closely. What he could make out of her slight frame looked emaciated. Her gangly legs seemed too long for the rest of her body. She gave him a shy smile, her teeth showing white and even. She's a pretty kid, he thought, she'll grow into a beautiful woman one day.

'Grub's up, Charlene.'

He waited until they had finished eating before he asked her 'What happened last night, Charlene? Why were you up here without any clothes?'

She tensed, her eyes darted around the room like a trapped animal looking to escape then her shoulders sagged, she looked down at the table, a defeated air about her. 'You promise you'll not throw me out if I tell yer?'

'I promise.'

'You won't believe me anyway; adults never believe kids like me.'

The Brat

'Try me.'

She hesitated for a long time as if wondering where to start. He watched her carefully as her face twitched, her fingers drummed the table, and her foot tapped the floor. She looked stressed and close to tears.

'Take your time, Charlene' he said, trying to sound gentle, but succeeding only in sounding gruff. Dawson wasn't good at gentle.

Finally, she shrugged and with a long sigh she said 'I'm a whore Dawes, a prostitute. Alexi says that's all care home kids like me are any good for.' Her voice was flat, her eyes blank 'I found something out, now they want me dead.'

The lump in his throat came unbidden and tears pricked his eyes, he struggled to keep his voice even. 'Who is Alexi?'

'Alexi Couscu, he's the boss bloke. The guy you beat up last night is his younger brother Serge. They have some takeaway shops in the Rochdale area with flats upstairs. Lots of us girls work for him.'

It took Dawson a few seconds to absorb this. He'd heard of paedophile rings, of course, but it was stuff you read about in the Sunday papers, wasn't it? In big towns and cities, yeah, but out here? On the moors? He cleared his throat 'so, what were you doing out here, naked? Why do they want you dead?'

She shrugged, the same blank look in her eyes 'kids who give trouble are sometimes dumped in lonely places and left to walk miles as punishment. But they were going to use me then kill me, that's why they took my clothes. I ran away.' She paused and looked at him speculatively 'Don't suppose you've got any weed?'

Dawson shook his head partly to answer her question, partly in stunned disbelief. This young girl believed her only use was satisfying the lust of perverts. He poured another coffee to give himself thinking time. Outside it was bright and sunny, daffodils were nodding in the garden. It was so normal, so every day. Yet here he was listening to a tale he would have dismissed as fantasy were the evidence not staring him in the face.

'OK, so let me get this straight, Charlene, you are in Local Authority care and you're a victim of a paedophile ring?'

'Yes Dawes.' she answered.

Dawson hated his name being shortened but hid his irritation.

'Where are your parents Charlene? Why are you in care?'

'Mum told me dad died in prison when I was a baby. She's a junkie an' goes with blokes to pay for her fix. They put me in foster homes, a lot of foster homes. The foster parents were nice but as soon as I got to like them, I was moved on. Mum would come out of rehab saying she was better. They gave me

The Brat

back to her a few times, but she always went back to the drugs and the blokes.'

'So, how old we're you when you went into care full time?'

'I was eleven, I hated it. I started robbing houses with some older lads 'an got caught a couple of times.'

Dawson knew nothing about the care system, he'd heard of foster care, of course, but how it worked was a mystery to him.

'So, when did you start seeing men for sex?'

'When I was twelve. I met a lad called Ali. He bought me presents, told me he loved me. When I slept with him for the first time it hurt.'

'How old was Ali?'

'He said he was sixteen, but I found out later he was twenty. Then he made me sleep with his friends and after a while he was seeing a new kid and he sold me to Alexi.'

'What does Alexi do with you, Charlene?'

'He sells us to blokes who like kids. They dress us up sometimes in sexy underwear, fishnet stockings and frocks. They get one of the older girls to do our make-up, then take us to see blokes all over the place. Some of 'em live in big posh houses.' She paused, then, as if excusing her abusers, she said 'it's not just me, they do that with lots of girls, some boys, too. They have older girls, a lot of them are from Romania or Lithuania, I think.'

'How do you know?'

'Some of them speak a bit of English, they work the massage parlours and other places. They're, like, prisoners or somethin.' They take us there sometimes to meet men.'

Pity, anger and shock coursed through him. He looked down at his empty plate, his face sad. Is this really happening, he thought? He had been working abroad at the time, but now he remembered reading about the Rochdale paedophile ring trials on the Internet. Lots of mostly Asian men had been arrested and jailed for long terms for abusing young working-class girls from Local Authority care homes. It looked like it had started over again only now it had been organised into a business. East European girls held in massage parlours meant people smuggling. Had he stumbled upon a serious organised vice ring?

'If they're making money from you, Charlene, why would they want to kill you? I mean, you're a pretty girl…' he broke off, not wanting to state the obvious that a certain type of man would pay big money to sleep with her.

'Cos I know about Detective Sergeant Swanson.'

Dawson's fingers raked his hair, a bemused look on his craggy face. Christ almighty, he thought, this is getting more bizarre by the minute. He stared hard at her, looking for any liars' giveaways in her body language. She sat across from him her arms now still

The Brat

and resting on the table, looking him in the eye, her manner relaxed.

'Who is Detective Sergeant Swanson and what has he got to do with this?'

'He's a copper who investigates child abuse n' stuff, only he is one of Alexi's best customers.'

'Really?'

'Yeah, he asks for me special. One night, when we'd finished, he took a shower. I went into his wallet to see if I could nick a few quid and I saw his ID with his picture.'

'How did he find out that you knew?'

'I tried to put the screws on him saying I'd tell his bosses if he didn't slip me a hundred quid. He just laughed at me and said who the hell would believe me, a runaway care kid with a bad attitude and convictions for stealing?'

'So, why does he want you dead?'

'He doesn't, but he told Alexi. Alexi went apeshit. He's been done for selling drugs and he's shit scared of being deported.'

So, her childish attempt at blackmail had backfired and had brought her to this. Dawson began to see how it might lead to someone wanting her dead if they were paranoid, still, best to check.

'How can you be sure they were going to kill you?'

She grimaced and her hands made tight fists 'when they do the long walk punishment, they don't take your clothes, they just dump you by the roadside miles from anywhere. They stripped me in the back of the shop then drove me up here and then off the road up a narrow track and got spades from the boot. When I asked what they were doing they said it was a surprise and told me to shut up and wait.'

He watched her very closely now 'and what happened then?'

'They moved away from the car until I couldn't see them anymore, but I could hear them digging. I knew they would screw me and kill me if I stayed there. The child locks were on, so I climbed over to the driver's seat. I ran off across the moors where they couldn't drive. I fell into a muddy gully and then I saw a car pass in the distance, so I ran and ran until I reached the road.' she paused looking at him her eyes sad 'and then you came.'

'Do you go to school, Charlene?'

'Sometimes, not a lot, I get bullied.'

'Have you a special teacher you can trust?'

She shook her head, 'not since the drama teacher left.'

Dawson was struggling to hide his emotions, his voice uncertain. 'What do you want to happen now, Charlene?'

'Can I stay here with you?' she asked hopefully 'I could work for you around the house, do washing an' cleaning, fuck yer, too, whenever you want it.'

The Brat

Dawson's elbows hit the table as his head fell into his hands, a despairing groan escaping him. 'Oh, dear Christ.'

The poor kid really believed that giving sexual satisfaction was the only use she had.

His heart pounded, and his body shook. Images flashed into this mind of the awful things he'd seen and done in Iraq. The stoning of barely pubescent girls who were rape victims called adulterers. The shattered bodies of dead men, women and children the victims of suicide bombers, IED's and stray bullets. He saw again the gunman run into the house and open fire through the window. He heard click of the grenade clip as he posted it through the window. He saw himself kicking the door open to see the terrorist dead on the floor along with the woman and baby she'd been suckling. It threatened to overwhelm him, and he took several deep breaths, evicting the awful images from his mind.

He looked up at last. She was staring at him, a frightened look on her face.

'You OK, Dawes?'

He sighed deeply, ignoring her question, pushing his trembling hands beneath the table. 'OK, Charlene' he said, forcing his face into a calm mask 'let's get a couple of things straight. Firstly, you can't stay here, full stop. I would be breaking the law by keeping you and, secondly, I don't sleep with under-aged girls, *ever.*'

Charlene looked desperate seeing the hope of escape snatched from her. 'Please Dawes, *please*' she pleaded. 'I'll be good, honest. I won't give no grief an' I'll not steal yer stuff an' I'll work real hard.'

His shoulders sagged as sadness threatened to swamp him. Dawson reached out and took her hand. She was shaking, her crumpled young face and tearful eyes saying more than any words could convey. Here was a child begging, pleading for her life. He paused before answering her, his heart aching. What could he say to offer her comfort, some shred of hope?

'Charlene, you are *not* a prostitute, you are an abused child, OK? The men you talk of were raping you, do you understand?'

'But I did it free and willing Dawes, I thought the men were my friends. They gave me money and presents, they said they loved me. I felt happy.'

Dawson shook his head, bemused by the enormity of what she was telling him. 'They were *not* your friends, Charlene, Alexi is a criminal selling you to perverts. All he wants is money.'

She started sniffling 'I know it was wrong, Dawes, but I just wanted to be loved, so I did what they told me. Now they want to kill me, and I'm scared.' Her tears flowed freely.

He stopped his questioning; she was becoming too distressed.

The Brat

In the past, when he'd had a problem to ponder, Dawson had gone for a walk over the moors to clear his head. In most cases, it worked.

He hesitated, could he leave her alone for a short while? He felt the need to be alone, to think. 'Look, Charlene,' he said 'I have the day off today. I'm going for a walk to think about this. We'll try to work something out, OK?'

She looked reluctant to accept this but nodded 'OK then, I don't suppose I can come too dressed like this and with no shoes.' She spread her arms and smiled sheepishly 'if my mate little Julie could see me now, she'd have a right laugh.'

He decided against a walk, Dawson needed to run, to purge his rage. He told her he'd be back in forty-five minutes in the meantime to sit still and read and, in the unlikely event of anyone coming to the door, hide and don't answer it.

He ran up the track through the plantation to the top of the hill overlooking the reservoir a mile away and two hundred feet below. Too fast, he told himself, you'll blow out. 'Bollocks' he said aloud as he plunged on down the hill. The wind rushing past him was warm with the promise of spring. The early green and winter brown grasses blended in a blur beneath his flying feet. The moors stretched away on all sides to the horizon, their desolate beauty and remoteness the reason he lived here.

Dawson came to a single-track road that wound its way around isolated sheep farms. On he ran for another two miles, the air tearing through his lungs, his calf muscles protesting. He slowed to a stop, beaten by the lactic acid build up in his muscles. He doubled up, retching against a dry-stone wall. He puked, splashing his trainers.

After a few minutes, he'd recovered sufficiently to turn around and jog slowly

back, an idea beginning to form in his head. It might work, it just might, if Joanne would go along with it.

He stopped on the hill overlooking his house, another thought assailed him, did those blokes get his car registration number? Could they trace him? Eastern European people traffickers were ruthless. If they believed he was a threat to their business helping the kid could be dangerous.

Oh, god, he thought, I really don't need this crap right now, I've enough damn trouble coping with my own shit and bodyguarding that bitch Jezebel. How the hell do I get rid this kid?

Chapter 2

Speaking in his native tongue Serge Couscu said 'I tell you, Alexi, when I catch up with that bastard, he's a dead man. My fucking head is killing me.' He was holding an ice pack to a pigeon-egg sized lump on his forehead, his half-closed right eye was black and blue. He groaned as he touched a tender spot a little too hard. 'damn and fuck the bastard.'

'Make sure you plan it right, then, brother or you could be the one to end up dead.'

Serge's mouth made a bitter moué 'you reckon?'

'Yes, I do reckon. I've seen a lot of pretend hard men, Serge, that one's for real.'

Serge winced as pain stabbed through his head; his temple throbbed abominably as he nursed his injuries. 'He got lucky, that's all, the bastard won't be lucky next time.'

Alexi sighed, a worried frown on his brow 'do you think that kid told him anything?'

'She might have, but would he have believed her? He probably just fucked her and dropped her off somewhere quiet as soon as he could. He wouldn't want to get stopped with a naked kid in his car, especially if he's married.'

The Couscu brothers were sitting in the staff room off the kitchen of the Kwik Kebab Kabin, their main fast-food takeaway. The place was dingy, the only window, uncleaned for a decade, admitted a dismal half-light. The room stank of ancient cooking oil. The tiles, once white, were now a grubby grey. Upstairs were thirteen-year-old Julie Smythe and a client.

So far there'd been no sign of trouble and Swanson hadn't rung so nothing had been reported to the police yet. Even so, they were nervous, wanting to be rid of the pair upstairs as soon as possible. They couldn't refuse this man, he was an old crony who brought them a lot of new clients.

They had no idea who Charlene's rescuer was, but Alexi had his vehicle registration number on his car camera. Maybe Swanson could find out.

Alexi Couscu switched his thoughts to the women the syndicate had brought to London. They were due to arrive later that day and he didn't want any difficulties with their reception. These things had to be done with care. OK, so the British authorities were fools in their eagerness not to offend ethnic minorities. One had only to play the race or religious

The Brat

card and they couldn't back off quick enough. This, however, didn't mean one could be careless. He had two convictions for drug dealing, one more offence and it was certain deportation. That would be the end of his lucrative life in the UK. Once they got their teeth into something, the British police could be extremely tenacious and almost impossible to bribe; Swanson being the exception.

Serge was another cause for concern. He was too blatant about the business, too ready to bring in unproven clients. True, he was ruthlessly efficient muscle, and he made a lot of problems go away, but then he created problems, too. Alexi sighed again and lit another cigarette. Maybe a radical solution was necessary.

'If Swanson can trace that driver' Alexi said 'we'll be able to deal with him. The kid doesn't matter that much, but it is safest to dispose of her, too. Kids grow up, and Charlene Keenan is bright and has guts.'

Serge dabbed his head again and flinched 'She'll die alright, the cocky little bitch.'

Swanson rang moments later not with any news but to book an appointment with Charlene. Alexi told him of the problem omitting that Serge had been bested in a fight. He told Swanson they'd taken her for a punishment walk. 'On the moors, she started jumping in the road when a car come, it stops, she gets in, the man I think he takes photo of us. He drives off fast before we can get her back.' he said, 'but I got his number.'

Swanson cursed, reluctant to get involved.

'He probably just screwed her; she'd have offered it quick enough if she thought he'd get her away. She'll probably turn up later today.'

'So, what you think we should do?'

'Do nothing unless you hear from me, the odds are you won't, especially if he's shagged her. He won't want to broadcast that, will he?'

'You think he shag her?'

'She's a pretty little bitch, there's not many blokes would turn her down if she offered and they thought they'd get away with it.'

Swanson judged everyone by his own abysmal standards. A career cop, he was regarded by his superiors as reliable but a bit one-paced. He had been passed over for promotion to inspector. At forty-six, he had no chance of furtherment. Now, he just made extra money where he could and looked forward to a prosperous retirement in Thailand. His long-suffering wife had divorced him ten years previously because of his fondness for using massage parlours. She knew he liked younger women, but she had no idea just how young.

'OK, we do nothing yet, now, which girl you want?'

'Charlene's friend, that cute kid, Julie, ain't it?'

The Brat

Alexi snorted, he'd have to cancel her assignment for this evening. 'And I suppose you want for free as usual? I run a fuckin' business you know.'

Swanson laughed sarcastically 'free shag and a kabab, too, Alexi. I keep a lot of shit from your door, my friend, remember that.'

Alexi Couscu put his phone away, his deeply creased face showing how far from reassured he felt.

'Do we know anyone else who can trace car numbers, Serge?'

Serge thought for a moment, scratching his stubble 'I know a man who runs a parking business, I think he can get numbers. Shall I ask?'

Alexi's lip curled, 'of course you should ask, idiot.'

That afternoon they thought they had the information they needed. Dawson Jukes was the car's registered owner but the address they had was in London. Jukes, like a lot of busy people, had forgotten to change it when he'd moved North.

Alexi sat thinking, trying to decide what to do for the best. On the one hand, Swanson said to leave it be as the risk was a minor one. No one believed runaway care kids, he'd said, especially not the cops. Alexi wasn't so sure, there had been arrests and convictions in Rochdale in recent years and heavy sentences meted out. It would be safer with the girl out of the way. Then Serge wanted vengeance, he would be a pain in the arse until he got it.

Alexi was the older and wiser of the pair, he knew that vengeance was a dangerous motivation, it distorted the thinking. People bent on vengeance often made bad mistakes.

'Well, brother?' Serge looked eager, his painkillers had kicked in 'I can be down there tonight, kill the bastard and be back by tomorrow morning.'

'We have girls coming tonight, Serge.'

'Can't you and Marcia handle it? God, there's only six of them.'

'No, I need you, this is more important than your damn pride.'

Serge's eyes flashed defiance 'since when did you give me orders?'

'Since you stopped thinking straight, arsehole' Alexi's shouted, 'you want to fuck the whole operation up just so you can kill some tosser who most likely doesn't matter?' he thumped his fist onto the table 'for fuck's sake man, grow up.'

Serge leaned into his brother's face, his eyes like daggers 'listen, cunt, that bastard Jukes is a dead man. No one fucks with me like that and lives.'

'What's going on here?' Are you two at each other's throats again?' Marcia Catanova took in the scene in an instant, 'what the hell happened to your face, Serge?'

'Nothing much, a fight with a punter.'

The Brat

Catanova's ice-blue eyes seemed to pierce Serge's soul, her face as hard as a brass cannon. A well-built woman, she had shoulder-length raven hair scraped back into a ponytail. She could have been beautiful but for her mouth which held a permanent sneer.

The brothers knew better than to lie to Catanova, twenty years as a high-class hooker had left her an excellent reader of men. She would detect any lie in a heartbeat. A word to her Russian boss and things would get very ugly. They told her what had happened.

Catanova listened intently, her arms folded under her silicon enhanced bosom, her face devoid of emotion. At thirty-eight her belly was still flat and taut; her mini-skirted legs were long and bare.

The tale told, Catanova stamped a Jimmy Choo clad foot in irritation, seeing through Serge's face-saving excuses of being caught off guard. This man Jukes had dealt with him in seconds; that made him dangerous. She knew Charlene Keenan, too, was smart and sassy, she'd had a run-in with her before. She'd tried to intimidate and humiliate Charlene and had failed.

'Maybe the risk is small as Swanson suggests, maybe not.' Catanova paused briefly then delivered her verdict. 'This Jukes man and the girl pose a risk, getting rid of them is necessary, but not by you. This is a job for a professional.' She sneered at them contemptuously. 'You two fuckwits couldn't even kill a kid for God's sake.'

She rolled her eyes, shaking her head. 'Swanson is to be kept in the dark. If he raises the subject, tell him you've taken his advice and dropped the matter.'

The Couscu's grunted their agreement.

'The expense of dealing with your problem will be deducted from your cut.'

They sullenly accepted her verdict, nobody argued with the Russian syndicate.

'Now, to business. What time will these girls be here?'

'The driver rang an hour ago, he's been delayed but says he'll be here by eight.'

Catanova glanced at her gold Rolex 'good, I'll go and find a restaurant that serves edible food.'

*

Serge Couscu had been drawing attention to himself lately. He had gotten into a fight with a drunk in the shop the previous month. Instead of simply throwing the man out, he had lost his cool and beaten the guy half to death. It made the courts and the media.

Child prostitution had proved a lucrative addition to the main business. Taking over from a few poorly organised perverts and streamlining it into a profitable business had been easy. The spin-offs were

The Brat

the hidden camera footage that produced an income on the dark web and, recently, blackmail.

The blackmail of a Member of Parliament, the private secretary of the Minister for Security, was coming to fruition. She had been cultivating him for months, arranging select parties, gradually gaining his confidence, providing him with eighteen and nineteen-year-old girls. She had been tasked with gaining top secret information, but she had to tread lightly. Not for the MP cheap thrills in brothels and massage parlours, he was far too sophisticated for that. She thanked god that University fees were so high and so many students were struggling financially, they made easy targets.

Her boss had made it plain that Moscow would not be pleased if she failed.

The drugs trade and the people smuggling for the adult sex trade were all going smoothly, and she would keep the child section that way, too, if she kept the Couscu brothers in line.

She made a phone call, Jukes and Keenan had to die and the sooner the safer. She knew just the professional for the job.

*

Six women alighted from a minibus with blacked out windows in the courtyard of a block of low-rise flats. The driver pointed and addressed them. 'Up there, girls, top floor, you'll be met.' He left without a backward glance. The girls looked around them dubiously; this didn't look like the nice hotel they'd been promised. Drizzling rain started to fall, and a chill wind blew. A man whistled from a walkway above and beckoned them. There was nothing for it but to gather their belongings and trudge up the stairs.

In the flat, the girls were herded into the living room by Serge who signalled them to be silent. They were made to stand around the walls. They were young, tired and confused.

'What is this place?' a small mousy girl asked, looking at the shabby wallpaper and dinginess of the place. Serge placed his forefinger on his lips and glared.

Catanova emerged from a bedroom hard of eye and square of shoulder, followed by Alexi.

She looked slowly from girl to girl assessing each one. Two of them were tall and lithe, they would possibly make lap dancers for the clubs. Three had average looks and height but the sixth girl was small and mousy. She was fingering a cheap gold cross around her neck, eyeing the two men nervously.

This was the part of her job Catanova relished, telling the girls that the non-existent domestic jobs they had been promised had evaporated.

'Listen in ladies,' there's been a change of plan.' She went on to explain the true nature of the work they'd be doing. She told them they would be

The Brat

entertaining gentlemen in massage parlours and houses of assignment as she termed the brothels. The interest rate on the money they'd been advanced for their fare, food, and accommodation all bore interest. It had to be repaid from their earnings. They would be allowed to send some money home. This last was not an act of generosity, it was to prevent their families from asking awkward questions.

The looks of shock and dismay on the girls' faces sent a thrill of pleasure through Catanova. She revelled in power over others.

The Mousy girl protested loudly, indignation burning in her eyes 'I am a good Catholic girl and a virgin. I will not do this filthy work' she shouted, 'go to hell.'

In the silence of the room Catanova's heels clicking on the bare floor sounded like pistols being cocked as she walked slowly around the table, deadly menace in her eyes. She towered over the hapless girl.

'So, you're a virgin, are you?' The terrified girl nodded dumbly. Catanova moved with the speed of a striking cobra. She grabbed the girl and threw her onto the table, pinning her by the throat. She pulled the girl's legs apart and thrust her hand up her skirt.

The girl screamed as a sharp fingernail tore her hymen. 'Why, so you are my dear.' Catanova's sadistic smile froze the souls of the watching girls.

She began thrusting her fingers hard and rhythmically ignoring the girl's screams 'There, see how easy it is? You can take two fingers already.' She turned to Serge, her voice as brittle as icicles. 'This young lady is a virgin, please cure her of that affliction.'

Serge Couscu smiled, his lips curling back tightly over his tobacco-stained teeth; his eyes glinted lustfully. He'd been hard since the girls arrived knowing one of them would become an example, a tool with which to intimidate the others. He slid down his fly zip 'happy to oblige Marcia.' He gripped the girl's thighs and dragged her to the edge of the table.

Tearing her underwear away, he rode the girl without mercy, her screams dying away to racking sobs as he continued thrusting. When he was finished, he put himself away with the air of a man who'd just taken a casual piss. The raped girl slid off the table into a heap on the floor moaning softly, the bloodstains stark on her milk-white thighs.

Catanova stepped over the girl without a downward glance, glowering around the ashen-faced women. The tallest of the girls, a twenty-one-year-old Lithuanian beauty, stood sobbing, her head bowed, a puddle of urine at her feet.

'OK,' Catanova hissed, 'any more virgins among you?' There was shocked silence 'Any of you cattle feel she is too good to put in a hard day's work to

The Brat

earn her keep?' Again, silence. 'Good. There's food in the fridge, tea, coffee, sugar, and milk. In the bedrooms, you'll find bunk beds. There are tampons in the bathroom, don't put used stuff down the toilet, if you block it, you'll clear it with your bare hands. Make yourselves comfortable, tomorrow we start training you.' She nodded at Alexi.

Alexi spoke, his voice emotionless 'The windows are restricted, if you do manage to open one fully, there is an eight-metre drop onto concrete. The front door cannot be unlocked, the letterbox is blocked, there are no other exits. There is to be no smoking. Place your passports, phones and any cigarettes, lighters, nail files and other stuff on the table. Anyone caught with contraband after tonight will be severely punished.'

The items were thrown on the table. Alexi went through the raped girl's belongings taking her passport. He found nothing else except a rosary and a small prayer book. He ripped the cross from the girl's neck and threw it all on the table.

Catanova poked the raped girl with her foot 'make sure this cow gets the morning after pill.'

Alexi nodded acknowledgement as he scooped the womens' belongings into a plastic bin bag. As he reached the door Serge turned around 'Shout for help if you like, the neighbours are all deaf mutes, one of them works for us. You'll be reported then God help you.'

Chapter 3

Dawson checked his phone; he had a one bar signal. He pressed his speed dial and waited until her voicemail kick in. 'Hi, Joanne, something urgent's come up and I need your agile brain, can you ring me when you get off shift?'

He hung up and looked at Charlene. She was on his laptop playing a game, seemingly oblivious of her surroundings. She'd been surprised because she couldn't get an Internet connection.

Dawson used his laptop to control his security system around the house and grounds, each device transmitted directly to the laptop. He could also fly his drone with it, too, should the need arise. He had installed his elaborate system because there was a chance his former employer would send someone after him. Abu bin Sultan bin Sayyid Al-Obaidi claimed he was a Sheikh of a noble tribe. That he had wealth, power and political influence was beyond dispute. He was utterly ruthless with a love of vendettas. He'd promised Dawson a quarter million-

The Brat

dollar bonus if he kept him alive for a year. This Dawson had done, foiling two attempts on the Sheikh's life.

The man had reneged on the bonus, pretending he'd no memory of his promise. Dawson had accepted this with seeming good grace; there was no point fighting battles he couldn't win. He hid a pinhole camera overlooking the sheikh's safe and when the office was empty, he opened it, taking only what he had been promised and then left the country immediately.

So, Dawson took precautions. Anyone approaching the house up the track would be detected at four hundred metres. Approaching from any other direction they'd get within two hundred metres. In the closet of his bedroom there was a steel cabinet where he kept his 12-bore pump-action shotgun. Three boxes of military grade magnum shells were locked in a small hidden wall safe.

That the house was isolated was what Dawson needed right now. The dreams that came unbidden, the horrors of war returning to torture him,didn't make him good company. He didn't want friends and neighbours dropping by to see how he was doing; he was doing fine if he was left alone. He could manage work because that was total focus, but he wasn't ready for the social side of life. He planned to re-join mainstream society, but in his own good time.

Dawson left Charlene to her games. She seemed relaxed and a bond of trust was being established. He'd caught her staring at him, a curious look on her face, on a couple of occasions.

She finally abandoned her games and sat next to him on the couch. He removed his headphones, the jazz abandoned. Clearly the kid had things on her mind.

'Why are you helping me Dawes, what's in it for you?'

'What do you mean, Charlene?'

'Well, every bloke I've met since I was twelve wanted me, yer know? For sex an' stuff. I've never met anyone like you before.'

Dawson scratched his head; he didn't know how to respond. He was quiet for a moment gathering his thoughts. 'OK, Charlene, what's happened to you isn't right. It's the instinct of normal men to protect women and girls, not use them.'

'So, if I was to come on to you, you wouldn't do nuffin?' She smiled and slid her hand up his inner thigh,

His reaction was explosive. Grabbing her hand, he threw it violently away, his eyes blazing. 'Stop that you little brat, you do that again and I'll thrash yer arse 'til you can't sit down.' His breathing was harsh, his chest heaved as he felt an almost overwhelming

The Brat

urge to slap her face. 'I've told you once, I don't sleep with kids, it's disgusting.'

Charlene recoiled to the end of the settee, bursting into tears 'sorry Dawes, sorry. I…I had to be sure.'

Oh, Jesus, he thought, the kid was testing me. His rage turned to sorrow; her childish test was understandable considering her past. Now he felt anguished.

He took a huge breath letting it out slowly. He arose and fetched a piece of kitchen towel giving his emotions time to rebalance.

'Here, wipe your eyes and blow your nose, we'll forget it, Charlene, OK?' Dawson burned with shame at his outburst.

He sat next to her and placed an arm around her shoulders, hugging her close. It felt strange to him to be comforting her, yet it seemed the right thing to do.

'There's things you need to understand, girl' he said quietly. 'I'm not some knight in shining armour, OK? I've been a mercenary soldier, a man of violence. I've done some bad things in the past, Charlene, terrible things, do you understand? I'm not a fit bloke to be looking after kids. I'm not a fit bloke to be around anyone, right now, that's why I live out here. You know about the dreams, but I also get dark moods and fits of temper. I'm sorry for the wrong I've done, but that don't change anything.'

He looked at her wondering if she understood, wondering if even he understood.

'What those blokes were doing to you was wrong, very wrong. If I can help put a stop to it then maybe it'll make up for some of the bad stuff I've done.'

Her face screwed up, she looked puzzled 'I don't think you're bad Dawes and I'm sorry I tested you, but I needed to know. Every bloke I've ever met has been a lying bastard. They'll say they love me or that they want to take care of me, they give me some money or buy me a cheap present but all they want is to use me.'

Dawson's heart was aching, this poor kid was a victim just like the kids he'd seen in Iraq. Why was it always the kids who suffered most? He pulled her tighter to him.

'Charlene, all I can do is my best to help you. Most likely it won't be enough. I know a couple of decent people who might help, but I can't promise anything beyond that.'

She wiped her eyes on the now soggy kitchen towel and looked up at him, her face calm. 'That's OK by me, Dawes. I know you can't make promises, but I know now you'll do yer best.'

A little while later Charlene made tea and he marvelled at the change in her demeanour. She poured for them. He couldn't believe the amount of sugar she scooped in hers.

'Good god, Charlene, leave some of that sugar for tomorrow.'

The Brat

'It's to keep me nature sweet' she quipped flashing him a bright smile. Now she was fully confident that she could trust him she was relaxed, playful even.

'You got any proper music, Dawes?'

'Yes, I've got Jazz, the best music there is.'

'It's shit, Dawes, now rap, that's lit.

'Lit'?

'Yeah, cool, amazing, yer know?'

'I do now and while we're talking, Charlene, I don't like my name being shortened to Dawes, OK?'

'Aw, don't be a boff, Dawes is cool' she playfully poked her tongue out.

'Boff?'

'Boring old fart, Dawes, Dawson is… well…it's dorky, not cool, in your language. Don't wanna be a dork, do ya?' She stuck her tongue out again and he laughed.

'You really are a cheeky little brat, aren't you?'

Charlene grinned, delighted 'Oh, yeah, brat, that's sick, mate. I'll be your brat' she punched the air 'Yeah' she said then added: 'you ain't too bad for a boff, Dawes.'

Dawson picked up on her mood and retaliated, poking his tongue out at her. 'Right, then, you cheeky little bugger, Brat it shall be, suits yer, too.'

Dawson knew he was fully trusted now but decided to take it slowly with her, easing information out of her gradually lest she clam up. She never volunteered information; she simply answered his questions as briefly as possible. It was as if she wanted to block out all the bad stuff in her life. He could understand that. He also blocked out the bad stuff as far as possible. If he was to be of help to her, though, he needed to know everything she knew about the organisation she was running from.

At ten thirty p.m. Joanne rang full of curiosity. Charlene was asleep so he took the call in his bedroom. He told her of his situation and broached the subject of Charlene's immediate future, could she stay with her and Jaineba?

There was a long pause, Dawson knew she was thinking hard. Joanne and Jaineba were a gay married couple who were going through the adoption process.

'How long for, Dawson?'

'A couple of days only, Joanne. I plan to get the press involved. I know a journalist at the Manchester Evening News, she's a bit of a crusader.'

'Can't she take her in?'

'She lives in a tiny one bed flat.'

'I see, but I don't want to become involved with publicity any more than you do, Dawson, and I'd have to run it past Jaineba first.'

'Does that mean you'll consider it?'

'Of course. She's a vulnerable young girl. There's a problem, though. Even if Jaineba agrees, we

The Brat

couldn't take her until the day after tomorrow as she is working away and I'm on your shift again.'

Dawson woke her bright and early next day. 'I have to go to work, Charlene…'

'Brat' she interrupted sleepily, rubbing her eyes 'I'm The Brat, remember?'

'Yeah, whatever. I think I've found you a temporary new home with some friends of mine, but they can't take you until the day after tomorrow.'

'I like it here Dawes, I feel safe with you. Can't I stay?'

He didn't have time to argue, so he marched her over to the Laptop. 'You asked why I have this setup. Let me show you.' He switched to the remote cameras and infra-red detectors and ran her through the security system.

'I've been involved with some very nasty people, Brat, they may come after me. If anyone approaches the alarm will beep. Check them out here. Now, we get a few ramblers passing by so don't panic but if they look or act suspicious run for the woods and hide, OK?'

Charlene looked at him quizzically 'you're serious, Dawes, ain't ya?'

'Damned right I'm serious, Brat, so pay attention to what I'm showing you.'

She ran her nimble fingers over the keyboard demonstrating just how competent she was. She went through everything he'd shown her without any mistake, zooming the cameras in and out. 'I'll be OK with this, Dawes' she said, 'If anyone comes near who looks dodgy, I'll be off, quick.'

'OK, don't worry too much, usually I don't see anyone for days on end here. Now, I'll get you some clothes and shoes while I'm out and pick up some more grub, too.'

She knew her measurements and shoe size. She exaggerated her bra cup size, sticking her chest out as she did so, even Dawson wasn't fooled.

He laughed, genuinely amused, 'I've seen more tit on an eel, Brat' he teased.

She grinned at his insult 'I'm growing Dawes, you cheeky tosser, now, give us a hug before you go.'

He was surprised at how quickly she'd placed absolute trust in him. Were all kids like her? He couldn't answer his own question.

He went to the garage and, before getting into his car, he waved goodbye at the hidden pinhole camera.

He was amazed at her ability to bounce back from the horror of her ordeal, or was she just putting on a brave front like he did sometimes?

Chapter 4

'Hey, you, I wanna McDonald's burger and fries, it's just across the street, go get it me.'

Dawson's polite smile hid his intense annoyance 'Sorry, madam, I can't leave my post.'

Jezebel Justiz responded with shocked disbelief; her voice rose to a screech 'What the fuck did you just say? I pay your fuckin' wages, asshole, you do as I say.'

Dawson's smile never faltered 'I'm your bodyguard, madam. I cannot leave my post.'

Joanne heard and came to his rescue, striding purposefully across the lush hotel suite her voice calm and appeasing 'Dawson has to stay in the vestibule madam, he'd be fired if he didn't. I'll have one of your people fetch it or would you prefer room service? They do great burgers here.'

Jezebel calmed down a little. She was in awe of Joanne who was a tall, athletic, self-assured ex Royal

Military Police captain. She had a calm face and placid manner born of her expertise in martial arts.

'I don't like the crap they serve here' Jezebel whined 'aw, forget it, I'll starve, it'll be good for my figure.' She glared at Dawson 'comes to somethin' when the hired help mouth off' she muttered.

Jezebel Justiz was the stage name of American Latino rapper Lola Chavez. Two years of fame had gone to her head so she behaved as she thought a famous diva should.

A short time later, Dawson went to the suite's kitchen for his half hour lunch break. He was far from happy with his situation. Jezebel had forbidden phones, cameras or any electrical device in the apartment. This including his earpiece and cuff communications rig. He had to call down to the lobby using the room phone to speak to the guy on guard there. It went against his security man's instincts, and all because Jezebel was terrified that her true personality might be revealed and ruin her carefully constructed PR image.

Dawson heaved a relieved sigh as he raised his coffee cup; it was good to sit down and relax away from the constant carping. He had read Jezebel's history. Two years previously, she'd been an unknown, flipping burgers in McDonalds by day and working cheap clubs by night. Now, she was an international rap star and a twenty-four-carat pain in the arse.

The Brat

Lunch over, Dawson returned to the hallway. Jamie, new, young and eager, was outside checking everyone who came to the door, Dawson had to do a second check of visitors in the hall, if they were female, he called Joanne. It was all part of the ego massage demanded by the self-important Jezebel.

He'd been back for a few minutes when there was a knock. Dawson put his eye to the spyhole. The man wore the livery of the hotel staff and held a covered tray. Dawson couldn't see Jamie but that was not unusual, he would have checked the waiter out then stepped aside to allow him access. Dawson opened the door and the man entered swiftly.

Giving him the once over Dawson noticed that although the man's uniform was smart, he was wearing dirty, down-at-heel shoes, all the hotel staff wore smart, highly polished ones.

'Hold it there, pal.' He reached for the tray lid.

The man looked panicked and barged past Dawson running toward the lounge and Jezebel. Dawson dived after him catching him just before he reached the star.

'Bitch' he screamed and threw the lid off the tray reaching for the glass of clear liquid. Dawson smashed the tray from his hands sending the contents of the glass flying away from Jezebel. It splashed over the carpet hissing and bubbling. He brought the man down with a neck chop, then rammed his arm up his back and sat on him. He looked toward

Jezebel, she was curled into a tight ball screaming hysterically, her feet kicking rapidly up and down, but he could see no injuries.

Then Joanne was there. 'It's OK, Jezebel, I've got you, you're safe now.' She lifted Jezebel, still screaming, and carried her bodily into the bedroom, slamming and locking the door.

'Jamie? Where the hell are you?' Dawson yelled. There was no reply. A moment later the hotel security people ran in, summoned by one of Jezebel's staff who'd pressed a panic alarm.

As he was being dragged away, the attacker shouted 'you never answer my emails, bitch, I send you flowers, you don't send thanks. Fuck you, you cheap burger flipping whore.'

The liquid fizzed on the carpet and the sleeve of his jacket was holed. Dawson recognised the pungent smell of sulphuric acid. Jezebel had had a narrow escape. But where the hell was Jamie?

Dawson was ringing the guy downstairs when there was a tap on the door, He put down the phone and went to the spyhole, it was Jamie, he was carrying a McDonalds takeaway box.

Marcus Weitz, Jezebel's manager, was a short, fat, obnoxious man, full of himself. He waved his fist in Dawson's face, his eyes rolling, the veins in his neck standing out like fat blue worms 'I'm getting her outta here right now, new hotel, new security team, the works. You fucking people are obviously

The Brat

incompetent. How the *fuck* could you let this happen?' he bawled 'Jesus Christ, we'll have to cancel tonight's gig. Have you morons any idea how much that will cost us?'

Dawson and Joanne were irked by the man's arrogance and blame shifting but their faces remained impassive.

Joanne spoke, her voice matter of fact, no sign of appeasement in her tone. 'Your client waited until my colleague here was on his break, she then sent me on a fool's errand checking the already checked procedure for tonight. It was then she personally ordered Jamie to go, via the back door, and fetch her a burger from across the street. That was strictly against our contract rules, sir.'

'Fuck your contract rules and fuck you, too,' Weitz bawled 'how the hell is she supposed to know that?' Your guy should have told her no. I'll have your fuckin' jobs for this, you'll never work security again.'

Realising Weitz was upset because his asset had been threatened, Dawson was prepared to be extremely patient, but the man was going too far. He went even further, poking a pudgy finger hard into Dawson's chest, drool spilling from the corner of his mouth. He leaned into Dawson's face 'I blame you for this you useless fuck, you're the head honcho here, just sitting on your fat ass instead of supervising these idle cunts.'

Dawson's temper finally snapped. He shoved the man out of his face and back into his seat with a speed that terrified Weitz. He gripped the man's lapel, drawing him half out of the seat. 'Now, listen to me, you obnoxious little turd, I'd told Jezebel emphatically that we were not to be used for errands but she's too full of herself to listen to anyone. Not even we can fix her kind of stupidity.'

Dawson felt Joanne's hand on his shoulder 'Leave it, Dawson, let me handle this.'

The flash of temper left him as quickly as it had arisen, Joanne was right, this wouldn't mend anything.

Weitz realised he was out of immediate danger. 'That was assault' he screeched, 'you got no goddam right to lay hands on me, you goddammed limey bastard. I'll sue your fuckin' ass for this.'

Ignoring Weitz, Dawson spoke to Joanne 'I'll be back at the office reporting to John. Can you look after her in the meantime? Deal with the police?'

Joanne nodded 'sure.'

When Dawson had gone, Joanne turned to Weitz, it was time for a cool head. 'I'll have a word with Jezebel, Mr Weitz, tell her how brave she's been and try and save your gig. She listens to me, maybe we can turn this into great publicity.'

Weitz was an angry, egotistical *little* man, but he wasn't stupid. Losing tonight's gig would cost a million plus and Jezebel wouldn't even talk to him.

The Brat

He calmed down almost immediately. 'OK, I suppose it's the least you can do, so go ahead.'

A single drop of honey catches more flies than a whole gallon of vinegar was Joanne's philosophy. There was no point in telling Jezebel how bloody stupid she'd been, that would achieve nothing. By using a combination of flattery, praise and logic she persuaded her that the publicity would be fantastic.

'Just think of the headlines, Jezebel. *"Brave superstar goes ahead with gig despite deadly acid attack. Refuses to let her loyal fans down"*. We could have it running on social media this afternoon.'

Jezebel loved the idea, but still played the martyr 'will you be there, Joanne?' she affected a small, frightened voice 'I couldn't do it unless you were right there in the wings watching over me, hun.'

Even though it would take her way past her shift time, Joanne agreed on condition Weitz got off Dawson's case. 'It wasn't Dawson's fault' she told her firmly 'everyone's got to eat sometime.'

'I suppose so' Jezebel reluctantly conceded. She'd already absolved herself of all blame.

Joanne told Weitz the gig was back on, but he still looked sour. She didn't trust him to get off Dawson's case.

'OK' he muttered 'That's something, I suppose, but that big bastard Jukes should'na touched me.'

It was time for her to be firm 'Listen, Mr Weitz, Dawson Jukes is not the only one who's had enough of your aggressive rudeness. Jezebel will only go on stage if I'm there and you get off Dawson's case, OK? Maybe you should reflect on that.'

Weitz's face twitched and he bit down hard on his lip. She had him by the balls. He hated anyone getting the better of him, especially a woman. But maybe there was a way he could turn the tables.

Chapter 5

John Babcock was a worried man and it showed in the tense lines of his face. His security company was relatively new and bad publicity was the last thing he needed.

'They've cancelled the contract, Dawson, so you won't be going with them to Glasgow.' His broad shoulders sagged, and worry creased his brow. At fifty, he considered this his last chance to build a business of his own to support himself and his family.

John's PA brought coffee and set it on the desk, leaving without her usual cheerful remarks.

John tugged his right ear lobe, his dark brown eyes downcast, 'I've been taking crap from her manager, Weitz. Almost an hour of earache. The bugger is threatening to sue us, though he hasn't got a cat-in-hell's chance, of course. I've had to fire Jamie, I know he was still a probationer, but he should have known better than to leave his post. When I refused to fire you, Weitz went mad but he can go and play with his arse.' John sighed 'I'm afraid, though, with the contract cancelled I'll have to lay you off until something else comes up, Dawson.' Then he brightened a little 'Joanne Shipley, for some reason, is still trusted by that bloody Justiz woman. She wants her to stay on to guard her at tonight's show.'

'Yeah, I had a call from Joanne on the way here, John. Jezebel won't go on stage tonight without her being there. If she doesn't perform it'll cost 'em huge money and fans, too, so stick your overtime rate for her way up.'

John nodded 'I will, that's something at least.'

At a loose end now, Dawson went shopping. He'd taken advice from Joanne as to what young girls like to wear. It took him a lot longer than expected as he fumbled his way through endless clothes racks assisted by amused saleswomen. At last, he was through and headed off home.

Charlene was in the bath singing her head off when he arrived. Singing was not her long suit, but at least it showed him she felt safe. Dawson opened a crack in the door and threw the shopping bags into the steam. 'Here you are Brat.'

When she emerged, she was in jean's, sweatshirt and Nike trainers. She was grinning from ear to ear. 'Pretty cool stuff Dawes, you're not a bad judge for an old fella.'

He glowed, basking in her approval. Dawson felt pleased. He neglected to tell her that Joanne had

The Brat

given him a list. *You silly old bugger* his inner voice said, *trying to impress a teenager with how cool you are? You're pathetic.*

After a steak dinner, Dawson asked her more question about her life. As well as helping older boys to burgle houses, she'd fallen under the influence of the wrong kind of older girls, too. They taught her how to shoplift and scrounge free food from takeaways. Running with the fast mob had seemed so exciting at first. Then, as she reached puberty, the grooming process started.

'Ali was a really good-looking lad. He bought me presents. He said I was beautiful and that he was in love with me.' She looked guiltily into Dawson's face 'a week after I let him have me, he passed me around his friends. Soon it was older men, and he was charging them money. He said his uncle would beat him if I didn't do it. He sold me to Alexi when he got a new girl.'

Her face looked pinched and drawn as she spread her hands in a helpless gesture 'I know I'm a bad person, Dawes, but I just wanted someone to love me.'

Her words cut into his heart like shrapnel and he reached out and pulled her to him wrapping his big arms around her trembling shoulders as she sobbed into his chest. She was releasing all the pent-up misery of her young life. He could find no words, being close to tears himself. He rocked her, stroking her hair with a huge clumsy hand until her tears subsided.

Half an hour later she was back to her old self. Dawson marvelled at the behavioural change. *It must be a kid thing* his inner voice said.

'Dawes, this place is crap. Your TV's broke, your music stinks, except for that Ella Fitzgerald woman, she's not bad but that jazz shit is boring. Ain't you got no rap?'

He forced a laugh 'I never watch TV, too much garbage on the news; maybe I'll get it fixed or buy a new one someday soon. When I get back here, Brat, I chill, I read, and listen to *real* music.' His thoughts tuned in briefly to the images on the news he couldn't avoid seeing at work. The barrel bombs in Syria, the refugees, the broken, dispossessed people. The ones burying their children. A tightness took his chest, and he shook his head forcing the images away. No, he didn't need a television.

'I like Jezebel Justiz, now she's a real rapper, she says it like it is.'

Dawson choked off a snort of derision before it escaped him. He was tempted to tell her the truth about her heroine but thought better of it. *Don't even think of going there, Jukes, you'll be answering questions all night.*

'How come you don't have a phone, Brat? Most kids your age are never off the damned things.'

The Brat

Her mouth twisted down as anger flare in her eyes. 'That bastard Alexi says we can't have them, he's frightened about social media.'

'So, how does he contact you about his dirty business?'

'He tells us when and where to be when we go for food or through the Kulaks.'

'The what?'

'Kulaks, they are older lads who have phones. We go down to a bushy bit of land by the canal every day around five, it's called the Meat Rack. We get picked for jobs. If you don't show they come looking for you and you get beat up.'

Kulak, the Russian word for fist. How ironic, he thought, they chose the title given to the brutal enforcers who kept their fellow peasants in line. He felt she was still only telling the half of what she knew, reluctant to even think about her life. He could see she was close to tears again, so he stopped the questions.

She turned the tables on him. 'Anyway, what about you, Dawes? You got a girlfriend?'

'No, Brat, not now.'

'You gay?'

'Would it bother you if I were?'

'No, not really, but I'd like it better if you weren't.'

'I'm not gay, Brat, and you're a cheeky little sod for asking. My last girlfriend dumped me when I went working abroad.' It was his turn to feel sad, thinking about Margaret made his heart lurch, he still had feelings for her.

Almost as quickly as the emotion came it passed. Dawson was uncomfortable talking about himself and didn't want to speak of Iraq so, to distract her, he asked 'do you know how to play poker?' It was the first thing that had popped into his head. *You crazy bastard Dawson Jukes.*

They sat at the table and he taught her five card draw poker. He was amazed at the speed with which she picked it up and her uncanny, intuitive grasp of strategy. Charlene was very bright, he realised, under educated perhaps, but highly intelligent.

Later that night Joanne rang with the news that she was on her way to Glasgow with the show. She had rung Jaineba who had agreed they could have Charlene for a few days. The bad news was her case had overrun; she'd be in London for another day.

He put his phone away 'looks like I'm stuck with you for another day, Brat.'

She beamed 'great, you can teach me more about poker, Dawes.'

Next morning he was up early, it had rained overnight, now the bright spring sunshine made the world look fresh and clean. He looked into the living room, Charlene's small head was tucked deep in the sleeping bag; she was gently snoring. He glanced at his phone. No signal. He went out and walked up the

The Brat

hill to where he knew the signal was good. He stood admiring the serene view over the counties of Lancashire and Yorkshire. The air tasted fresh with the tangy smell of fresh herbs; a deer walked past a hundred metres away pausing briefly to inspect him before continuing unhurriedly on. He drank in the beauty for another minute then checked his messages.

There was one from John. *Have you seen Facebook? Twitter? Have you seen what Weitz has done? We need to talk. Please be at the office for 9:30.* Dawson checked the local news site. The first thing that hit him was the headline. **Jezebel Justiz in deadly acid attack. Bodyguard flees**.

"A brave Rap star was left to fight off a deadly acid attacker in her hotel suite yesterday afternoon while her bodyguard is said to have fled to save his own skin, leaving her to fight for her life. After carelessly allowing her attacker access to her suite, the man, named locally as Dawson Jukes, allegedly fled for his life when the attacker produced a phial of lethal acid. Jukes, who was hired to protect Ms. Justiz, so far cannot be contacted. The Manchester agency Babcock Personal Protection Ltd, owned by a Mr John Babcock, denied the claims and said he wasn't in touch with Jukes for the moment. Babcock said the claims were "a pack of lies" told to ramp up publicity. He said he'd make a full statement after consulting his legal team. However, we have seen the acid burns on the carpet of Jezebel's hotel suite proving the incident really did happen. Police have detained a twenty-year-old man under the mental health act."

There was a picture of the carpet. The article went on with lie after lie saying the brave star had insisted that her gig went ahead that evening despite her ordeal as she refused to let down her adoring fans.

There was a photo of Jezebel with Dawson, his face circled, standing close behind her.

Dawson stopped reading, a sick feeling in the pit of his stomach, a sour taste in his mouth, the bright morning suddenly made dark. That slimy bastard Weitz had got his revenge and a load of sensationalist free publicity, too. Joanne had not even been mentioned. Christ, he thought, what a crock of shit. He hurried down the hill to the house his innards tense. Charlene was still asleep. He left her a note: "Hi, Brat, I've been called away urgently, make your own breakfast and don't burn the house down. Keep the place tidy. Back soon, Big hugz, Dawes."

He grabbed his car keys and left.

Chapter 6

As a result of Catanova's phone call, a Russian man called at Dawson Jukes' old address in London. The door was answered by an elderly woman. The man said he was an old friend and was trying to trace Dawson Jukes with the news that a close relative had died. The lady couldn't help but gave him the address and phone number of the agency who were responsible for the letting. They in turn could only tell the man that Mr Jukes had moved to the North West of England with his job leaving no forwarding address. They couldn't release his phone number under data protection laws.

This had taken most of the morning and Catanova paced the floor of her living room clicking her fingers, stopping to check her phone every few minutes. She wanted this over with quickly before it could reflect on her. Any threat to business, no matter how small, had to be eliminated either through bribery, coercion, or murder. This kid knew too much, and she had shown initiative and defiance.

After some high-profile cases, kids like her were now being listened to. Also, her hatred of Charlene was personal. She'd probably told this guy Jukes about what she'd done to her.

At last, her phone rang 'Yes?'

'He moved months ago, he's up your way somewhere, North West of England was all I could get.'

'OK, come up. If he's here it won't take me long for me to find him.'

Alexi Couscu rang minutes later 'We know where Dukes lives, Marcia, We have a client in the council tax office. We can deal with him.'

'It's in hand, Alexi' she sneered 'I don't trust you two as far as I can spit.'

'I love you, too, Marcia' he said then gave her Dawson's address and hung up.

*

Dawson sat in John Babcock's office for the second time in twenty-four hours, his insides squirming, his face looked calm. The gentle tapping of his right foot on the floor the only clue to his tense inner state. This was not his field of expertise. Threats from men with weapons he knew and understood how to deal with, this Internet stuff was beyond his ken.

John looked sick and Dawson couldn't even guess the impact this story would have on his business.

The Brat

'Even when we prove the story false, a lot of damage will have been done, Dawson' John said 'it's all trial by media these days. Christ, I could really do without this.'

'Yeah, John, and the chattering classes believe everything on bloody Farce Book and Witter' he deliberately mispronounced the names expressing his contempt for social media. 'What worries me, John, is that this shit has a worldwide reach and there are people to whom I do not wish to be remembered.'

Dawson had changed his appearance as much as possible since returning to England. He'd used some of his earnings to have his broken nose fixed and he'd shaved off the full beard and moustache he'd worn when in Iraq. His once shoulder-length hair was now a neat crew cut. Now his picture was all over social media and his new face shown to the world. He wished now he'd changed his name, too.

John had recalled Joanne and was waiting for her to get back from Glasgow so they could call a press conference. A solicitor had been consulted to evaluate the situation to see if a defamation lawsuit was a viable proposition.

'It's a mess Dawson and no mistake.'

Joanne rang John. 'Hi, I've just crossed the Scottish border, I'll be there in about three hours, OK?'

'How did Jezebel take your leaving?'

'She was not best pleased; she had a rant then went into a super-sulk.'

'My heart bleeds for her.'

Joanne said 'I challenged Jezebel on the wildly inaccurate stories. **She** blamed it all on Weitz, saying she knew nothing about it until it was too late. I asked would she now go public with the truth and she clammed up.'

'Where's Weitz now?' John asked.

'He's gone AWOL; he's not answering his phone and Jezebel said she couldn't do anything before consulting Weitz.'

'What a bastard, I'd like to get my hands on the lying bugger.' John, normally a very calm man, was almost beside himself with rage. He hung up, his face tight and tense.

Chapter 7

By mid-afternoon Charlene was bored. She'd played computer games for hours. Earlier, she'd made herself a lunch of sandwiches and a beer from the fridge. Dawes would give her a bollocking for drinking alcohol and she looked forward to it. It would show that he cared.

She decided to wash her used crockery and put it away. He was a neat person, he washed up immediately after their meals and put everything back in its place. He had insisted her sleeping bag was rolled and stowed away, too.

This kind of tidiness was alien to Charlene. He was the opposite of her mother who never put stuff away then blamed everyone else when she couldn't find her shit. A warm, secure feeling ran through her when she thought of Dawson. He had protected her when she needed protection, even showed her affection.

She put the beer bottle in the bin and tucked his note into her pocket. She looked around the neat house with a satisfied smile. Yeah, he'd be pleased. The thought of pleasing her Dawes felt good.

She contemplated doing the basket of washing he was obviously going to do that morning until he was called away. She examined the washing machine; she'd never used one before. It was a huge one like the ones in the childrens' home and looked complicated. There seemed to be dozens of different wash settings and temperatures and dryer settings, too. If she got it wrong she'd look a right dork. The last thing she wanted was to look stupid in his eyes. Charlene decided to leave well alone.

The rain that had marched in vertical sheets across the moors, row after row for the last hour suddenly stopped and the sky became clear again, the sun inviting. Charlene gazed out of the kitchen window over the paddock to the trees two hundred metres away. She felt the loneliness of the place crowd in around her. She could hear a bird singing nearby and she wondered vaguely what type it was. She felt strangely nervous never having been out of big towns before.

Her thoughts returned to Dawson. He'd passed her test, scaring the life out of her in the process. His craggy face was hard to read. Ugly, she thought, but if I'd had a dad, I would have loved it to have been Dawes. Embarrassment flushed her cheeks. That she had offered him sex seemed so very wrong now.

The Brat

Her mood switched to anger as she recalled the days when her mother was out of her head on drugs or bringing men home so she could earn her next fix. What had she done to deserve this life? Other kids were dropped off and met at the school gates by loving parents who embraced and kissed them. They were whisked off in comfortable cars to safe homes where they were loved and cherished by their families. Why wasn't her life like that? Why did no one love her? Huh, you need to ask, stupid? She thought, it's because you're a liar, a thief and a whore, yup, you steal and you're a whore, just like your mother. 'You're just no fuckin' good Charlene Keenan' she whispered 'You deserve all you get.' The tears pricking her eyes were those of anger not self-pity.

She wiped her eyes on her sleeve, sniffing loudly. I'm a care brat, she thought, some kids are, that's all there is to it.

Charlene smiled to herself, she liked the soubriquet Brat, it conjured up images of a tough, street wise kid in her mind. Yeah, she was Dawes' Brat, at least for now. The thought cheered her immensely.

Charlene's thought of her friend Julie Smythe, she seemed so frail and vulnerable, lost in the world of vice and street life. Where was she now? What was she doing? Was she still sniffing glue?

Anthony Milligan

Charlene checked herself, shaking off the dark thoughts. She thought instead of the advice Mrs Alnwick her care worker gave her. *Feeling sorry for yourself won't alter your situation, Charlene. Accept what is and work to change it.*

Yeah, right, with bastards like Alexi and Serge Couscu on her case it was never going to be easy. But she also knew that Mrs Alnwick had once been in her situation. She was a tough woman, a survivor, maybe with Dawes help she'd be a survivor, too. The thought cheered her.

Charlene decided to go for a walk now the sun was shining. She'd feel better for it and Dawes hadn't said she couldn't. She was halfway to the back door when the laptop started beeping. She hurried across and clicked on the camera icon that was flashing. A tall, gaunt man was leaving a big Volvo that was stopped around the bend from the house. He looked around him slowly then spoke into a small black hand-held radio. If he'd been a social worker, he would have had a woman with him. He looked sinister as he eyeballed the area.

As she continued watching, the man leaned into the back of the car and withdrew a sawn-off shotgun.

Charlene drew a sharp breath as her hand flew to her mouth. She watched wide-eyed as he loaded the weapon then tucked it under his short car coat. He pulled a long handgun from under his shoulder and worked the slide. It looked like a scene from a

The Brat

gangster movie, but she knew this was deadly serious. The man started walking up the lane towards the house. She switched cameras. He stopped again looking carefully around then cut into the woods to approach the house from the side.

She was about to follow Dawson's instructions and bolt for the woods when another icon started beeping and flashing. The sensors covering the back of the house had picked up movement.

She zoomed in to the treeline. Two men were lurking on the edge of the woods at the far side of the paddock. One of them had a radio like the man on the track. She was trapped.

*

Vladimir Buchovski crept stealthily under the living room window and crouched, listening. There was no sound of movement, or of any TV or radio.

He waited; these things had to be done carefully. After a few minutes, he made his way around the house slowly, stealthily, listening under every window. He was sure there was no one home but he was a thorough man. Every possibility had to be checked.

He tried the back-door handle. It was locked. The lock was a five-pin mortice, an old design. He took a bunch of rakes out of his pocket and set to work. Three minutes later he stood in the kitchen. He walked carefully through the house working his way soundlessly around each room the shotgun to the fore. He stopped at the steel gun cabinet. Catanova said her bent cop had told her Jukes held a shotgun licence. He went back to the kitchen.

'Come out come out wherever you are' his voice was a soft singsong, low and full of menace. 'Are you in here little girl? He started to open cupboards in the kitchen base units whistling softly to himself 'if you're in here I'll find you so why don't you come out and meet Uncle Vladimir? Uncle Vladimir is a nice man, he has money and sweets for good girls. Bad girls get punished.'

He moved on throughout the house repeating himself as he searched every room again.

After a look in the attic, he moved outside to the garage and the shed that housed the Calorgas tank. Finally, he came back and leaned against the sink. He took out his phone. He spoke in Russian to Catanova, it was not a happy conversation. He then made a radio call.

'You two can come in now and we'll go back to the car, they're not here. A short time later the two men came into the kitchen 'wipe your damned feet' he snarled.

Buchovski sneered at them 'I don't suppose you saw anything in the woods?'

'No mate, nothing.'

The second man reached for the laptop. 'This'll fetch a bit.'

The Brat

Buchovski smashed his hand away 'Cretin! You touch nothing.'

The man jerked back angrily cursing 'what the fuck?'

'Have you noticed nothing about this house you dammed fool?'

'No, nothing special, and I've done a few hundred burglary's in my time.'

'And how many times have you been to prison?'

The man was defiant 'only once, I got two years. I hit an old bloke when he caught me in his house. I left DNA when my knuckle split. Just bad luck.'

'I have assassinated twenty-two people and never even been a suspect. Why do you think that is?'

'I dunno. Lucky? Bent cops lookin' after yer?'

Buchovski's fist flew hard into the man's guts. He gasped and collapsed

'The reason, *imbecile*, is because I'm careful. Look around you.' Buchovski pointed, his hand making a wide sweep 'this house is immaculate, no crockery left in the sink, everything tidy and put away, the bed is made, there's not even a speck of dust. This is the home of a single man, he is extremely tidy, obsessive I'd say. If we move anything, he'll know someone has been here. I will come back later, after dark, then I'll catch him. I won't need you for that.'

The second man stood sullenly watching this exchange, there was something implicitly evil about Buchovski, he scared him.

'We gave you two idiots two hundred pound each just to watch and report if anyone came out of the back door, that's all. If you touch anything, I'll kill you.'

As they left the house the downpour started again. Buchovski pulled up his collar and jogged back to his car his companions stumbling behind him.

Buchovski had no intention of sitting in the woods waiting. After dark, he'd be able to see the house lights from the track then he'd be in business. He swore inwardly, why had he listened to her?

He rang Catanova again. 'He's not home and he must have taken the kid with him. I'll clear out now and come back later.'

'Why don't you wait?'

'Why don't you shut the fuck up and stop telling me how to do my job?'

He heard her sharp intake of breath 'I'm paying top dollar for this job Buchovski, a little respect wouldn't come amiss.'

'I'm doing you a big favour lady; this is a rush job. Normally I don't do rush jobs no matter how easy they seem. And another thing, these two lunatics you gave me are next to useless. One of them even tried to steal his bloody computer.'

'Did you look at it?'

The Brat

'No, he's an obsessive so it would require a password. It's quite possible he'd know even if I only lifted the lid. I moved nothing. He won't know I've been. His voice hardened, he didn't like his methods being questioned, especially by a woman, no matter how well connected she was. She had briefed him that the target had the kid with him, that he was a loner and out of work. He would certainly be sitting at home. She had been wrong and now he had to return to this god-forsaken place again instead of getting back to London.

His voice took on a hard tone 'leave this to me Marcia and do not interfere. I'll let you know when I have completed the task.'

Chapter 8

It was late afternoon when Dawson arrived back home. Conferring with solicitors had taken a long time. Joanne had told her version of the story as had Dawson. A press release was distributed, and social media posts were made but it was too early to tell what effect their efforts might have.

On the track Dawson braked, his knuckles whitened on the wheel and he leaned forward, alarm bells ringing. One of the sticks he'd placed across the wheel groove was broken and there were fresh tyre marks in the mud. He drove another hundred metres, that tell-tale twig was still intact. Someone had driven to within three hundred metres of the house.

Dawson had been in a hurry that morning and almost decided against setting the tell-tales, now he was glad he did. Whoever it was had reversed down to where they could turn around, that was over seventy-five metres. Anyone who'd accidentally taken a wrong turn would have continued to the

The Brat

house to where there was bound to be a better turning place.

Had Charlene followed his instructions to run and hide? Was she waiting for his return? Why had she not moved to a position where she could see his car turn up from the road? His fingers drummed the steering wheel as he pursed his lips. After half a minute, he got out of the car and lifted the spare wheel. From the well beneath, he took a shortened adapted scuba divers spear gun and loaded it with a spiked bolt. He entered the woods.

The house was in the tree shaded gloom of early evening yet there were no lights on. He made his way to the side of the house keeping out of sight. There was no sign of life. A feeling of dread swept over him, but he resisted the urge to rush in shouting her name. He crept along the wall and turned the corner to the front door.

The door was locked so he used his key and pushed it open an inch. He ran his fingers around the frame feeling for wires. An old Iraqi trick was to booby trap a house door to catch your enemy just when his guard is down as he thinks he's made it back home safe. Nothing, there was no sound. He crept in and checked the rooms one at a time finishing in the kitchen. He opened the laptop and checked. 'Oh Christ' he said aloud, 'the bastards must have her.'

'Dawes? Is that you?' her voice was muffled 'Dawes, fer fuck's sake help me out of here.'

His face lit up as relief flooded through him, 'where the hell are you, Brat?'

'I'm in the washing machine cramped to fuck, give us a hand yer ugly git.'

She sounded annoyed and relieved in equal measure. He opened the door and saw the washing moving then a hand stretched out followed by her face. He eased her out slowly, gently. It was obvious she was suffering awful cramp.

After half a minute's oh-ing and ouching and a few choice expletives, she was free. He picked her up and laid her on the table.

'Oh, god, Dawes' she said 'rub me legs will yer? I thought I was a goner in there.'

It took a full ten minutes before her circulation was fully restored and she could get up. Now it was time for questions.

'OK, Charlene, take your time and tell me everything that happened.'

'They came to kill us, a Russian guy and two English blokes. The Russian reported to Marcia, she's real bad news.'

'How do you know the guy was Russian and who's Marcia?'

'I've slept with Russian blokes; I know it when I hear it.'

'And Marcia?'

The Brat

'He used her name three times on the phone. She's an evil bitch, even Alexi don't give her no lip. She made me do things to her with me tongue, you know, down there.' She looked down at the floor shamefaced, her cheeks flushed. 'I hated doing that lezzie stuff.'

Dawson's eyebrows shot up, he'd heard of older women seducing under-aged boys, but young girls? Christ! Was there no end to the depravity this kid had been subjected to?

She went on to tell him everything she'd heard. 'I tried to run like you said but he had two blokes out back, waiting in the woods. The Russian bloke searched every cupboard I thought he was going to look in the washing machine, he was stood right next to it for ages. I nearly shit meself Dawes. He said he was coming back after dark.'

Dawson stared at her, feeling sheer admiration. She had realised in a flash that she had nowhere to run and that the place would be searched. She had snatched up the washing he'd left and squeezed herself into the family sized washer/drier, a feat both he and the Russian would have thought impossible and covered herself with his laundry. That was bloody quick thinking under pressure.

'Wow, I didn't think anyone could possibly get in there, Brat, it's such a small space.'

Fully recovered now she dropped over backwards into the crab position then, grabbing her ankles, she pulled her torso down to the floor until her head was between her feet. She grinned up at him.

'I've always been bendy. I can get through tiny windows in downstairs toilets that people leave open.'

He looked at her disapprovingly, 'yes, well, let's not go into that, we need to pack your stuff and get out of here.'

It was almost full dark now, so time was short. There were more questions, but they would have to wait. Dawson considered laying in ambush for the killer but that would mean having to shoot him. He would not expose Charlene to that, and his flashbacks would return in their full horror. No, the best option was to get her out of there right now.

'Go pack Charlene, there's a rucksack under my bed.' He left the house and ran down the track to his car. Jumping in, he drove up to the house. She was already at the front door, rucksack in hand. She didn't have much to pack.

At the track's end, they turned left onto the Isle of Skye road and headed towards Oldham. In the distance the lights of Manchester sparkled from horizon to horizon like diamonds on black velvet. Aeroplane landing lights on final approach to Manchester International Airport seemed to hang stationary in the sky for ages before swooping down like birds of prey.

The Brat

A car, it's lights on main beam, came around a bend towards them fast. Dawson flashed his lights to warn the other driver, but he didn't dip until he was almost past them.

'Stupid bugger' Dawson mumbled as the big Volvo sped past and continued up the hill.

'Oh, shit, Dawes, that was him, that was the car.'

'You sure, Brat?'

'Fuckin' right I am.'

'Stop that foul language, you hear?'

'Just move yer arse will yer, Dawes? The bastard looked right at me.'

Dawson hadn't seen the man through the oncoming headlights glare, but Charlene was certain. That was enough for him.

'OK, hang on, Brat.'

*

In the Volvo, Buchovski was about to dip his headlights for the approaching car when he got a glimpse of a young girl in the front passenger seat. He kept on main beam despite the other driver flashing him. The man was the target whose face was all over social media. He slammed on his brakes as the Mercedes disappeared round the bend.

Buchovski knew he was outgunned for speed, but the road eventually became a series of dangerous bends down steep hills that dropped away above the Dovestones reservoir. He had an eye for these things and a trained memory. Did Jukes know he was following him? Probably not.

There was a fair bit of traffic in both directions now so the Merc wouldn't be able to use its superior speed advantage even if Jukes knew he was being followed. Also, Buchovski was a Spetsnaz trained driver. He smiled, and tapped the 6P9 Pistolet Besshumnyj under his arm, the touch of the 300mm long double suppressed weapon gave him a warm feeling. He was the consummate professional; his targets would not elude him. He turned around in a field gateway and pushed the pedal, a bleak smile played about his mouth. This would be easy. Sod Marcia's instruction to bury them, his car was untraceable and his London alibi solid. Yes, he would enjoy this.

The Brat

Jaineba Shipley nee Thomas had the fine features of her Guyanese roots. She was tall and willowy and elegantly dressed in a light grey business suit that been sculpted millimetre perfect to her lithe figure. On the couch she put her arm around Joanne's shoulder looking deep into her eyes.

'Sweetheart, you know we're taking one hell of a risk with this, don't you?' She spoke with a refined West Indian lilt. Her large brown eyes were filled with concern 'If this guy Dawson Jukes can be perceived to have abducted this girl, we could be charged with assisting an offender.'

Joanne stroked her thigh gently 'Jaineba, darling, I've worked with Dawson on quite a few jobs now, he's a genuine bloke. If he says this young girl's life is in danger, I believe him. He only wants a safe place for her for a couple of days until he can find a social worker and an honest cop who'll protect her.'

Jaineba's mouth drooped under her creased brow, she looked far from being reassured.

'I'm a barrister, my love. If we get caught up in any wrongdoing, I could be struck off. Boom, end of career. We'd have to sell this place, probably my car, too. It's a hell of a risk.'

A weak smile struggled to Joanne's lips 'please, Jaineba,' she pleaded 'I've already told him yes. He'll be on his way over real soon. Please, just let's hear what they have to say, that's all I ask. If you decide against it, I'll accept that without question.'

Jaineba had agreed earlier when Joanne had first asked her but was now having second thoughts, her career and their whole future could be at stake.

She shrugged her shoulders in resignation, Jaineba found it difficult to refuse her wife anything 'Ok, Joanne, I'll go that far, now, how about a drink? I'm bloody parched.'

*

Dawson put half a mile behind him before glancing in the mirror. There were no lights behind. Then there was a lorry, big and wide, bumbling downhill in front of him at fifty-five miles per hour. He pulled out. Oncoming lights of another lorry were chugging up the hill, it was too close.

'Come on, for God's sake' he muttered. The oncoming lorry was being followed by a long convoy of cars held up by the slow mover. Overtaking was impossible. Then headlights appeared behind him closing rapidly.

The car behind closed to within five metres of the Mercedes and stayed there for a few seconds. Shooting at a moving vehicle from a moving vehicle through toughened glass whilst driving was purely the stuff of movies Dawson knew. If the guy, believed himself undiscovered, he would probably try a bump-stop.

Sure enough, the Volvo closed the gap and rammed him. The impact was not hard enough to

The Brat

destabilise either vehicle but if Dawson had been unaware of his purpose, he'd have pulled over, so he braked and indicated to pull in.

The uphill traffic continued to stream past. The blocking lorry was now three hundred and fifty metres in front of him. Dawson floored it, the Volvo responding instantly. With metres to spare before hitting the lorry, Dawson stamped on the brakes.

The Volvo's nose dipped as the driver braked hard, but the move had caught him off guard. He hit the Merc with a jolt. Dawson saw the airbags explode into the driver's shocked face. Blinded, the man lost control and slid sideways into the crash barrier.

Dawson breathed a sigh of relief 'That should hold him for a bit, Brat.'

There was no response. Charlene was staring white-faced through the windscreen her eyes like saucers. He patted her shoulder 'don't worry, Brat, we'll beat him.'

The road finally cleared, and Dawson overtook the lorry but to his dismay, there was another huge truck quarter of a mile further on disappearing round a sharp bend.

'Have we lost him Dawes?' Charlene asked, her voice shaking, she sounded as scared as on the night he'd found her.

There was no point lying to her. 'It depends on how damaged his car is. We'll see.'

She shrank into her seat whimpering.

It was several minutes before the Volvo picked them up again. The driver was pushing his car hard. The sharp bends were appearing in earnest now, making top speed difficult.

'He's back with us, Brat.'

Charlene started to cry. 'Jesus, Dawes, do something fer fuck's sake, *please.* Don't let him get us.'

He wished he'd said nothing. What could he say to her? He glanced in his mirror 'listen, Brat, that guy behind us is a good driver but he's cocky. He thinks he's better than me. He's not, OK?'

Then there was no more time, the Volvo had a clear run, and the guy was taking enormous risks speeding around the sharp bends. Dawson could see the car sliding but the guy was up to it, controlling the slides to his advantage. Well, two could play that game.

Dawson shot around the lorry in front pulling back in as an oncoming car braked hard and swerved, horn blaring as it flashed past. Dawson took the next two bends on tortured tyres. Charlene was screaming now, her hands over her eyes, but he ignored her.

'Oh, shit!' he said aloud as he rounded a bend. There was a huge tanker two hundred metres in front. His heart sank.

The gap closed. He could see the other driver, now, his white teeth bared, jaw tense.

The Brat

Dawson saw the man pull a long-barrelled gun and knew what he intended. He swerved the Merc right to overtake now a gap had suddenly appeared in front of him, but the tanker driver pulled into the centre of the road, sticking a one fingered salute out of his window, cruising on, barring the way.

The road was too narrow, squeezing past was impossible. Dawson blared his horn frantically jinking left and right and flashed his lights. He received the same aggressive response. Obviously, the tanker driver thought he was thwarting a couple of boy racers. Great sport for a bored truck driver.

Ahead, Dawson saw what their salvation could be. An empty layby made the road just wide enough. He pulled the wheel over right, then, when it seemed he must hit the steep roadside bank he swung hard left, slamming on the hand brake. The Merc's rear wheels locked, tyres screaming their smoking protest as the car slewed around in its own length. Braking hard, Dawson released the handbrake then shot off in the opposite direction. He swore in his mirror as he saw the other driver perform the same manoeuvre with expert skill. They were now travelling in the wrong direction, but Dawson had gained several hundred metres on their pursuer.

Charlene had pulled her knees up into her chest in the foetal position, her head was down, and she was howling.

Dawson considered going back to the house and getting his shotgun. He quickly dismissed the idea. They could have someone waiting to ambush them. Their pursuer was alone, but there were three men recorded on his laptop that afternoon. It was a risk too far.

Again, he was hampered by slower traffic. The road was a popular shortcut to Sheffield and the M1 Motorway, at this time of night; a lot of people were commuting.

The Volvo was gaining again as he pulled almost suicidal overtaking moves.

A large empty viewing point was signposted where people stopped off in the daytime to admire the scenery. Dawson drove in and spun the car around. Turning back onto the road, he drove straight at the oncoming Volvo, 'let's test the size of your bollocks, sunshine' he growled.

In the oncoming car Dawson saw the man pull down the sun visor but it was clear from his shielding hand that he was still being dazzled. With feet to go the Volvo driver chickened out. There was a cannon-shot bang as wing mirrors collided. For once there was some clear space and Dawson sped on

A Sunday driver bumbling his way timidly around the bends with seven cars queued behind him was Dawson's next problem. He glanced in his mirror. He was not the only one with problems. Steam was streaming from under the bonnet of the Volvo. If he

The Brat

could just get past this next obstruction, they may yet survive but the Volvo showed no sign of slowing, closing to with feet. The chasing driver swung left and then right clipping the rear of the Merc at an angle, trying to destabilize it. Dawson was up to it and straightened his car out.

The would-be assassin was losing his cool now. Dawson watched as the man drove up close, leaned out of the window and fired.

The Merc's already battered wing mirror exploded into a thousand silver shards that glistened in his one remaining headlight. Dawson swerved crazily left and right. This bloke was either lucky or a bloody good shot. He was almost at his wits end, now. Shaking this man off seemed like an impossibility. He'd practiced chase scenarios and done it for real a couple of times in Iraq, but this guy was in a different class.

Ahead, Dawson saw a slender chance, he instantly decided to take it before his pursuer's aim improved. He pulled out alongside the line of the seven cars and accelerated fiercely. The oncoming truck was closing fast. To his left was a faint gleam of water as the last glimmer of twilight struck the Dovestones reservoir far below. A cliff descended to the road on the right, an almost vertical drop on the left. There was no escape. The oncoming headlights grew larger, almost blinding him, the Volvo was hard behind. He was nearing the front of the line now as the lorry loomed like a primeval monster, horn blasting. Disaster was two seconds away. The Sunday driver saw the danger and slammed his brakes on, creating a gap for Dawson to squeeze into. The Volvo tried to follow and almost made it.

The lorry smashed the Volvo's rear end spinning it like a toy. Out of control, it hit the cliff on the right of the road then shot across the road narrowly missing the Sunday driver and careered over the safety barrier, turning end over end.

In his mirror Dawson saw the massive fireball as the Volvo's ruptured fuel tank exploded. He slowed to a reasonable speed 'we've lost him, Brat. For good this time.'

'I've wet myself, Dawes.'

He drew a deep breath then burst into loud nervous laughter as sheer relief coursed through him. 'Kids' he said, shaking his head in wonderment 'she's just escaped a murderous maniac and the first thing she worries about are her damp drawers.'

The speed limit changed to forty as they approached the bottom of the long descent. He turned right on Hollings Lane before the traffic island at the bottom. He wound his way through camera free country lanes not wanting to give anyone an easy time of tracking him. There would be people with footage on their dash cameras, of course, and the Police would inevitably catch up with him, but he

The Brat

needed a little time before that happened. Caution was now of utmost importance.

He brought up his Satnav route planner. They needed a supermarket, somewhere he could buy her some fresh clothes. He found what he was looking for and, using the quiet streets, made his way there. They parked in a back street and walked across the carpark.

Before she went to the toilet with the rucksack to change herself Charlene asked, 'you got any money Dawes?'

Sure, what do you need?'

She hesitated 'monthly stuff, you know?'

He gave her twenty-five pounds 'buy yourself some new jeans, too. Will that be enough?'

'Yeah, thanks.' She took the money and left 'see you back at the car, Dawes.'

He didn't like leaving her even for a minute unsupervised, but he also didn't want to embarrass them both by hanging around while she was choosing tampons. She came back to the car after twenty minutes full of smiles and handed him a pork pie, unwrapping one for herself. They sat munching away like hungry wolves swapping the occasional smile. She then delved into the rucksack and produced two cans of coke.

He frowned, a feeling of suspicion growing in his mind 'how much were the jean's, Brat?

'Twenty quid, why?'

89

And did you buy your hygiene stuff,'

She grinned 'sure' and produced a large pack of tampons which she waved in his face, laughing as he reddened.

'So, your stuff plus two pork pies and two cans of coke, what did that come to?'

'She gave him a mischievous smile 'they were on special offer.'

He reached for the rucksack and opened it. It was full of sweets, candy bars and a couple more pies and two more tins of coke.

'You didn't buy all this with a fiver, did you?'

'Course not, I nicked it' she beamed 'it's a doddle in these places if you go through the tills and pay for some of your stuff. You just need to know what you're doing.'

Dawson's face darkened and he threw the remnants of his pie onto the dashboard.

'Jesus Christ, Charlene.'

Charlene knew she was in trouble as it dawned on her that people from his world did not approve of stealing.

'If you had said you wanted that stuff, I'd have given you more money, no problem. What if you'd been caught, you silly little bugger?' He slammed the wheel with the heel of his hand 'they would have had to call someone from social services. What then? You'd be taken back to the very people you're running from.' His voice rose, he was striving to

The Brat

keep his temper, 'for a bright kid like you, that was a bloody dumb move.'

He was shouting now, 'am I wasting my time helping you? Bloody hell!' he brushed his hand over his hair and took several deep breaths to dispel his exasperation.

Her voice was quiet, full of contrition, there were tears brimming in her eyes 'I'm really sorry Dawes, I didn't think. I was so buzzed up at escaping that guy. I just did it because I was excited and because I could. I'll never do that again, I swear, and I'll not touch your friends' stuff, either. Please Dawes…'

He looked at her and shook his head, expelling a deep breath, his anger dissipating. Maybe he shouldn't be so mad at her, she was only a kid and she'd been exposed to a life where criminal behaviour was the norm. Was he expecting too much of her? Yeah, probably, he thought. He could see she was trembling, on the verge of breaking down completely. The adrenaline of the last half hour had worn off and the shock of the chase was catching up with her. He drove off, there were things that still needed saying but he'd give her a little time to restore her composure.

Finding a quiet street next to Heaton Park Dawson pulled over. His voice was calm now 'OK, Charlene, let's forget about that stuff you stole' he paused, eyeing her carefully. 'You must want to know where we're going and how I'm going to help you.'

Anthony Milligan

She looked like a scolded puppy, her face angled downward, staring up at him though long eyelashes 'will you call me Brat again, Dawes, please?'

He smiled, 'OK, Brat, you're forgiven, now listen up. I'm taking you to stay with two women. One of them is a good friend of mine. You're going to have to be on your best behaviour. These women are nice, you may even think they're posh, but they're not snobs and they are not fools either, so don't try anything clever, OK?'

'Do they have any kids my age?'

'No, they're a gay couple.'

Her reaction was instant 'I'm not staying with any fuckin' muff munchers' she spat and reach for the door handle.

Dawson grabbed her arm 'Listen to me, Brat, would I put you in any danger? These are kind and caring women. They're certainly not attracted to girls your age, or any other women for that matter' he sighed 'and don't use that vile term again. They are married gay women, OK?'

The fear was still in her eyes, but she was no longer trying to leave the car.

'Look, come along and meet them, if you don't feel comfortable we'll think of something else.' His face hardened 'there's every chance they won't like a snot-nosed little bugger like you.'

'OK, then, but if they're big and butch, there's no way Dawes. I'll be off first chance I get.'

The Brat

Dawson groaned 'You won't be a prisoner for God's sake, you can leave anytime you like. The only reason I'm taking you there is for your own safety until I can get something sorted for you with the authorities, some place where you'll be permanently safe.'

'OK,' she agreed, 'I trust you, Dawes, but what about Alexi?'

'I'll be visiting the Couscu's and this Marcia woman. They'll be *persuaded* to leave us alone.'

She gawped at him with open-mouthed disbelief, 'Christ, Dawes, they'll kill you. I saw a punter once who'd bashed a girl's face so she couldn't work. They broke both his arms.'

Dawson's eyes danced with amusement 'don't worry about me, Brat, I know what I'm doing, but don't tell the ladies, and maybe keep quiet about the chase tonight, OK? We don't want to put them off.'

He checked the car's rear end; the damage was not as bad as he had expected. They had lost the bumper and had a dented boot panel. Importantly, they still had one working light cluster. They drove off, the rest of the journey into Manchester was taut with worry in case the police stopped them, but they made it. Dawson stuck to the quieter roads, using the satnav's alternative route function but not entering their precise destination.

They parked in a side street two miles from Joanne's Didsbury address and walked a few blocks before hailing a taxi.

The house was a large, graceful Edwardian red bricked semi on a broad tree-lined street.

'We were expecting you sooner' Joanne said smiling.

'Traffic trouble' Dawson told her 'may I present Ms Charlene Keenan aka The Brat?'

'That's not very nice Dawson Jukes' Joanne admonished him, 'I'm sure Charlene's a very charming young lady if you treat her like one, you great oaf.'

They laughed as Charlene looked from one to the other, puzzled.

'Come and meet my Jaineba, Charlene, dear.' Joanne turned and led the way to the lounge. Hesitantly, Charlene followed.

In the spacious, beautifully appointed room Jaineba Shipley, rose from her armchair extending her manicured hand 'Hi, Charlene, I'm Jaineba, pleased to meet you.'

Charlene was awestruck, Jaineba was stunningly beautiful and dressed like a model in a long flowing yellow silk robe dress that complimented her ebony skin perfectly. She looked around the room the like of which she'd never seen before. These women were not at all what she'd imagined. They were

The Brat

stylish, elegant, well-spoken and exuded friendliness.

Joanne produced a large pot of tea and a plateful of butterscotch biscuits. She poured the tea and pointed to the biscuits 'help yourselves folks.'

Charlene snatched three biscuits like they were about to be taken away. The women exchanged looks but said nothing.

Jaineba smiled warmly 'Charlene' her voice was gentle, but her barrister's sharp mind was fully focused. 'I believe you've been having some serious trouble lately; I'd like to hear what's been happening to you in your own words. Could you do that, do you think?'

Charlene looked from Jaineba to Joanne then at Dawson who smiled and nodded reassuringly.

She started speaking, quite shyly at first, but with growing confidence as she went on. No one challenged her and Jaineba smiled encouragingly. The longer she spoke the more the women's faces grew sad and serious.

Charlene told her story in simple words that had a compelling ring of truth to them. She told of the father she had never known dying in prison, of her mother's descent into drugs and prostitution. Then the series of foster homes from the age of four. Of constantly being returned to her feckless mother after she'd supposedly been cleaned up. Her mother had quickly relapsed into her chaotic lifestyle. There were her mother's many boyfriends, too, who came and went. Some of these men treated her kindly, most ignored her, one sexually abused her. Later, she was taken into care when her mother did a spell in prison. She admitted to running away when she felt unhappy and of stealing to survive, of being returned and absconding again and again. She described her seduction and of being drawn into the world of child prostitution. She spoke animatedly of her refusal to take drugs 'I smoke a bit of weed sometimes, yeah, everyone does, but I told the bastards I'd only work if they stopped trying to shove drugs on me. No way am I ending up like my mother.' She told it all without a hint of self-pity, pausing only to remember names and places.

When she had finished Jaineba wiped her eye. 'Would you excuse us for a moment, please? She reached for Joanne's hand and the two women went hurriedly into the kitchen.

'What's up Dawes? Have I blown it? Do they think I'm a slag?'

It was the first time Dawson had heard her full harrowing story and he, too, was choked up. He coughed, trying to release the lump in his throat 'No, Brat, far from it. I think you just made yourself two good friends.'

'They're alright, aren't they, Dawes? They're not what I expected lesbians to be like.'

The Brat

In the kitchen, Joanne and Jaineba embraced, tears were streaming down Jaineba's cheeks. 'Good god, Joanne, is this really still happening to our disadvantaged children under our very noses? It's almost beyond comprehension.' She took a piece of kitchen towel and wiped her eyes then blew her nose. 'I thought this had all ended in 2012, when those men were convicted. How can it still be going on now?'

Joanne, as hard and worldly as she was, brushed a dewdrop from her nose with her sleeve 'I've worked with abused women and girls in Afghanistan. A lot of them were considered as of less value than cattle. Captured women were used as sex slaves, they usually died a brutal death. Dealing with it never gets any easier.' She looked at Jaineba lovingly 'It's hard my darling, but it still happens, I'm afraid.'

'But this is England, 2017, we're supposed to be a civilised nation, how *can* this still be going on here?'

Joanne took Jaineba's hand 'From what Charlene said, I believe it's even worse now than it was before those convictions. When the Russian Mafia organise something, they do a thorough job, and they are ruthless.'

'Russian Mafia? Surely not.'

Joanne shook her head 'Well, I can't be certain, of course, but there being older Eastern European women kept in locked houses, forced into prostitution, and this Russian woman Marcia

Catanova being involved, I'd say it has all the hallmarks.'

'But I thought they only operated in Russia?'

'Oh, dear, sweet Jaineba, you inhabit such a cosy corporate world. All those rich companies suing each other in courteous courtrooms before civilised judges. You see every shade of human greed, yes, but I have lived in a much different world.'

Jaineba looked pained 'It's not all about suing.' she sniffed defensively, 'mostly, it's advice on company law, mergers, takeovers, corporation tax and floatations, it's very intricate.' She looked peeved 'It can be extremely stressful, you know.'

'Sorry Jaineba, I'm not trying to put you down, my love, it's just that I've had to deal with some very nasty types. Take poor Dawson out there, he saves a silly woman from an acid attack caused largely by her own stupidity and what does she do?'

'Yes, I've seen it on social media, lunatics saying they'll hunt him down and bathe him in acid. It'll make him unemployable, won't it?'

'Not for long, we've got a few things in hand. Anyway, we digress, we must do what we can for this poor child, agreed?'

They returned to the lounge, Joanne telling Charlene she could stay for as long as she needed to. Jaineba admitted she was no expert in childcare law, but said she'd make enquiries among her colleagues.

The Brat

Dawson advised them the fewer people who knew Charlene was there the better. He gave Charlene a goodbye hug, she clung to him pushing her head into his side reluctant to let him go.

He closed the front door behind him knowing that he had to help, knowing also that he could be killed or arrested at any moment.

Chapter 9

Marcia Catanova paced the floor of her penthouse apartment, her brow deeply lined, mouth a tight, hard line. Her mind was spinning. That bloody idiot Buchovski had failed, getting himself killed in the process. Now there was publicity and wild speculation in the media. They'd found a sawn-off shotgun and a pistol in his car. Not any old pistol, oh, no, a bloody 6P9 for God's sake.

The rare Russian pistol with two built-in suppressors was specifically designed for the quietest of assassinations. Only the top echelon had access to it. That Buchovski was employed as a chauffeur at London's Russian Embassy was an added embarrassment. Dmitry would be incandescent.

Footage from several car cameras appeared on the local TV news and on social media. The car being chased was registered to one Dawson Jukes whom the police were anxious to trace. The police were also

The Brat

interested in the whereabouts of his metallic grey Mercedes Benz S350. Jukes had recently been linked to an alleged bodyguarding scandal involving the rapper Ms Jezebel Justiz. She alleged that he abandoned her to face an acid attacker alone.

All that, though it would bring enormous pressure from the Embassy, was not her main concern. It was a failed operation and Dmitry Nikoli Petronovski did not accept failure. He would want to know why she ordered the hit without first consulting him. Then, of course, she'd have to make good the fee. Buchovski had been expensive, $60,000 US for the pair paid up front at his insistence. He'd boasted that he never failed and hated killing clients who reneged on the balance after the job was done.

Then there were those two idiots she'd hurriedly recruited as back-stops to report anyone running. How much did they know? Would they keep their mouths shut? They were a loose end that she could deal with herself.

Catanova now saw her response to Charlene's insolence for what it was, a knee-jerk reaction based on emotion, not logic. Swanson had been right. No one listened to these kids and the cops were far too busy chasing hate crimes or doing headline-grabbing community projects.

After the arrest and conviction of a group of mostly Asian men on child sex charges, the media dropped the issue. The cops, too, had gone back to sleep. Job done, move on. This could wake them up again.

That kid, that bloody kid, her mind seethed. She was just a cheeky little bitch who had mouthed off calling her a fuckin' pimp's whore. She'd force-bedded her to humiliate her, threatening to hurt her friend Julie if she didn't comply. Now, it looked like a bad idea. She'd have to grovel to Dmitry, to offer restitution, to admit failure. There would be consequences.

Could she fix matters herself? This Jukes bloke was an enigma. Her sources were able to tell her that he was ex-military and that he'd done close protection work in Iraq. Normally obtaining a soldier's service record was easy but his was shrouded in secrecy. Ministerial authority required to access his file meant only one thing, he had worked on the dark side, he was something special. That he'd outdriven Buchovski pointed to that. Had the kid mentioned her? When she'd thrown her out the next morning, Charlene looked like she just wanted to forget the whole episode.

That she'd forced the girl to perform sex acts on her didn't matter. Dmitry couldn't care less if she were being buggered by baboons as long as she did her job. But the Jukes bloke would take some explaining. Who was he? What was the kid to him? Why was he involving himself in the affairs of a throwaway street urchin?

The Brat

Being totally amoral, Catanova could find no answers.

Catanova's thoughts went around and around in her head. Was killing them herself worth considering? If so, how could she accomplish it? She hadn't got long; the weekly conference was three days away.

In the event she didn't get her three days, Petronovski sent for her. His office was in his home, a modern mansion set in four hundred acres on the Wirral peninsular overlooking the widest part of the river Mersey.

The hour was early, the sun not yet up. Petronovski was dressed like an English country squire, a Purdey side-by-side double-barrelled shotgun over his arm. 'Walk with me' he commanded.

'I can explain, Dmitry….' she began.

He held a finger to his lips for silence and started walking through the grounds. He loaded the shotgun as they walked. For five minutes they walked on in silence, Catanova was quaking inside. If the bastard was going to shoot her why was he prolonging it? Surely, he wouldn't shoot without listening to her explanation.

They were alongside a coppice, a pair of startled pheasants flew up and he dispatched them with deadly speed and accuracy, that they were not in season meant nothing to him.

'Fetch them' he handed her a game bag and pointed to the fallen birds.

Catanova obeyed. The corpses felt warm and heavier than she expected, blood dripped from their mouths onto her shoes, disgusting her. Fear and revulsion spread through her as she returned with the kill.

He took the bag from her, slung the strap over his shoulder, then reloaded the Purdey, sliding the cartridges in with exaggerated care before snapping the gun shut. He walked over to a fallen log signalling her to sit next to him, his face unreadable.

'If there's one thing I cannot stand it's weak excuses for failure' Petronovski's voice held no emotion, his grey eyes as were as cold as tombstones. 'In view of your status and former excellent performance I rang Moscow for clearance to execute you rather than take the decision myself. They considered my request then asked me to be patient, to give you another chance. It would seem you've fucked the right people there. Make no mistake, though, Marcia, they left the final decision to me.'

Catanova remained silent knowing that any interruption would annoy him. Looking into his stony face she knew that death was one wrong word away.

'Come with me' he got up and walked into the woods. In a small clearing two men stood arms

The Brat

loosely at their sides behind them a freshly dug grave. He pointed 'get in.'

She looked at the men, they were large and fit looking ex-Speznaz types, escape would be impossible. Terror gripped her heart.

She climbed into the grave on trembling legs, it was barely three feet deep. The woods smelled of spring, the freshly dug earth, rich and fecund. There was an odour she had not smelled since she was a girl on the farm on the Russian Steppes. She wondered vaguely if some animal would dig her corpse up, then she wondered at her thoughts.

Despite her terror, she glared defiance at him. She would not plead.

'Lie down.'

A sudden surge of anger consumed her, and she screamed 'no. Fuck off, Dmitry, fuck you to hell' she spat, her voice ringing through the woods shrill and hate-filled 'I could run this operation better than you, that's why you want me dead, you fucking arsehole.'

His smile was bleak as he slowly raised the shotgun. She closed her eyes and lowered her head. He fired twice.

She opened her eyes again, wondering why she was still alive. She collapsed to her knees.

Petronovski beckoned the men who lifted her out of the grave, then he ordered them to return to the house.

Catanova stood, her trembling knees barely supporting her, hands shaking, her mind in turmoil. She'd heard of mock executions, never realising the terrible impact they had on the victims. Her legs gave way and she fell onto her hands and knees vomiting.

He reached down and helped her up 'you're not out of the woods yet' he told her with a twisted smile, revelling in his ironic pun. 'You performed well and passed my test, had you pleaded for your life you would now be dead.'

She wiped the puke from her lips on the back of her hand 'why?' it was the only word she could manage.

Petronovski started walking back to the house 'When I gave you the North West area two years ago, certain people expected you to fail. You didn't. You increased the turnover in drugs and prostitution one hundred and twenty percent. You discovered that child prostitution here was an amateur business run mainly by a few perverts. You organised it into a profitable arm of our vice trade. I was impressed.'

He stopped and turned to look her in the eye 'then for some reason you fuck up' he screamed, his face becoming aminated for the first time since they had left the house. 'You bed a young heterosexual girl sending her off the rails for God knows what reason. Where's the profit in that?' Then you order a hit without consultation, getting one of our best operators killed. Have you any idea of the

The Brat

embarrassment that caused me?' It was a rhetorical question.

He resumed his walk, his manner returning to his customary chill calm. 'Explain.'

She told him about Charlene discovering Swanson's identity, of her escape from the Couscu brothers and of Dawson Jukes' intervention. 'It should have been a straightforward execution' she said, 'it was supposed to happen at his house, quick and quiet, bodies buried, no clues, not roaring around country roads like some American gangster movie.'

They reached the house, Petronovski handed his game bag and gun to a servant. 'Fetch tea.'

They retired to a palatial drawing room where he waved her into an armchair. Tea served, Petronovski offered her lemon from a Georgian silver salver, which she declined.

After the servant had withdrawn, he looked at her keenly 'did you mean what you said about being able to run the entire division better than me?'

'I was angry. I thought I was about to die.'

'Answer my question.'

'No.'

'Good, I like ambition in my senior executives, but you are not yet ready, believe me, Marcia.' They drank in silence for a moment, an antique French clock began striking the hour. He glanced at his watch.

'You bedded that young girl at your place. That was a foolish thing to do. She now knows where you live and can describe the inside of your apartment. That could lead to trouble.'

'I'll deal with it, Dmitry.'

'Yes, you will. Also, you will repay Buchovski's fee by close of business this afternoon. I didn't order my men to refill that grave.

She looked into his soulless grey eyes; how many executions had this man ordered in his sixty years? 'Yes, Dmitry.'

'Do not underestimate this Dawson Jukes man. The girl, too, is reported as highly intelligent and spirited. You tried to intimidate her, but you failed, didn't you?'

'Yes, Dmitry.' Catanova's face burned red at the memory. The concierge who had been present when they entered her apartment building was still on duty when she let Charlene out in the early morning. The girl had run down the street a little way then turned and screamed 'you fuckin' dirty dike bitch, I hate you' before running off.

Petronovski finished his tea and arose, the interview over 'You have one week to clean up this dung pile. I remind you again, that grave remains open.'

Chapter 10

After Dawson had left Charlene with Joanne and Jaineba he went to collect his car. He now had more time but fewer resources. He couldn't risk going home and his car stood out like a bulldog's balls with its back end smashed in. He drove to Manchester airport and parked in the long-stay carpark in a corner bay, the vehicle's back end to the wall to hide the damage. Next, he drew £500 from the cash machine in the terminal building. It was the maximum cash amount his bank allowed in a single day.

It was ten thirty p.m. and he was dog tired. He hired a car with a lot of hassle because he was paying in cash. Finally, after arguing with an obtuse manager, he managed it. He drove down the road into the Northenden district, his head fuzzy with fatigue.

Spotting a nondescript B&B with a vacancy sign he pulled in. The owner was an Indian woman in her mid-fifties who eyed him suspiciously 'No luggage?'

'The Airline lost it; I'll pay cash up-front.'

She immediately doubled her price 'ninety pounds please.'

'Your sign says forty-five.'

'All those rooms are taken. Ninety pounds please.'

He was too tired to argue 'The breakfast will have to be bloody good' he snapped, shoving the notes into her ready hand. She showed him his room. He stripped and got into bed; sleep came immediately. Tomorrow he'd be busy, very busy.

He arose at 6 a.m. and showered, He switched on the TV, the local news announced they were looking for him. Hearing mumbling, he opened his door. In the hall he heard the landlady on the phone 'yes, I'm sure it is him.'

Breakfast would have to wait. He came up behind the woman as she replaced the phone. He leaned in her face baring his teeth 'If you remember my car reg, lady, you'd better up your fire insurance, I'm not a lone operator, understand?'

The woman shrank, terrified, he tore the page from her guest book, she knew what terrible vengeance Manchester gangs could extract. She bobbed her head 'OK mister, OK, I've forgotten you.'

Outside he started the car. He felt deep shame for frightening a lone woman, but he needed some time to work. He checked his phone, there was a message from Joanne sent late the previous night. *"She's a perfect angel, but why did you buy her so few*

The Brat

clothes? Off on a girls' shopping trip tomorrow morning. Coffee in town?"

He smiled; Charlene must be behaving herself. He texted back: "Too tight-fisted to spend on the kid. Sorry, no time for coffee."

*

Margaret Jennings was a journalist working at the Manchester Evening News, she was also Dawson's ex. His call came as a surprise. she agreed to meet him later that day in a quiet Northern Quarter restaurant for lunch.

Margaret was mystified. She knew he had been back from Iraq for months now, yet he had made no effort to contact her. Now, he reckoned he had a story of a scandal but would give no details over the phone. She'd seen the social media hoo-ha surrounding him and she didn't believe a word of it.

Margaret was intrigued to know what lay behind the allegations; it smelled of a possible exclusive on Jezebel Justiz.

Dawson kissed her cheek and they hugged, genuinely pleased to see each other. They sat in the furthest booth in a dark corner. Lunch was an amiable affair catching up on old times. The meal over, she became serious as he related the recent happenings.

Margaret's eyes looked sad 'so, child abuse has reared its ugly head again. I thought the police had cleared it all up.' She placed her hand on his arm 'you'll have to tread very carefully, Dawson. If you start throwing accusations at this Sergeant Swanson, his copper colleagues will close ranks. The reputational damage would be great, so they'll bend over backwards to protect him.'

'We've got Charlene's testimony, surely some of the other kids will testify too?'

She shook her head 'only incontrovertible evidence will suffice, Dawson, and that would be difficult to obtain. Street kids make notoriously difficult witnesses. A lot of them are too fearful of their abusers to speak out, others tend to embroider stuff. That leaves them wide open to experienced defence lawyers.'

'I see.'

She felt glum, watching his hopeful face slowly lose its enthusiasm, his eyes looking sad. 'Major investigative journalism is extremely expensive, Dawson, and the M.E.N is a small regional paper and not a rich one these days.'

'I see.'

'I'll run it past my editor and see what she says, but, with so little evidence, I'll be struggling. In the meantime, I know of one senior police officer who is dedicated to this task. She's Chief Superintendent Elise Elwin, and a voice crying in the wilderness.'

Margaret looked at his lived-in face, his anxious eyes, and felt the old pangs of wanting him, feeling

The Brat

the weight of his body on top of hers. Why did he choose to live such a bloody dangerous lifestyle? She pushed the thought aside.

'Also, I can put you in touch with Shakina Hussein, she's a social worker who is anxious to protect these children. Like all her kind, she has a huge workload, but she'll do her best for you.'

She glanced at her watch, 'I have to get back soon so spill the beans on Jezebel Justiz, what really happened?'

She was disappointed but not surprised when he told her lawyers were involved and he had been advised to say nothing.

*

After Margaret had gone, Dawson sat at the table nursing a coffee, his earlier mood of optimism was now a tattered remnant. In the cold light of day what real evidence had he got? The word of a semi-feral child and an alleged attempt on her life by some Russian mystery woman. He needed something concrete, something that would put these people behind bars. He sighed; it was going to be far more difficult than he imagined. His inner voice said *"well, give it up man, you've nothing to gain and you can't save the whole bloody world."*

'Bollocks to that' he muttered aloud and drew a stare from a passing waiter. He paid the tab and left.

Anthony Milligan

Dawson walked across to the Arndale Centre and bought a car charger for his phone and a cheap pay-as-you-go phone. He'd be harder to find if he used that. His cash was getting low now, so he drew another £500.

He rang Shakina Hussein, using Margaret's name to get through. He gave her the outline. She asked him to come into the office later that day after her shift finished 'is six o'clock OK?' she asked.

'Sure, see you then.'

He met her at her office entrance, a small thin woman with intelligent dark eyes and world-weary look. She was dressed in a hijab, anorak, jeans and trainers. Her smile was warm, but her eyes were wary. They went for a coffee nearby.

After he had explained the situation Shakina's eyes looked sad and tired 'We know it's still going on, of course, from the kids we meet. What I didn't know was the scale and organisation behind it, if what you say is true.'

He arched an eyebrow.

'Oh, I'm not calling you a liar, Mr. Jukes, it's just that I'm finding it difficult to absorb the full horror of it all and I've been a social worker for fifteen years.'

'The thing is can you find Charlene a place where she'll be safe?'

'I'm not her social worker but I can find out who is. If she's a serial absconder, we could be wasting

The Brat

our time. Childrens' homes are not prisons. If a child runs away there's not much we or their carers can do. Only serious offenders are sent to secure accommodation, but Charlene doesn't fall into that category.'

They left the café and went their separate ways, Shakina went home to cook the evening meal for her family, her day far from over.

A short time later, Dawson parked outside the gothic splendour of Rochdale Town Hall, he rang Greater Manchester Police and asked for an appointment with Chief Superintendent Elise Elwin. The civilian phone operator wanted to know the nature of his business. He simply told her it was regarding child abuse and refused to elaborate. Elwin wasn't on duty and he was advised to call next day after nine a.m. Dawson texted his new number to the people he thought should have it then switched off his old phone. If he was up against the Russian Mafia, they had huge resources and could locate him through it.

At a loose end until the next morning, Dawson left the car parked and walked around the town, getting a feel for the layout. The main shopping centre depressed him. Bookmakers' shops and charity outlets seemed to be the main occupiers of the high street interspersed with shuttered frontages of closed businesses.

The Couscu takeaway was slightly out of the town centre. On Drake Street, a tram trundled by looking garishly new against the backdrop of the tired Victorian buildings. What people he saw, though, looked cheerful enough as they went about their business.

He found the Kwik Kebab Kabin. Outside, a delivery man was making adjustments to his moped. Dawson walked around the back looking for cameras. There were none that he could see but kept his head down, his face under the long peak of an old baseball cap he'd taken from his Merc.

The shop had an open yard with a smelly overflowing waste bin. The shiny black Toyota looked out of place there. Dawson had never been an overly cautious man, Should he just barge in fists flying? He paused, pondering.

He saw Serge Couscu leave the back of the restaurant, both hands full of food takeaway bags. The guy threw them in the back of the four by four and climbed in the driver's seat. Why was he doing a delivery when he had a man standing idle out front?

Dawson slid into a nearby yard and waited until the four by four had gone past. He looked at his watch it was too early for the takeaway to be open, so where was he going with all that food?

Hurrying back to the main street, Dawson was in time to see the Toyota stopping at the traffic lights

The Brat

two hundred metres away. As he reached his car, he saw the vehicle turn left. He quickly followed. It was not a long journey.

He watched from his car across the street as Couscu carried the bags up the stairs of some dingy flats. He reappeared on the top floor walkway, stopped, looked around him, then let himself into one of the flats. Two minutes later he came back out, locked the door, tested it with a push, and made his way back to the Toyota.

Dawson watched him drive away, it had been no ordinary delivery for sure. He waited for five minutes to see if there were any more developments then he made his way to the flat. He lifted the letterbox, but it was blocked. The deadlock looked of top quality and he had no rakes anyway.

He knocked the door, waited a minute then knocked again. There was no response, so he went to the window. The blind was down, and he could see nothing. He tapped the glass with his keys, waited, then tapped again more insistently.

After another minute, the blind moved at one end and a frightened face appeared.

'You OK, love?'

The mousey girl spoke in a language he didn't understand, the double glazing muting her voice. He signalled with his hand to ask if she wanted out.

She nodded vigorously.

Anthony Milligan

Dawson thought hard, he couldn't kick the door in without making a lot of noise. If Couscu had friends here, he could be in trouble. He tried to indicate to the girl he was going for help. That posed a problem.

If he rang the police, the odds were the Couscu brothers would get to know long before a raid could be organised and move whoever was in the flat. However, he knew who had the key.

On the drive back to the Couscu's shop Dawson's anger and frustration ate at him, 'Just who the hell do these bastards think they are?' he muttered.

Noticing his fuel was low, he stopped at a garage to fill up. It was then he got an idea. He bought a petrol can and filled it.

Time, he thought, to spread a little fuckery.

The town hall clock was striking five as he got back to the shop. It was open but there were no customers inside. The delivery man was gone. Dawson made his way to the alley behind the premises. The black Toyota was parked in the yard. The back door stood open; the smell of stale cooking oil wafted into his nostrils.

Walking into the back of the shop he saw Serge with his back to him. He dropped him with a neck chop following up with a kick to the guts.

Serge groaned loudly, alerting Alexi who came out of a preparation room, knife in hand.

'What the fuck…?' He launched himself.

The Brat

Alexi was slow and Dawson deflected the knife thrust easily. He splayed his fingers, ramming them into his enemy's eyes, feeling them squelch.

Alexi screamed and dropped the knife as his hands flew to his face. He twisted away, staggering into the wall. With the man's back to him, it was easy for Dawson to kick through his legs crushing Alexi's groin on his instep and instantly ending the fight.

Taking his time Dawson removed a lace from one of Alexi's trainers and cut it in half.

He pulled Alexi's arms behind his back and tied a clove hitch around the base of each of his thumbs with barely two inches separating them. Next, he took the man's right leg, tucking his ankle behind his left knee in a figure of four. He raised the left foot and pushed it towards Alexi's head trapping the right foot in the crook of the knee. Taking the tied thumbs, he pulled them back, arching his prisoner's back as he hooked the shoelace over the left foot, immobilising the man completely.

He followed the same procedure with Serge who was beginning to regain his wits. He started shouting for help.

Dawson silenced him with a kick to the guts. 'Yeah, I'd better do something about that' he said and took the socks off each man in turn. He stuffed one sock into their mouths and tied it in place with the other one. He retrieved the Toyota's keys from Serge's pocket then lowered the roller shutter front leaving by the rear, driving the Toyota back to the flat.

As he entered the flat the occupants drew back in fear, eyeing him warily. 'Any of you speak English?' he asked.

His question was greeted with silence as the girls glanced at each other then at the open door behind him.

The mousy girl spoke 'who are you? What do you want?'

'I've come to help you, to take you from here. You are free, you understand? Free.'

'This is a trick, yes?'
'No trick, I've locked up Alexi and Serge, now you are free. Come with me.'

'You a policeman?'

Dawson was worried that one of his captives might free himself and get help, he didn't have time to explain.

He shrugged, spreading his hands 'No, I'm just a man who hates Alexi and Serge.' He expelled a loud breath 'look, I ain't got all day. You coming or staying?' He turned and left; behind him he heard the girls burst into loud, rapid conversation. As he reached the Toyota the first of the girls emerged from the flat. Now what the hell could he do with them?

It took just a few minutes for the girls to gather what few possessions they had and join him.

The Brat

'What's your name?' Dawson asked the mousy girl.

'Irena Adamkute, from Lithuania. Where are we going?'

'To the authorities, you'll be looked after.'

'We go to jail?'

'No, Irena, you'll be looked after, that's all I know.'

'What's your name, mister?'

'My name is not important. You're safe now, that's all you need to know.'

Ten minutes later Dawson stopped by the war memorial opposite the town hall and pointed to the police station. 'Go in there, tell them what happened, tell them the Couscu brothers are locked in their shop, you understand? They need arresting quickly.'

Irena started to ask another question. Dawson cut her off abruptly. 'Look, girl, you're free, I can't do any more. I have to go now, just tell the others where to go. You are not in any trouble. Now for Christ's sake just piss off.'

He leaned over and opened her door, she got out slowly and the others followed.

'Thank you, mister, God bless you.'

Dawson drove off, freeing these girls was bound to piss off some seriously bad people. Ah, what the hell, he thought in for a penny, in for a pound.

He retrieved the petrol can, from his car and drove the Toyota around the back of the town hall where there were acres of empty parking spaces. Stopping well clear of the building, he poured the fuel into the vehicle and spilt a trail for fifteen metres tossing the can back towards the car. He lit the trail and walked away hearing a satisfying whoosh as the vehicle went up in flames.

Reaching his car, he drove off in the direction of Manchester, releasing a satisfied sigh. 'Now, that's what I call spreading a little fuckery' he mused aloud.

Chapter 11

In Joanne's house Charlene sat at the computer, she couldn't believe what was being said about her beloved Dawes. 'Who put this crap up here, Joanne?' she asked, an angry frown spoiling her pretty face. 'I'm a fan of Jezebel's, I can't believe she'd say this shit.'

Joanne knew Charlene would find the stuff but to deny her access to the Internet would have been cruel to her way of thinking.

'None of that nonsense is true Charlene, Dawson would never abandon those he looks after. I was there at the time, so I know it's all lies. It was her manager, a man called Aaron Weitz who did this to gain cheap publicity.'

'What a lousy basta....sorry, the nasty man.'

Jaineba looked up from her magazine and smiled broadly 'you're coming on, Charlene, good effort. For what it's worth I think he's a lousy bastard, too.'

That night Charlene lay awake thinking. She felt angry and disappointed with Jezebel, wondering why she didn't tell the truth about Dawes. Dawson was the bravest, kindest man she'd ever met. He had saved Jezebel and he gets shit thrown at him.

It rankled Charlene deeply. She didn't have any social media accounts and even if she posted that Dawes was a good guy the trolls would still be just as nasty. She fell asleep wishing there was something she could do.

Next morning Joanne gave Charlene lessons in maths and English and was surprised at her ability and enthusiasm. They went on for four hours until Joanne said it was time for lunch. Afterward, Joanne had close quarter combat practice at her gym. She took Charlene with her.

Charlene sat awestruck as she watched Joanne being put through her paces by a thin, older oriental man. She was so graceful, yet so fierce in her practice. Charlene was scared and thrilled at the same time. Maybe she could grow up to be like her? Not the lesbian bit but to be able to fight like that would be great. What if Joanne was straight and married to Dawes? What if she were their daughter? At first the fantasy thrilled her then harsh reality made her feel sad and empty inside. She told herself it was crazy to dream such silly dreams.

After her session, Joanne came over smiling 'Sorry if you were bored Charlene, but I have to keep in practice for my job.'

The Brat

'Bored? No way! Can you teach me some of that stuff, please, Joanne?'

Joanne smiled, 'It takes years to learn Charlene not hours' then her face turned serious. 'I could teach you a few simple strikes, though, I've got a couple of hours.'

Charlene felt her heart soar and her face lit up 'great, I'll be able to make the bullies pay.'

Joanne's face went serious 'The moves I'm talking about could possibly kill, Charlene, this CQC stuff isn't a sport, there are no rules except win. You must never use this stuff to bully others, you must never go looking for a fight, OK?'

Charlene's face went contrite she was scared that Joanne would change her mind. 'I promise, Joanne, honest.'

Joanne taught her about throat chops, eye gouging, 'If you stamp on the ankle of a downed opponent you can break it. If they can't stand, they can't fight, Charlene.' She showed her vulnerable areas like the kidneys, liver, and spleen warning her that a hard strike could rupture the organ causing heavy internal bleeding leading to death. She taught her several ways of striking the male testicles. 'A man with badly bruised balls rapidly loses his enthusiasm for rape' she told her.

Joanne made her practice in slow motion. 'If you learn in slow motion your subconscious mind will learn accuracy.' Joanne was surprised at the girl's ability and athleticism, as she performed every move taught with ease. When the session was finished, Joanne went deadly serious. 'Practice in your room when you get up and before you go to sleep Charlene.'

She grinned, nodding eagerly. 'You bet your arse…. Oh, Sorry, Joanne, yes I will.'

Joanne looked stern 'don't be getting the idea that you're now an expert, Charlene, because you're not.' She placed both hands on her shoulders and stooped to look into her eyes. 'Never use this stuff unless you have to, Charlene, it could get you into a lot of trouble' Joanne's face grew less serious. 'But if you have to use it for real then don't hold back. Ninety percent of fights are won by the person who strikes the first blow. Don't give warnings and never make threats. Use it.'

It was a supremely happy child that left the gym. She couldn't wait to tell Dawes. Later, in her room, Charlene practiced the moves Joanne had taught her in front of the mirror, feeling her confidence rising.

Tired at last, she flopped on her bed. She thought about Dawson and her happy mood evaporated. Dawes could get hurt or even killed looking after her, it would be all her fault she told herself. Maybe she should get out of his life forever then he'd be safe. It was a thought that filled her with sadness and a tear fell onto her cheek.

The Brat

The other person Charlene thought about was Julie, her friend. She worried about her because she was so young and alone. She was only just thirteen but looked even younger. The other kids used her to run errands, fetching drugs, booze, and cigarettes. Alexi sold her to men who paid a high price for her childish looks, red hair and pale skin.

Julie had run away from a comfortable middle-class home because her parents were always fighting. Her dad drank and beat her mother. Her mother snorted cocaine to cope with life. There were terrible rows. She was being used as a weapon by them both. Her mother had gotten drunk one night and told her she couldn't leave her father thanks to her. If she didn't have to stay for her sake, she could start a new life. That's when Julie had run away and ended up under Alexi's control.

Charlene longed to see Julie, to comfort her and protect her as best she could. She was still a little child at heart, she had even run away with her teddy bear.

Maybe she should go and see her even at the risk of being caught by Alexi. Still thinking of her friend, she fell into a dream haunted sleep.

Chapter 12

Catanova sat at her desk, staring through the window with unseeing eyes. She'd heard the news that the Couscu's had been arrested and bailed. It seemed the sex slaves wouldn't give evidence against them fearing for their families back home. The six women had stated a desire to be sent home as soon as possible. The investment was lost and her relationship with Dmitry further soured. But what really scared her was that she would be next in line for a visit from Dawson Jukes.

She rang Petronovski 'this guy Jukes is a fucking maniac' she said, her voice shaking, 'the Couscu's are shitting themselves in case he goes back. God, Dmitry, I need some protection, the concierge at my place couldn't hold the bastard.'

Petronovski told her to calm down 'this could be exactly the opportunity we need. I'll send Ivanov over tomorrow morning to keep an eye on you.'

Catanova felt a little better knowing help was on the way but where to start? What action first? Word

The Brat

had also come that William Berg and John Nugent, the men she had hurriedly recruited to assist Buchovski, had been drinking and talking of a burglary they planned to do soon at a house on the moors. They were looking for an older car, one that would be easy to steal. Maybe there was an opportunity to kill three birds with one stone? She made some phone calls, arrangements were made.

She wished now she hadn't gone behind Dmitry's back. She'd done so because she knew he would never have sanctioned the killings. This is what happens, she told herself, when you allow your emotions to take over from common sense.

Self-analysis was something Catanova rarely did but now she thought about her motivations. Why did she hate Charlene Keenan so much? The truth dawned on her. The kid was very much like she had been at that age, tough, fiercely independent and mouthy. Charlene refused to do drugs apart from occasional cannabis, nor would she drink much alcohol, terrified she'd end up like her mother. She was highly intelligent with a 'fuck you' attitude. Too clever for her own good, she thought. Well, little girl, I'm cleverer than you, a lot cleverer.

A car was placed in a pub car park in Bury and Berg and Nugent made aware of its presence through an acquaintance. The car disappeared. The trap was set.

The following morning, Catanova received a phone call, the burglary was planned for that afternoon. She left Ivanov watching porn on her computer and made her way to Dawson Jukes' house dressed in a baggy dark boiler suit. Arriving early, she slipped on a full-face balaclava as a precaution. she would stay out of sight in the woods, there could be hikers in the vicinity who might get a glimpse of her. With Ivanov's sawn-off shotgun in her hand she crouched, waiting, watching.

At two thirty Berg and Nugent arrived, parking out of sight of the house they sneaked up the track and cut through the woods.

From her hiding place Catanova watched the pair approach the house. She smirked at their body language that shouted "we're up to no good" as they ducked and bobbed looking all around them furtively as they crept up to the front door. They knocked and waited barely thirty seconds before they started to work with the crowbar. She came up behind them.

'Turn around you two.' The crowbar fell with a thud as the startled pair spun. She signalled them to move away from the door with a wave of her weapon.

Sullenly they obeyed. 'We thought you lot had no use for it anymore' said Berg nervously 'it seemed like a good opportunity; we'll piss off if you like.'

She stood with her back to the front door and eyed the two men briefly. 'Thank you, gentlemen, you

The Brat

have been most useful.' Catanova grinned before shooting Berg in the chest. As he spun and dropped, she aimed at Nugent who screamed in horror. Belatedly, he turned and tried to run. Laughing, she allowed him to get ten metres before she shot him in the centre of his back. He jerked, his hands flying in the air as he pitched onto his face.

Catanova felt a surge of joy as she inspected her handiwork. Both men had died instantly. That was one less problem for her to worry about. She made her way through the woods back to her car. She knew the cops would start looking for Jukes in earnest now. Once he was in custody, she'd know where to find him. She knew the killings wouldn't stick and that he'd soon be released. Ivanov would be waiting when that happened.

By three forty-five she was back in her flat, weapon cleaned, parrying Ivanov's crude advances. She hated him but he was Dimitry's favourite thug, so she had to be careful around him. She knew she'd have to bed him eventually, but she would put it off as long as possible. It was a price worth paying for protection against Jukes.

Ivanov was pawing her again 'Pietre, slowly please, I'm not one of your whorehouse harlots. I'll make dinner tonight and afterwards we'll do it properly; it'll be worth the wait, I promise you. Besides, I need a bath after this afternoon's job.'

Ivanov looked sour; he'd wanted her for a long time, but she'd always rejected his advances. She was too high status just to grab and screw. Now he had the upper hand, and she couldn't refuse him.

'OK' he conceded 'but you'd better make it worth my while.'

He needed to cool down now 'I'm going outside for a smoke, I'll not move from the entrance door, so you'll be safe.'

*

Dawson drove to see Joanne, Jaineba, and Charlene, to give them an update on the care situation. Jaineba was at work when he got there.

'You know Marcia's address don't you, Brat?' he asked, 'I need to visit the lady to tell her fortune.'

Charlene said she didn't know the actual address but could lead him there.

Joanne was dead against this and said so.

'I'll stay in the car, Dawes, I'll just point it out as we drive past. I don't want to see that evil bitch ever again.'

Joanne reluctantly agreed 'just don't let this poor girl anywhere near that evil woman, OK?'

Arriving at the apartment building Dawson was dismayed to see a large man smoking outside the front door. He was watching every man that passed with suspicion. This presented a problem. He could

The Brat

hardly approach the bloke and thump him in the street.

'It looks like she's got some heavyweight protection, Brat.'

Charlene appreciated his problem at once. 'You got any money on you, Dawes?'

He was puzzled 'Yes, a couple of hundred, why?'

'Lend it to me and I'll get rid of that bloke.'

'Oh, no way, Brat, I can't let you near that goon.'

'Look, Dawes, the street's full of people, there are two blokes in that parked builder's van, and you'll be watching me, too. That big bastard ain't going to start nothin' with me, is he?'

'So, what's the plan?'

She looked him in the eyes, her face set hard. Gone the vulnerable child replaced now by a worldly-wise young woman. 'I ain't telling yer, it's something I can do, and you can't, now, gimme the money before I change my mind.'

He drew his wallet and reluctantly gave her the money. 'I'll be watching closely, at the first sign of trouble I'll be there, OK?'

Charlene left the car and walked up to the man. He looked at her puzzled.

'Excuse me, Mister, I think I know you' she said quietly. The traffic noise made him bend forward 'what was that?'

Charlene threw herself at the man, wrapping her arms around his neck 'No, no, I'll not have sex with you, leave me alone, leave me alone' she yelled. People passing stopped to stare. In the builder's van the two men stopped munching their sandwiches and looked across. 'Please, please help me' she screamed sounding distraught 'he's trying to force me to have sex, I'm only fourteen.'

Ivanov was stunned, 'What the fuck…? Piss off you little bitch.' He pushed her away and she fell to her knees only to rise again screaming hysterically.

People were stopping and staring, some reached for their phones to film the incident. The builders left their van and were crossing the broad pavement. Ivanov turned to the gathering crowd 'she's lying, the kid is lying' his voice sounded panicked.

'The burliest of the builders asked 'what's going on here, kid? Has this bloke upset you?'

Charlene was well into her act now; real tears were streaming down her face 'He's trying to take me in here for sex, mister. I'm only fourteen and I'm scared.'

Ivanov was recovering from his shock now 'I'm guarding this building, it's a ruse to get rid of me' his Russian accent was very pronounced as he desperately tried to explain himself. The builder hesitated and looked at Charlene. She pulled the bundled notes out of her pocket 'he tricked me into taking this money now he says I owe him sex.' She threw the money at Ivanov's feet 'I don't want your filthy money, pervert.'

The Brat

The builders had seen enough 'you dirty bastard' the biggest one spat, the second builder moved around the side of the Russian. A middle-aged woman in the crowd joined in

'I've heard of you foreign perverts coming here after our children' she shouted then ran in and swiped him with her handbag.

Ivanov was in meltdown now 'she's lying he screeched, the little bitch is lying.'

'Where would a young kid like her get all that money you evil bastard?' The builder hit Ivanov in the jaw, his mate added another to the side of his head. The crowd was cheering them on as Charlene scooped up the cash and scurried away.

Ivanov turned and fled pursued by an angry mob.

Dawson had stepped out of his car. He couldn't hear all that was going on, but he got the gist of it. He was in open-mouthed admiration for a few seconds then made his way across to the building. The concierge was leaning out of the open door gawping at the goings-on as Dawson pushed past him.

'Hang on a minute, sir, you can't just come in here.'

Dawson kept walking 'sorry mate, it's an emergency' hurrying past the lift, he went into the stairwell, taking the stairs two at a time. The sixty-four-year-old concierge tried to follow, but gave up after the first floor, wheezing and holding his chest.

Arriving at the penthouse twelve floors up, Dawson saw that the door was a good quality one but with only one lock. He pushed the top and felt it give. Putting his foot at the bottom he pushed, it also gave slightly. Great, not bolted, just hope there aren't too many of them in here. He placed his kick expertly.

The door crashed open as splinters flew from around the lock. He rushed in just as Catanova emerged from the bathroom. She aimed a karate kick at him which he deflected easily. Grabbing her throat, he squeezed her Adam's apple between forefinger and thumb fending off her flailing arms. Through the lounge, he saw a patio door leading on to a small balcony. He forced her backwards over to it. Sliding the door open he shoved her across the balcony until her back met the rail. He continued to push her slowly over until she could arch no further.

The rail dug hard into Catanova's back, her feet slipping as she scrabbled to hold on, her terrified eyes locked on his and saw no mercy. Desperately she tried to force herself upright, but he held her easily, like her honed body was no stronger than a child's. He eased the pressure on her throat, but he kept her there, one small push from death.

Dawson spoke with icy calmness 'you, lady, are beginning to boil my piss. Lay off Charlene and lay off the kids. This is the only warning you'll get. Come after me or mine, you're dead. Understand?'

The Brat

Wide-eyed she nodded, her constricted throat not allowing her to speak.

He released her and dragged her into the room throwing her onto a settee.

'Who do you work for anyway? Who is so fucking sick they'd sell young kids?'

She rubbed her throat, sense beginning to return, speech hurt like hell 'people who are much more powerful than you, Jukes' she croaked 'you'll be squashed like a bug you bastard.'

'Well, in that case, maybe I should kill you now.'

She assessed him rapidly. She knew men and this one would kill, sure, but not in cold blood. 'If you were going to kill me, you'd have done it already.'

'My guess is Russian mafia' he told her 'I used to belong to a powerful organisation, too. I still have excellent contacts. Know this: Even if I'm killed, you will not survive, OK? Your destruction is guaranteed. You have been warned.' He took her little finger and watched her horrified face as he bent it back until it broke. He left her shrieking and rolling on the floor, clutching her hand to her chest.

He arrived at the lift just as it stopped, and the doors hissed open. A soaking wet Ivanov looked up in surprise a split second before a hard-edged hand chopped him across the throat. He went down clutching at his windpipe gagging and choking.

'Don't worry pal you'll not die' Dawson tore the guy's hand from his throat and bent his pinkie back until he felt the satisfying crack of bone. He grabbed the man by the collar and belt, dragging him out of the lift. Ivanov was on his knees and elbows clutching his throat, his little finger hanging uselessly. Dawson swung his right foot hard between the man's spread legs catching him full in the balls. Ivanov rolled into the foetal position with a choking scream.

'Not your lucky day is it, pal?'

At his car, Dawson saw he'd got a parking ticket. He was retrieving it when Charlene came up behind him. 'Hi Dawes, how did it go?'

He turned to see her, eyes sparkling, a huge smile on her angelic face. 'It went very well, Brat, thanks entirely to you.'

'Did you kill the bitch?'

Dawson studied her face, he realised she was serious. He shook his head in disbelief, this kid was revealing surprise after surprise 'would it bother you if I had?'

'Hell, no, I'd go out and get smashed.'

'Killing people is a last resort, Brat, not a first one. I gave her a bit of attitude adjustment therapy, that's all. If she has any sense, she'll back off.'

'Do you think she will, Dawes?'

'Not for a minute, now, get in the car we need to be gone.'

They drove off, she handed back his money. 'I was good in drama classes at school, Dawes, it was my

The Brat

favourite subject. They teach you how to project emotions and how to use props n' stuff.'

He grinned broadly 'I'll tell you what, Brat, for that performance, I'm going to open a savings account for you with that money, how's that?'

Her face lit up like a Christmas tree, excitement at her recent adventure bubbling over 'really? Wow, Dawes, that's fuckin' sick.'

He frowned; the language sounded so wrong coming from the mouth of a young girl. 'You're going to have to learn to stop using that language, Charlene' he said sharply, 'it really doesn't sound good.'

Her mood of joy instantly evaporated 'you're pissed off with me, now, aren't you?'

He thumped the steering wheel in frustration 'there you go again. Look, Charlene, I know you've lived a rough life with some very dodgy people, but will you promise me you'll try to improve your language, eh?'

'OK, Dawes, I'll really try hard. I haven't smoked ganja since I met you. I hate drugs, they ruined my mum's life. I don't want to end up like her but sometimes I needed it to sleep with those smelly old men. It made it easier, you know?'

He glanced across at her, was she acting now? Making the noises she thought would bring sympathy? He decided she was being straight. 'OK,

Brat, that's fine by me, as long as you *try*, I'll forgive the odd slip-up.'

As they approached Joanne's house, she said 'better not tell the ladies what I did Dawes, they wouldn't be happy with you for letting me, and I don't want them to think I'm a slag.'

He smiled broadly at her; his former annoyance completely melted. This kid really had some smarts 'I think you're right, Brat, I think you're right.' His smile beamed but, in his heart, Dawson was a worried man. He'd kicked a Russian bear in the balls, and some seriously violent and well-organised criminals would be out for revenge.

Catanova practically screamed down the phone 'I tell you, Dmitry, this guy Jukes is barking fucking mad. I thought I was dead.' Petronovski went to speak but she rushed on 'he and that fucking kid set a mob on Ivanov, claiming he wanted to fuck her. He had to swim a canal to escape. He got back as quick as he could but ran into Jukes. The bastard half choked him, broke his finger just like mine, and pulped his bollocks. He was taken away by ambulance.'

*

Petronovski's mouth tightened and his eyes narrowed. He lit a cigarette as he listened with growing dismay, Ivanov was his best man. How could this have happened? Who the hell was this Jukes guy who had walked into their business and created mayhem? It was all her fault, of course, and she would pay with her life, but not yet. Not until these problems were cleared up. He'd have to become personally involved now. Clearly, Catanova was incapable of containing the situation, however, she might yet make a useful scapegoat.

'Why wasn't Ivanov in your flat?'

'Because he wanted to fuck me, and I wanted a bath. He went downstairs for a smoke.'

A loud, impatient grunt silenced her, Petronovski had heard enough 'I'll speak to my people, somebody must know about this guy and how to get to him.' he paused, allowing the silence to grow then he said 'you have created these difficulties Marcia and you have mishandled the situation from the start. I am a patient man, but my patience is wearing thin.'

There was desperation in her voice now as her hand tightened on her phone, she winced as her splinted finger came under pressure, her face screwed up tight 'I will handle it Dmitry, believe me, I will.'

'Your grave remains open' he intoned and hung up.

Petronovski was a worried man, this could reflect badly on him if he was not careful. Moscow didn't accept excuses for failure. Catanova was his protégé so her failure would be treated as his. The recent contract to recruit spies and carry out executions was extremely lucrative, but only if successful. The only saving grace was that it was Moscow's request to give her a second chance, not his. She would have to die now whatever the outcome, and finding a replacement would not be easy, still, it must be done. He took out his encrypted phone and called Moscow.

Chapter 13

Dawson walked into Greater Manchester police headquarters with solicitor Moshe Bergman and was promptly arrested on suspicion of murder. It was a shock for both himself and Bergman. He had been expecting to be questioned about the driving incident. The young solicitor pushed his John Lennon spectacles up his nose and looked from his client to the Detective Sergeant, a worried look on his long pale face. Detective Sergeant Griffin, the arresting officer, seemed quite aggressive and took no action when Dawson told him he had an appointment with Chief Superintendent Elise Elwin.

In the interview room, Dawson was reminded of his rights. The interview was being conducted slowly and methodically until Dawson said, 'I take it you've been into my house looking for clues?'

Griffin acknowledged that they had. 'We obtained a warrant, Mr. Jukes, it was all done legally.'

'I'm sure it was, I'm also sure you are unable to obtain access to my laptop.'

'The Laptop is with the computer experts now sir being forensically analysed. Why is that important to you?'

'Because it contains footage from my security cameras, the real murderer will be on it.'

'I was on that search sir, and neither I nor any crime scene officer saw any security cameras.

'Dawson smiled 'you probably did see one of them. Two hundred metres down the track there's a crow in a tree, it has realistic feathers that flutter in the breeze. Its head moves to follow what it sees. It can flap its wings, it can even caw.'

'And why would you want it to attract attention to itself?'

'So that an intruder looks towards it and I get a full-faced shot of them.'

Moshe Bergman spoke 'officer, Mr Jukes is trying to be helpful. If the computer can be made available, I'm sure he'll access it and perhaps we'll obtain valuable evidence.'

Griffin looked irked, like a man who was losing control of the interview. 'we'll see' he said stubbornly.

'I would have thought the sooner the better, officer, your time is valuable.'

Griffin scowled 'OK, I'll see if the computer can be made available. Interview suspended at 1404 hours.'

The Brat

The laptop was produced. Dawson rapidly accessed the footage. The murderer was there, a tall figure in a baggy boiler suit with full face cover walking up the track to disappear into the woods. Then, half an hour later, the two victims arrived looking about them as they approached. The figure was seen again, the men moved out into the front garden where they were shot.

'That person certainly doesn't look like my client Detective Sergeant, as you can plainly see Mr. Jukes is a large, muscular man, that figure looked slim despite the baggy suit.'

'That's for the forensic analysts to decide, sir' Griffin told the lawyer.

'Can you account for your movements around that time, Mr. Jukes?'

'No.' He didn't want to disclose that he'd been with Charlene and Joanne at the time. Only if it became vital later would he do so. He knew what was coming next.

'Really?'

'I've been moving around a lot; certain people want me dead.'

Griffin inwardly agreed that the figure in the video footage was highly unlikely to be Jukes. In fact, he thought it could be female judging by the hip movement although the figure appeared to be taller than the average woman. Forensics would give him the height to the nearest centimetre later.

'OK sir, we'll move on to other matters for the moment. We recently recovered your car from Manchester airport following our investigations into a fatal road incident. Several motorists have provided footage of your car being driven in a highly dangerous manner. As a result of this dangerous driving, a motorist, who appeared to be racing you, crashed, receiving fatal injuries. What have you to say about that, sir?'

'He was trying to assassinate me because he had been instructed to do so by the Russian mafia.'

Griffin raised an eyebrow, his mouth went into a tight thin line 'and why do the er… Russian mafia want you dead, sir?'

Because I know of a corrupt police officer who is working with them and providing information. He is probably doctoring his reports to aid child prostitution. There is also a racket in foreign women being brought into the country to work in massage parlours and brothels.'

'And you have evidence of this activity?'

'Recently there have been women freed in Rochdale as you know. It was me who freed them. As for evidence of child prostitution, I have evidence from one child who would be willing to testify.'

'Then why don't you hand over this so-called evidence and let us be the judge of that?'

'Because you've already judged it, officer, otherwise you would not have used the term 'so-

The Brat

called.' Dawson was tiring of the bullshit. 'It's common knowledge that the car chasing me contained a pistol and a sawn-off shotgun. He wasn't out shooting rabbits, was he?' Griffin remained impassive. 'Also, you know that a bullet shattered my wing mirror. Do you reckon I did that myself?' Before Griffin could answer, Dawson turned to the one-way mirror 'Would you please come in now, Chief Superintendent Elwin?'

Griffin looked surprised and took a sip of water to cover his confusion. The door opened and she came in. Elwin took a seat, her face unreadable.

'I believe you know the whereabouts of a child who is a victim of sexual exploitation, Mr. Jukes?'

'I do, she's safe for now.'

'How did you first encounter her?'

Dawson explained, leaving nothing out except his treatment of the unholy trio.

Elwin was silent for a moment then she said, 'are you aware that concealing this child is unlawful?'

'Mr. Jukes is acting in the child's best interests; she was a passenger in his car when the attempted assassination took place. My client was not the only target.' Bergman, who had a daughter himself, had been horrified but not surprised by the details he'd been given.

Elwin looked stern 'I think we professionals are best placed to protect her, Mr. Bergman. I must insist that her whereabouts be disclosed at once or charges may be brought against your client.'

Dawson's patience snapped, he leaned across the table, eyes blazing 'Look, lady, how many times have you stood before the TV cameras mouthing platitudes, eh?' he was practically spitting now. 'Lessons will be learned, procedures will be altered, blah, blah bloody blah! And yet it still goes on, children in official care slip through the net time and time again. You move on alright but bugger-all changes.'

She blanched visibly at his vehemence. The truth of what he said was not lost on her, either. Her force was overstretched, the social services even more so. However, she must be seen to be following the party line on camera.

'Mr. Jukes, we are quite capable of ensuring her safety, we have safe houses, she can be accommodated.'

'Even if you took her immediately to a safe house, your corrupt officer would know the locations of them all, Charlene will be abducted and murdered. I will not take that risk. I intend to keep her safe until social services can guarantee a place of safety.'

It was an impasse, Elwin secretly agreed with Dawson. She had known for some time that things were far from right in Rochdale. She'd put him in a cell for a few hours to see if that softened his position, but she had serious doubts that it would.

The Brat

Three hours later Elwin took Dawson his meal. The custody Sergeant's eyebrows went up a bit at the sight of a senior officer performing this menial task, but that didn't matter.

'This is off the record Mr. Jukes' Elwin said. 'I know that there is corruption in the force, our sexual health team isn't stupid. The street girls talk to them. Getting reliable evidence, though, is another matter.' She sighed, 'I believe you are doing what you think is best. I can only stress to social services the urgency of the case, I cannot put pressure on them.'

He believed her; Margaret was no fool. If she said this officer was sincerely trying to make a difference, she was. Still, he wouldn't mention the name of the corrupt officer, the risk of him getting to know was too high.

'As you know, Chief Inspector, I'm a professional bodyguard, I have experience in close protection. I believe I'm Charlene's best hope right now. I am not anti-police, I know you are sincere, but I will not risk Charlene's safety simply to comply with faceless bureaucracy.'

She paused for a moment assessing him carefully then changed the subject 'have you come across the names Dmitry Nikoli Petronovski or Marcia Catanova?'

'I've heard of Marcia Catanova, she molested Charlene. Who is this Petronovski guy?'

'A Russian businessman who lives in Cheshire, we suspect he's behind a lot of organised crime here in the North West. One of his interests is brothels and massage parlours. Marcia Catanova is thought to be one of his senior lieutenants.'

Dawson made a mental note of the name, he would look him up.

Elwin looked at him quizzically 'We have recent intelligence that a vehicle was burned out in Rochdale and two takeaway owners were assaulted and tied up before being arrested. Catanova, too, was also assaulted in her penthouse the following day. Her bodyguard was hospitalised by a large man answering to your description. This was your doing, of course.'

'No comment.'

She was curious having done background checks on him. She knew he had worked in Iraq as a highly paid minder, but she had not been able to access his military record. She was told her investigation did not reach the required threshold. If a murder inquiry wasn't a high enough priority, then what the hell was? The man fascinated her.

'I must warn you, Mr. Jukes, that you are working against the interests of some highly dangerous people. I urge you to be most careful about what you do next.'

The Brat

Dawson smiled bleakly 'yeah, like being shot at and damn near driven off the road. Don't worry, I'll be very watchful.'

'I'll have you released under investigation. You'll not be on bail and no conditions will be attached.' She gave him her card 'That number will put you through straight to me, should you obtain any more evidence on the child abuse, bring it to me only.'

Dawson stood outside the police station's rear entrance and looked around, the place was busy with police vehicles coming and going. He had an idea there would be someone watching the front. The back alley was narrow, there was no convenient place to watch from. He switched on his phone. There were three voice messages, one from Joanne, one from Shakina Hussein and one from Margaret. He took Hussein's message first hoping for news of a safe berth being found for Charlene. 'Hi, Mr. Jukes, Shakina here, I reported our conversation to my department head as I am obliged to do. She was not impressed and went to court this morning and obtained a place of safety order for Charlene. You have been ordered by the court to hand her over immediately to social workers. Failure to do so will make you liable to arrest.' She went on the explain that a POSO could not be challenged for twenty-eight days. 'I'm sorry Mr. Jukes but my hands are tied.'

His heart felt heavy as he opened Joanne's voicemail. 'Dawson, ring me as soon as you get this. Charlene's gone.'

Chapter 14

Charlene took the tram to Rochdale and made her way to the meat rack. No one had seen Julie for a couple of days. She searched the usual haunts in vain. After combing the town centre and the local parks it was almost time for the Kulaks to arrive. There was one last place she could look, the abandoned warehouse. Two kids had been badly hurt there the previous month when part of a wall collapsed, the whole place reeked of decay, so no one used it anymore.

'Julie? Julie, it's me, Charlene. Are you in here?' The weak sunlight slanted through the roof and the gaps that were once windows. The place stank of urine and faeces. She was startled as a gust of wind sent dust and debris falling to the floor a few feet from her, raising even more dust. A rat scurried close by causing her to shiver with revulsion. 'Julie, girl, if you're in here give us a shout.' There was a faint moan from the far corner, Charlene strained her eyes and caught a slight movement. 'Oh, Julie.'

She made her way over broken machinery parts and fallen girders fearing that at any moment the creaking building would fall on her. Julie was lying on an old mattress, a plastic bag clutched over her mouth and nostrils. A strong odour of solvent pervaded the area. 'Oh, Julie, what the fuck are you doing, girl?'

Julie looked up through hazy eyes 'Hi, Shar, can't take it anymore, mate. I just want out; I want to be dead.'

Charlene was close to tears as she looked at her friend's small, wasted frame. Her once beautiful red hair was a tousled mess, and her face and clothes were filthy. She raised her gently and held her to her bosom, rocking her like a baby. Tears were running down Charlene's face, 'You're my best friend, Julie. I've come to help you. I know a bloke, a great bloke, he'll help us.'

'Someone you're fucking?' she slurred.

'Dawes is not like that, Julie, he wants to help. He's kicked the shit out of some of them already.'

But Julie hadn't heard her, she'd drifted off on a sea of fumes. Charlene threw the bag aside and tried to lift her friend, but she was a dead weight. She got her hands under her arms and began to slowly drag her. It was hard work, the rubble-strewn floor snagging on just about every part of Julie's body and clothes. Finally, she got her out and pulled her into a clump of bushes out of sight of the canal towpath.

The Brat

She'd heard of the kiss of life but had only a vague idea of how to perform it. She bent over, blowing air into Julie's lips.

'You fancy her that much, eh?'

Charlene whipped around to see Jason Blunt, one of the Kulaks, a large mixed-race lout of around sixteen years.

'We've been looking for you for days, bitch, Alexi will pay me big time for you.'

Charlene looked around desperate for a way out, if she could get past him onto the towpath, she stood a chance. He was strong and heavy but an over-fondness for smoking skunk made him no runner.

'They said down the meat rack that you were back. Looking for your next fuck are yer, whore, or is it her you fancy?' He sneered as he saw her eyes darting left and right.

'You think we're stupid? Mark's on the bridge, there's a ten-foot wall behind you That only leaves me. You coming quiet or do I have to hurt you?'

Charlene gritted her teeth, she was scared, and her insides fluttered but she'd be damned if she'd give up tamely. She remembered what Joanne had taught her. Could she do it? Julie moaned softly. Charlene made her mind up 'You'll have to drag me, wanker.'

Blunt looked surprised and lunged for her. Charlene stepped inside his grasping arms as she stiffened her spread fingers. She rammed the two middle ones hard into his eyes, following through as she'd practiced. The effect amazed her. Blunt reeled back screaming, his hands flying to his face. Joanne had said that's what would happen, but she was still surprised it worked so well.

Blunt fell to the floor howling 'Mark, Mark.' She stamped hard on his ankle, but she was not heavy enough to break it, still, she could tell from his scream of pain she had hurt him badly.

'Fuck you, arsehole' she screeched.

*

Standing on a footbridge over the canal some fifty metres away, Mark Bailey heard Blunt scream and yell his name. A chill ran through him, the kid must have used a knife or something. He started running towards the sound as Charlene burst from the bushes and sprinted in the opposite direction back towards the meat rack.

She burst onto the scene as a bunch of kids were deep in conversation. 'Whoever grassed me up is fuckin' dead when I get 'em' she shouted and then continued her run.

Bailey realised he wasn't going to catch her and pulled out his phone.

Charlene was out on the main road now but knew she was not out of danger. She looked around, she needed somewhere to hide until it was dark. She had left the phone Joanne had given her behind because she thought they could track her by it. Now, she

The Brat

wished she hadn't. The Kulaks would be out on mountain bikes looking for her. The tram was her best bet to get back into Manchester, but they'd think of that and have people watching for her.

She ran on further up the street. A boy raced past her on a bike, she slowed then breathed a sigh of relief as he threw the machine down outside a newsagent's shop and went inside.

It was an opportunity she took. Grabbing the bike, she pedalled off swiftly as the owner's despairing shout sounded behind her.

Charlene knew she could access the canal towpath further down the road. The Rochdale canal ran into Manchester city centre. They wouldn't think she'd return to the canal. Not straight away at least, but it was many miles to Manchester.

After ten minutes furious pedalling, she stopped and adjusted the saddle, her efforts would be more efficient now. She steadied her pace a little but was still going too fast in her desperation to escape. Every few hundred yards she glanced behind her seeing only a couple of dog walkers and a few adult cyclists travelling at a moderate pace. The Canada geese hissed at her as she passed, and a graceful swan cruised up to meet her hopeful of a free hand-out. A Grey Heron took off and flew a hundred metres down the canal. It was a quict, peaceful place, only the sound of her hissing tyres and her own breathing intruded.

She peddled on, wondering if she should leave the towpath and risk getting lost in the myriad side streets. She decided to stay on the towpath, she knew where it went. But how long before they figured it out? How long before pursuit began?

*

In Rochdale, Alexi took the call from Bailey, his anger a throbbing entity in his chest. 'Get out, look for her,' he spat 'two hundred pounds for whoever brings her to me.'

Bailey hit his phone spreading the word among the Kulaks, 'fifty quid for whoever brings her to me.'

He had an idea. Charlene had been talking to Julie, maybe she knew where she was going, where she was staying. He ran back to the canal warehouse where he found Julie sitting up on the grass, looking bemused, her eyes hazy. He grabbed her arm twisting it viciously, 'Where's your friend live, bitch? Where's she going, eh?'

Julie looked confused 'Dunno, she never said.'

'Don't bullshit me you lying little bastard, she's your best mate, she must have told you.'

Julie's face twisted, 'told yer, I dunno, you're hurting me, leave me alone.'

Bailey hauled her to her feet, dragging her to the canal where he threw her down, thrusting her head under the water. He held her until the bubbles

The Brat

streamed up, her feet scrabbling on the towpath. He lifted her out. 'Where the fuck is she, bitch?'

Julie was terrified as she coughed out a mouthful of filthy water, her face stark, her eyes bulging 'I dunno Mark, honest' she spluttered.

As he started to push her head back towards the water she screamed 'Please Mark, I don't know.'

'Bollocks' he growled and ducked her again, this time for longer. The bubbles stopped and her arms and feet ceased their helpless thrashing. When Bailey dragged her out again, she was not breathing.

'Fuck, now I'll never know' he mumbled. He looked around carefully, there was no one in sight. He rolled his victim into the canal where she slowly floated away face down.

Bailey walked away with no more regard for Julie than a drowned rat. As he reached the meat rack his phone buzzed.

'I've found a kid who said a blonde girl nicked his bike. He said she was heading towards the canal.'

Bailey's dark eyes glinted in his rat-like face, in front of him, one of the junior Kulaks leaned on his bike awaiting orders. He grabbed the machine and adjusted the saddle.

'I'm borrowing this.' The lad gave him no argument.

Bailey thought about what he would do in her situation. She wouldn't want to peddle around the streets, too many other kids might see her. There was a Kulak at the tram stop looking out for her, so she hadn't ridden there. The canal made perfect sense. He smirked as he took off.

After a short ride along the towpath, Bailey saw two young guys fishing. 'Hi lads, have you seen a young girl on a bike pass this way? The little bitch just nicked my brother's bike.'

One kid looked up 'yeah, about fifteen minutes ago, riding like the clappers, damn near knocked into us.' He pointed down the towpath 'Yer'll need to be quick.'

'Thanks mate' he said, a smug smile of satisfaction on his face as he rode off in pursuit. She would look behind her for a while then, when she saw no one following her, she'd slow down. She couldn't sprint all the way to Manchester, it had to be around fifteen miles.

The bike Charlene had stolen was a child's bike with twenty-four-inch wheels and fifteen gears, the one Bailey had borrowed was adult sized with twenty-eight-inch wheels and twenty-one gears. He set off at a fast but sustainable pace, the towpath flying rapidly beneath his wheels.

*

Charlene had looked behind her at regular intervals for the first fifteen minutes of her desperate ride. She'd gone off far too quickly and now the lactic acid burned in her calves and her thighs shook.

The Brat

She considered dismounting and taking a rest but elected to slow right down instead, that way she'd still make some progress whilst recovering.

A while later she passed a man riding sedately towards her, his white cycle lamp flashing. It was almost completely dark now.

'You should get some lights on that bike, young lady' he said as he passed.

She cycled on feeling a little stronger now. Then from behind her came a shout of annoyance. Charlene looked back in alarm the man was standing on the towpath waving his fist at a dark figure pedalling furiously towards her. Her heart sank.

*

His phone rang, 'Any sign of her yet, Dawson?' It was Jaineba, her voice reflecting the anxiety she felt,

'I'm afraid not Jaineba. They've fished a young girl's body from the canal just now, but it wasn't Charlene. I only got a glimpse, but she had red hair poor kid.'

'Oh my God' she said, sounding deeply shocked 'that's awful, Dawson.'

'Yeah, it is. I've found this so-called meat rack place going by the number of beer cans, nitrous oxide canisters and general detritus lying around. There's a fire still smouldering but there's no one here. I'll get back to you later Jaineba.'

Jaineba killed her phone and turned to Joanne who looked worried sick. 'I wish she'd have taken her phone, Joanne, or at least some more money. I gave her twenty pounds this morning, two fives and a ten, she only took a fiver.'

'She won't get far on that for sure Jaineba but, on the positive side, she's a very resourceful girl and, from what Dawson says, she's extremely streetwise, too.'

Jaineba poured them both a stiff drink and they sat on the settee too worried to even think about dinner.

*

Dawson made his way back to his car. He drove slowly past the Kwik Kebab Kabin, the shutters were down, a notice on the window said closed for refurbishment. He drove around the back. The door was closed, and a new external bar and padlock had been installed. The brickwork above the door had acquired a security camera. He drove on.

Dawson had reported Charlene missing using the direct number to Elwin. She was incandescent and sounded off about how he should have left it for her and the social services to handle.

'If anything happens to that child, Mr Jukes, I guarantee you'll do time. If you have any idea where she might be, tell me now.'

He could understand her anger, he'd hold himself responsible, too. The thought made his heart ache.

The Brat

He still believed his course of action had been the correct one, if only the strong-willed little bugger had confided in me, he thought. She didn't because she knew he would not have approved.

God, this is a bloody mess, another Dawson Jukes clusterfuck, your life's full of 'em. Dawson silenced his inner voice, 'Spilt milk' he muttered, but where the hell was he to look next?

Chapter 15

On the towpath, Charlene whimpered with fear as the shadowy figure loomed larger. She pedalled furiously but he was catching her rapidly. She glanced back again as she reached a lock. Pedalling up the slight cobbled incline felt like climbing a mountain. She reached the top as he caught her and swiped her around the head sending her tumbling.

Bailey was on her in a flash, his eyes gleaming with satisfaction. 'Gotcha bitch.'

He sat on her, his hand over her mouth, pinning her down. He took out his phone and thumbed a speed dial. 'I've got her, Alexi, you want a look?' Bailey turned his phone around to show Charlene's terrified face.'What you want me to do with her? I could drown her like that mate of hers, we're on the canal towpath and there's nobody about.' Charlene was both angry and terrified at the news he'd murdered little Julie. She struggled fiercely and freed her face briefly, screaming to no avail, her hands pushing the gravel uselessly.

The Brat

Bailey clamped a large hand over her mouth again 'it won't be possible to get her back quietly boss.' Bailey said 'I got no transport.'

Couscu wanted to kill her himself but he had to be practical. 'Yes, yes, drown her, but I want to see it happen. Keep the line open, OK?'

'No problem Alexi, just have my money ready when I get back and it's a grand now not two hundred, I've got the film rights.' He laughed at his own sick joke.

'Right bitch, time to die.' He pulled her to her feet and started to drag her to the edge of the lock. She struggled wildly and started screaming. Bailey found it impossible to film, drag her and keep her quiet all at the same time. He got behind her holding his hand over her mouth. Pulling her tight against him, he thrust with his hips pushing her to the water's edge while holding the phone in front to film himself in the act of murder.

Charlene was petrified, she desperately tried to resist him but was being pushed inexorably towards the lock, her feet finding no purchase on the loose gravel, Baileys gloating laugh adding to her terror.

From somewhere in the recesses of her panicked mind Charlene heard Joanne's urgent shout "use it."

From a place beyond thought Charlene thrust her hips hard to her left, her right hand chopped down, slicing into her attacker's balls. Bailey let out a startled cry and released his hold on her, going into a crouched position two feet from the water's edge gasping and clutching his injured balls. He was desperately trying to regain his feet when she kicked him as hard as she could in the hip, sending him tumbling into the fifteen-foot-deep lock.

Bailey surfaced, flailing wildly and screaming for help. Charlene realised that he couldn't swim but his wild thrashing was bringing him near the edge. One hand reached up desperately trying to grip the stonework, his head a foot below.

Charlene resisted the urge to turn and run, if Bailey got out he would catch her again. It had to end here.

She picked up his bike and with all the force she could muster, threw it down on his head. The sprocket hit him full in the face, the frame slipping over his shoulders. Her would-be killer sank back and went down entangled in the bike frame; the weight dragging him to the bottom.

The surface boiled briefly with his last breath then all was still. She watched and waited for several minutes. The water remained calm, there was no sign of him. She picked up her bike to leave 'Fuck you, Bailey, that's for my Julie you bastard' she said. It was then she heard a faint anxious voice coming from a few feet away 'Hello. hello Mark, what's going on? You speak, please.'

The Brat

She saw Bailey's phone balanced precariously on the edge of the lock and made a grab for it but her trembling hand knocked it into the water. She swore inwardly.

Charlene picked up her bicycle again and mounted it, but her legs were trembling violently and refused to pedal. She pushed the machine slowly until, a quarter of a mile further on, she collapsed and lay on the grassy edge of towpath under some overhanging bushes sobbing as shock took its toll.

Her thoughts turned dark. She was a jinx for everyone she met. She'd caused Dawes and the ladies nothing but trouble and now her friend Julie was dead all because of her. If she had stayed away, Julie would still be alive. It was all her fault. Maybe she should just end her life and be done with it. That bastard Alexi would probably get her in the end anyway.

Her head was full of confused thoughts, she saw Dawson's face and then an image of Joanne and Jaineba their faces lined with worry saying, 'come back Charlene, please come back.' She couldn't think straight; her misery was all consuming.

Charlene had no idea how long she'd lain there stupefied, but dawn was breaking when a concerned voice asked, 'are you all right, love?'

She looked up to see an old West Indian man with a Jack Russell on a lead. He had a kindly, wrinkled

167

face and sad eyes. His dog came over and licked her face. She pushed it away even as he jerked on the lead.

'I'll be alright in a bit mister.'

The old man made a clucking noise with his tongue 'I don't think so love, you look done in.' He took out his phone and hit a speed dial as he raised it to his ear, he said 'I only live fifty yards away; I'll get my missus to bring a blanket then we'll get you indoors and cleaned up.'

A short conversation, then an old woman appeared carrying a duvet. Charlene allowed herself to be wrapped and guided to their house, the old man bringing the bicycle.

Charlene allowed the old lady to wash her hands and face with a sponge while the old gentleman made a cup of strong, sweet tea.

'I've put a drop o' dark rum in it dear, the good stuff from Jamaica' he said gently, 'it'll perk you up real quick.'

She drank deeply, gratefully, the hot, richly flavoured tea scalding its way down her throat.

'You're a runaway, aren't you?' The old man's eyes looked kindly, but they were also very shrewd.

'I need to tell someone I pushed a man into the canal, and he drowned. He was trying to kill me.'

The old man's eyebrows shot high. He looked stunned by this unexpected announcement, then he gave a slight smile 'all in good time my dear, all in

The Brat

good time. Why don't you tell me what happened while my Millie heats some soup?'

She was so tired now and felt unable to relate her whole story, so she said 'Yes, I ran away from a children's care home. I know too much about some bad people. They sent someone after me. I pushed him into a lock. He couldn't swim. Will they send me to prison?'

The old man's smile was gentle, his voice soft 'No my dear, it sounds like self-defence to me. No one will send you to prison just for defending yourself.' His smile broadened and he patted her shoulder 'don't you worry now, you're safe here, Millie and me will take good care of you.'

Charlene didn't know when it happened, but soon after she finished her soup, she drifted off into an exhausted sleep. When she awoke it was full daylight, the couple were sitting watching her.

'Is your name Charlene Keenan?' the old man asked.

She looked surprised 'Yes, how did you know?'

We rang social services and described you. They've been looking for you, they're sending someone round soon.'

'You didn't ring the cops, then?'

He laughed 'no, they will want to talk to you, of course, but first, you need a social worker my dear, you've had a very traumatic experience. The man in the lock hasn't surfaced yet, I've been and checked but, no matter, he won't be going anywhere.'

The smell of grilling bacon came to her and she felt ravenous. Apart from last night's soup, she hadn't eaten in over a day. She looked towards the kitchen of the small, terraced house.

'That smell is your lunch young lady. Bacon and eggs on toast. I hope that's OK?'

They sat in the neat kitchen eating. 'I'm Cyril, Cyril Alleyne, my wife is called Millie. You were too tired to take anything in this morning, Charlene, so we just let you rest.'

He looked at her with sympathetic eyes 'I, too, ran away when I was a child. My father was a drunk who beat me all the time. When I grew up, I saw no future for myself at home, so I came to England on a ship called the Empire Windrush many, many years ago now.' He smiled, his careworn face gentle 'things can look very bad at times, Charlene, but dark times always pass, you'll see.'

Charlene was moved to tears by this caring old couple's compassion. There were decent people in the world, her life was worth living. Millie gave her a motherly hug then some tissue to dry her eyes.

Half an hour later two social workers arrived to collect her.

The most dangerous, chapter of her life was about to begin.

Chapter 16

Petronovski received a call from Moscow with instructions he didn't like. He was to capture Jukes and question him about his military history before killing him. For a long time, the Kremlin had suspected the presence of a highly secret military unit belonging to the British Army Intelligence Corps. The British, of course, denied its existence. Yet, when certain suspicious things had happened, all known operatives of MI5 and MI6 had been accounted for and ruled out. The Special Air Service didn't do political assassinations, so the only other logical answer was some unknown body. The Army Intelligence Corps was the obvious suspect.

'You see, Dmitry, our friends in the FSV are most concerned. Over the years, several important operations have come to nothing in mysterious circumstances. Key people have disappeared, others have met with accidents or have supposedly committed suicide. These events have all been very convenient for the West and a damn nuisance for us.'

Petronovski scowled, why the hell had the organisation gotten itself involved in foreign politics? It was bad enough having to deal with this sort of shit at home but over here it just got in the way of business. 'Does this unit have a name?'

'We call it the Ghost Platoon because there's never a shred of evidence left behind. We suspect your man Jukes is a former member, hence his highly classified file. Only two such men have come to our notice in the last twenty years and the other one is dead.'

There were many ways of assassinating someone quickly and quietly and Petronovski was familiar with most of them. Capturing a man and making him talk was much more difficult, it required organisation, facilities, equipment, and a prolonged operation. All these things added to his expenses for no gain.

'You'll have to be careful how you extract the information, Dmitry, he'll be a tough man trained to resist torture, he could die before we have the information if it's not done properly.'

Petronovski thought for a moment 'He seems to be protecting a young girl, a runaway whore of ours. Maybe he would talk if she was being tortured.'

'An excellent idea, see to it as soon as possible please. I cannot stress enough the importance our friends in the Kremlin place on this.'

The Brat

This last statement Petronovski knew was code for *your life will be in danger if you screw up.*

'By the way, Dmitry, what have you decided about the Catanova woman?'

'I will dispense with her services once this episode is over, she has made too many mistakes.'

'OK.' The phone went dead.

Petronovski sat deep in thought. Jukes was probably travelling, using a different name, never sleeping in the same place two nights together. It would be always somewhere in or around the Greater Manchester area. If he was a trained agent, he would be damned hard to locate even with his face splashed all over social media so recently. He wouldn't have the girl with him, a lone man with a young girl would draw too much attention. So, he must have left her with someone he trusted, but who? Who were his associates? He worked as a bodyguard through an agency as revealed by the Jezebel Justiz incident. He should have them visited and their employees' files examined. He picked up the house phone 'send Ivanov to me.'

*

Ivanov did his research carefully. Jukes had no social media accounts, but his agency would have records of who he worked with and his next of kin. If this could lead him to Jukes that would please him immensely, he owed him a slow death.

Ivanov selected Yuri Yegorov as an assistant for this job, the man was a psychopath and most useful when persuasion was needed. He rang a British associate and instructed him to make an appointment with Babcock fearing his Russian accent might alert his target. It took a day to do the research he needed. An appointment was made for five pm the next day, a Friday.

Moulton House was a mundane office complex on Princess Street in Manchester. It was the kind of place you could rent an office by the month. It housed mainly start-ups and fly-by-night companies. The rents were reasonable so John Babcock, as a start-up business, had based himself there. The staff consisted of himself and his secretary Lisa Wilson. A five o'clock appointment was not very convenient for John but with the Jezebel Justiz fiasco costing him several cancellations, he needed to generate any business he could. He told Lisa she could go at half past four, but she insisted on staying. 'It won't give a good impression if you have to make the coffee yourself, John.'

At five sharp the door buzzer sounded. Lisa went to the spyhole to see a smartly dressed man in an expensive suit carrying a briefcase. She opened the door, Mr. Manley?'

Ivanov smiled, nodded and stepped forward, she stepped back to allow him entry. Suddenly there were two of them as Yegorov sprang from the

The Brat

corridor. The two pushed their way in and Lisa found herself staring down the suppressor of an automatic pistol. Yegorov passed them and barged into the office, pistol pointing.

'What the hell....?' Babcock jumped to his feet.

'Shut up and sit-down Mr. Babcock' barked Ivanov as he pushed Lisa into the room. 'This can go easy or hard, your choice.'

John Babcock sat back in his chair, a feeling of dread in his heart 'OK, whatever it is you want, we'll cooperate, please, don't hurt Lisa.'

'I want your employment records and your work schedules for the last twelve months.' He tossed a memory stick onto the desk. 'And before you think of downloading some other files instead, let me show you something.' He slid his phone from his pocket and showed John the screen. It was video footage of his house taken that morning as his wife Jaqueline was loading the kids in the car for the school run. 'I believe this is where you live. 51 Herons Nest Rise in Hale Barns, No?'

'Yes.'

'Your wife, son and daughter are safe, as long as you cooperate.'

Babcock took the memory stick and inserted it, he keyed in the code word then turned the screen so Ivanov could see it. He downloaded the required files and returned the memory stick.

'Your man Jukes, does he socialise with any of your staff?'

Yegorov leered at Lisa and grabbed her breast 'Is he fucking you, baby?'

'Leave her alone you bastard, you've got what you came for. He looked back at Ivanov. 'Jukes is a loner, he lives out in the sticks, he's not the socialising type.' He knew they intended to kill them now, if they were after Jukes it was a serious business. Babcock knew Jukes had been in Military Intelligence doing highly secret work, but he knew no details. He himself was ex-22nd SAS with vast experience in close personal protection.

He tried delaying tactics 'What do you want with Jukes anyway? Perhaps I could help?'

Ivanov wasn't fooled 'I don't think so, he wouldn't tell you he's screwing a fourteen-year-old now, would he?'

Babcock slid his right hand from the desk onto his knee. It was still in sight of Ivanov so as not to alert the man, but it was nearer to the knife on the magnet under his desk. If he could take one of these bastards out, he'd die a bit happier.

John's family had instructions of what immediate action to take in case of his suspicious death. Jaqueline and the kids would clear off to France, tout-suite, not even stopping to pack. They had been married while he was still serving in the Regiment. She knew that hard decisions sometimes had to be

The Brat

taken and she accepted it. Mourning would have to wait.

'I don't believe you; Jukes is no Paedophile.'

'Believe what you like.' Ivanov had a self-satisfied smile on his lips as he put his weapon away. His splinted figure got caught on his jacket, killing the smile. He sneered at Babcock 'you were 22nd SAS, I believe? I was Spetsnaz, we were much better than you.' He turned to Yegorov 'Kill them.'

Yegorov eyes glinted their perverse pleasure 'ladies first' he said and slowly, deliberately, swung his weapon away from Babcock to point at the terrified Lisa. He was thumbing back the hammer when Babcock's knife flew into his neck.

Babcock didn't wait to see the effect he grabbed his desk and overturned it in a lightning move, sending it crashing onto Ivanov's foot. He dived over the desk and onto Ivanov as the man reached desperately for his weapon.

Babcock punched Ivanov hard in the head, but Ivanov was a tough man and well trained, he took the blows and concentrated on pulling his gun. His damaged hand made it slower than normal, but he got it free. Babcock managed to knock it down sending the bullet that would have killed him into his upper thigh instead.

The door chime sounded, and a man's voice called 'Hi, cleaner, can I do in here?' Then 'Oh, shit!' To William Broadbent, office cleaner and veteran infantryman, the smell of burnt cordite was all too familiar. The hairs on his neck bristled as he turned and fled. Ivanov managed to take a hurried shot and missed, his splinted finger making his grip unsteady, his normally deadly aim made clumsy by Babcock on top of him. He wrenched himself clear of Babcock and took off after Broadbent, with is accomplice dead, and things getting out of control his thinking was now panicked. He had to kill the witness. Babcock's wound would keep him there, but the witness must be taken out.

Broadbent hadn't far to run. In the next office, his wife was cleaning when he burst in and slammed the door. Fearing this pursuer would fire through the door, William grabbed his startled wife and pushed her down behind a desk covering her with his body.

Ivanov threw himself against the door, but it didn't budge. He sent three speculative rounds through it before realising his mistake.

In Babcock's office, Lisa stood staring horrified at the corpse of Yegorov and the halo of blood spreading around his head, too shocked to even scream. Babcock managed to roll, then pull himself upright and stagger to the outer door, slamming it. Shutting Ivanov out was their only chance of survival.

Ivanov dashed back, but he was two seconds too late.

The Brat

Babcock hit his phone and sent a pre-set message to his wife. *Red light on, go.*

He hopped over to Lisa, putting his arms around her shoulders and guided her to his chair before dialling 999.

In the corridor Ivanov cursed and fired a shot into the lock, Bullet fragments and pieces of metal flew. Some hit him in the face stinging and narrowly missing his eyes. The lock held. Ivanov cursed and wiped the blood streaks off his face, another five seconds was all he had required. He'd left the killings to Yegorov because he knew the man enjoyed it and it paid to stay on-side with a psychopath.

Ivanov heard voices down the corridor. A man and a woman, their backs to him, were locking their office for the weekend. Any second, they would turn and see him. Escape was now the Russians priority; he donned the long-peaked baseball cap he'd entered the building wearing and hurried away. He had the information he required but Petronovski would not be happy. The empty briefcase was still in Babcock's office, but he knew there were no prints on it.

*

John Babcock slid his trousers down and inspected his leg. It hurt like hell, but he'd been lucky, the bullet had cut a shallow groove down his thigh, ugly but not life threatening. No major damage had been done. The wound made him feel weak and nauseous, but his job was not done yet. He rang Dawson Jukes and told him briefly what had happened. They've got the names and addresses of all our operatives Dawson, they asked who you associated with. I told 'em you didn't.'

Dawson thanked him and hung up. He rang Joanne and told her. She was mortified.

'Oh, God, we'll have to move out tonight, Dawson' she said. 'Poor Jaineba, she's not used to this sort of stuff, she'll be terrified.'

'Is there anywhere you can go for a few days?'

Joanne thought about it for a moment 'Jaineba has been talking about visiting her family in Guyana for ages, maybe this would be a good time.'

'What about Charlene?'

'She's in a secure unit with social services, she couldn't say where, and she says she was missing us but she's getting help.'

Dawson sat in his hotel room planning his next move. He'd kicked the can down the road to see who would chase it, now he knew, and his friend was wounded, and Lisa had almost been killed. Cold anger took hold of him, Who the hell did these Mafia bastards think they were? He would bring their whole rotten empire down or die trying.

His phone rang. 'Hi, Dawson, can we meet for dinner tonight?'

The Brat

He didn't really feel like it, but Margaret wouldn't have asked him unless it was important 'Sure, where?

They met at Mr. Thomas's Chop House, an old Victorian pub on Cross Street. Her news was as bad as he expected. Her editor had said she needed more evidence to get her teeth into before she could commit a large slice of her tight budget to an investigation.

'So, basically, we ran a "Has it started all over again?" speculative piece but we had to be careful about what we said. Those articles don't carry much weight without hard evidence.' She looked down-in-the-mouth. 'Sorry.'

'I see,' said Dawson bitterly, 'so, if I can obtain proof positive and hand it over you, she'll write it up while bigging-up the paper for its dogged investigation?'

Margaret laughed, showing pearly white teeth 'we're not that bad Dawson, and besides, you'd hate any personal publicity. Now, shall we order?'

He smiled fondly at her. She was just as beautiful as he remembered. God, how long had it been? Around twenty months. There had been Mona in London, she was nice, and the sex had been great, but it didn't work out. He'd been her bit of rough, but what she dreamed of was a polo-playing prince.

He stretched his hand across the table and took hers. She smiled at him; her large hazel eyes, enhanced by subtle makeup, made his heart race. 'You're still as beautiful as ever, Margaret' was all he could manage.

'You're not too bad yourself big man.' She looked hard into his eyes 'is there anyone else, Dawson?'

'No, there was, briefly, but it's been over quite a while now. You?'

'Two since you left, nothing serious, the last one turned out to be a scrounger, he got the boot a month ago.'

Their food came and they ate with a minimum of small talk. Afterward, she said 'have you got any more information I could use? Anything at all?'

He breathed in her high-octane perfume 'I could 'tell-all' as you Journo's say over breakfast tomorrow morning if you like.'

Her face lit up with a huge grin 'Hell, yes, I thought you weren't going to ask.'

'And if I hadn't asked?' he queried with a grin and a mock cocked eyebrow.

'I'd have bloody well raped you' she laughed.

They took a cab to her Spinningfields flat. She poured them each a generous glass of Malbec and they sank onto the sofa, eyeing each other with undisguised lust. God, he had missed her.

They sipped their wine, the sexual tension building. 'Before we start anything' she began.

'No, after we've finished starting something' he interrupted and pulled her to him. She responded

The Brat

fiercely, biting his lip then thrusting her tongue deep in his throat as her hand slid up his thigh, pulling down his zip.

He pushed her gently backward, his hand teasing her nipples. Clothing was rapidly discarded as they dragged each other to the bedroom. Taking hold of his penis she marvelled at its length, her fingers failing to close all the way around his manhood. She groaned with desire, spread her thighs and pulled him on.

Twice more before dawn they made wild, uninhibited love until her bed resembled a battlefield.

When morning came, they took a shower together washing each other tenderly, spontaneously arousing each other once more. She moaned softly forcing her hips into him. He lifted her onto him, she wrapped her long, slender legs around his waist as he entered her secret folds for the fourth time.

After they dried each other off they lay on the bed-wreck. She smiled the smoky-eyed smile of a sexually satisfied woman and stroked his face 'God, I've missed you, Dawson Jukes. What did we used to call these sessions?'

He grinned widely. 'You remember, you little strumpet, it was you who named them. A knock-down, drag-out fuck fight, wasn't it?' he laughed, feeling better than he had in months 'it always ended in a draw as I recall.'

After breakfast, they sat with coffee. It was Saturday and she didn't have to be anywhere. 'My editor is not unsympathetic, Dawson, just give us some hard evidence. Before, it was mainly Asian men grooming and abusing underage girls to satisfy their lust. Now you're saying it's well organised and done for profit.'

'If you believe me when I tell you it's going on then surely that must be enough to investigate further?' he said irritably. He hadn't told her of the agency incident as he wanted her to enjoy their love making. She'd find out soon enough.

Margaret sensed his deep frustration and stroked his hand, speaking softly 'with your background, Dawson, you know the criteria for prosecution is high and, Elwin apart, there's no appetite for it on the Chief Constable's staff. High command is beside itself with worry lest some ethnic or religious group label them with some damned woke "ist" or "ism."

This was getting him nowhere. He changed the subject. 'Have you ever come across the name Petronovski?' he asked her.

'No, why?'

He told her where he'd heard the name and she said she'd see if they had any information in the files.

*

After he left Margaret, Dawson felt deeply depressed, gone the euphoric mood of the bed

The Brat

chamber; he thought hard about his next move. On the one hand Charlene was safe now so, in theory, he could simply walk away and lie low for a while and hope it would all blow over. Even as the thought occurred to him, he dismissed it. His enemies would hunt him down, he had done them too much harm.

It occurred to him that Petronovski and co must have protection at an extremely high level. Detective Sergeant Swanson could not provide the kind of cover they would need to work with impunity. Having professional assassins on call with access to sophisticated suppressed weapons cost big money.

Maybe I should ring my old boss he thought, there might be a political element to all of this, if there is, maybe the old firm would get involved, god knows I can use the help.

He checked out of his hotel before lunch and collected his car.

Recalling the number long stored in his memory, Dawson rang and asked for the duty officer. After a thorough security check, he was connected. 'Dawson my boy, how the devil are you?' asked Major Bernard 'Dinger' Bell.

They chatted briefly about old times then the Major became serious 'So, what's the reason for the call, Dawson?'

He explained concisely then asked if they knew of any political or military connection that would make it their business.

The Major rattled his keyboard for what seemed an age. 'The man Petronovski was a colonel in the FSV until he retired five years ago. He disappeared for a year then resurfaced as a sort of demi-oligarch and sought asylum in Britain. He claimed he was on the run from his former masters. He provided us with a little genuine medium-level security stuff and a parcel of high-level bullshit. It cost MI6 a lot of wasted time and money chasing it down. By the time we'd sussed him he had permanent leave to remain in the country.' Bell read on 'It says here he has a finger in a lot of criminal pies, Drug distribution, prostitution, modern slavery, too, but nothing we can prove. He has a highly-placed friend in the Russian embassy, one of their many military attachés that he doesn't believe we know about.'

'Does he have any family here, a girlfriend perhaps?'

The Major did a brief check 'No immediate family here. An ex-wife in Moscow and a drop-out son somewhere who seems to be a permanent backpacker. He uses a couple of trusted Russian whores based in Liverpool when he needs to. He likes being whipped and pissed on, nothing too extreme.'

'I was looking for an Achilles heel, Major, some way to get to the bastard.'

'You and MI5, too, Dawson. If you do find anything be sure to let us know.'

The Brat

Disappointed, Dawson realised that, except for the kinky sex, he knew next to nothing about his enemy.

That the Russians would be using all their resources to hunt him down was a certainty. He drove to an airport Hotel and had his car collected by the hire people then he caught a tram into Manchester and hired another one. There was no point in making it easy for them to trace him. Maybe he should do the unthinkable and go hunting them, starting at the top.

He took a chance now and drove close to his home. He had equipment there he used for work that would be useful now. He watched the place from the top of the hill hidden in scrub. Two hours after sunset he made his way cautiously down. The house looked a mess. The police had broken his front door down to execute their search warrant. It was now boarded up. He went around the back and entered but didn't switch on the lights. Using a masked torch, he found what he wanted. He was not surprised to find that the police had taken his shotgun.

He found his thermal imaging camera, laser microphone, and recorder. His drone and control box plus night vision gear and binoculars. It was quite a haul, but he managed it back to the car taking the direct route. Now to find Petronovski's mansion by the River Mersey and do a survey.

Next day Margaret rang. She had found something in an old file. 'Petronovski likes to act the English country squire, Dawson, hunting, shooting, and fishing. I've found an old copy of the Country Squire Magazine He's a member of the local hunt, he likes to shoot anything that moves, and he goes fishing on the river Dee. She went on to read the article. 'Sorry, I don't suppose that's much help' she said.

He thanked her and tried to make another date, but she refused 'you're still living a dangerous life, Dawson, my nerves couldn't handle it.'

Her answer, half expected, was a huge disappointment but he knew better than to argue with her. He'd just have to stay dumped; anyway, he had work to do.

Dawson set himself up on a rise on the edge of woodland, overlooking Petronovski's mansion. He burrowed into some bushes to make a hide, then flew his drone up to three hundred feet and sent it over the house and grounds filming the layout. He brought it back after ten minutes. What the footage revealed didn't surprise him. The house had security lights and cameras in abundance. In the stable block at the rear two horses' heads were visible above the half doors. Behind the stable a paddock with another animal grazing. The whole house and gardens were surrounded by a two-metre-high wall with a second gate leading out to a wooded area on the right and open fields to the rear that ran down to the Mersey.

He switched to the Infra-red. The expected heat sources showed up plus another near the gate. He looked through his binoculars, nothing was visible

The Brat

from where he lay but the ground sloped away on the far side of the drive. He sent the drone out again and discovered a low door set in the slope with steps leading down by the main gate so, there was an underground bunker, not the standard fixture for an average country house. The flight had also revealed that the whole of the grounds was crisscrossed with light beams. The place was like a fortress, getting into it would be near impossible even with his experience. So, other means would have to be found.

He was about to leave when he saw activity at the front door. A Range Rover with blacked out windows pulled up and a man came from the house loading fishing tackle into the back then climbed behind the wheel. A couple of minutes went by then two men came out of the house. He recognised Petronovski from the magazine pictures. The other was Ivanov. They got into the rear seats and the vehicle took off up the drive. From the bunker, a man appeared as if out of the earth and raised a shotgun in salute. Dawson ran for his car.

The lanes were quiet, so he had to hang a long way back. He would have lost them had he not known they were heading for the river upstream. It took the guesswork out of some of the turn decisions. After five miles, the Range Rover turned into a country car park. Dawson drove past catching sight of the party unloading fishing creels and rods.

Half a mile further on he found a place to park and made his way to the river. A path led along the bank through woodland in the direction he needed to go. He walked casually, his binoculars around his neck. He stopped at intervals to watch birds, then carried on. He passed a notice telling him the fishing was private and that poachers were always prosecuted. Then there he was, Petronovski wading in the river casting with expert ease. Ivanov was a few metres away casting inexpertly.

Dawson studied the pair through his field glasses. The bulge under his left arm told him Ivanov was armed. Now, where was the driver? The answer to that question came a second later.

'What the fuck are you up to, pal?'

Dawson turned, sizing up the man pointing the shotgun at him. He was a sneering, cocky bastard, but a lightweight.

Adopting a quizzical look Dawson asked 'what's your problem, mate? Birdwatching illegal is it?'

The man was not fooled, he recognised Dawson from the media pictures his boss had made him study 'Jukes, ain't it? My boss wants to see you, pal.' He motioned down the path with the gun. 'Move.'

Good thought Dawson, if his boss wants to see me, this clown isn't going to shoot.

'Don't think I will, mate.'

The man's eyes widened in surprise then he moved quickly, but not quickly enough. He altered

The Brat

his grip on his weapon and swung the butt at Dawson's head. When it arrived, Dawson's head wasn't there. He had swayed back allowing the butt to pass within inches of his face. Using both hands he grabbed butt and barrel and twisted the weapon savagely, wresting it from the man's grasp. In one smooth movement he sent the butt upwards, smashing into the man's jaw.

Dawson bent over the groaning man 'I've a mind to shove this gun up your arse and let you have both barrels, you cocky bastard. Why does your boss want to see me, anyway?'

The man was slowly regaining his senses, he rubbed his jaw then spat out a bloodied, broken tooth. Dawson stepped back allowing him to sit up.

'I dunno, I'm only his chauffer' he groaned and sank back on his elbows 'all I know is he wants to see yer bad.'

Dawson broke the gun and checked the load; it was bird shot. Too light to reach the men in the river and do any damage, but maybe enough to put the wind up them. He aimed low and fired the choked barrel. The shot splashed into a wide area of water around the men. He had the satisfaction of seeing both men drop their rods and grasp their legs, hearing them howl in pain and surprise. 'Now they'll want to see me even more' he told the Chauffer, 'you tell that Petronovski bastard he can stop looking for me, I'll be finding him soon enough.'

Dawson gave the man a sharp rap in the forehead with the gun butt then bent and broke his right-hand little finger. This was now his calling card. He knew it would piss them off big time and angry people made mistakes. He took the gun with him along with six cartridges from the man's pocket, they might just come in handy.

He reached his car, the exhilaration of his recent encounter now faded. The truth was he was still no nearer to stopping these men. Now, he had wound them up even further he risked a bullet in the head at any moment. They had a lot more resources than he did. For starters he'd buy a car but register it under a false name. But what the hell was he to do next? Other than getting Charlene to safety, he'd achieved nothing of value save winding up Petronovski. He needed to plan, to stop acting impetuously.

He returned to his hide to continue his vigil.

Chapter 17

Charlene cried herself to sleep on her first night at her new secure care home, feeling utterly miserable. She was away from her Dawes and the ladies. Though she'd known then only a short time they had made a great impression on her. That they genuinely cared for her just for herself was obvious.

The police interview hadn't been too bad. She was not questioned in a police station but in a special suite designed to be non-intimidating. A senior looking policewoman questioned her gently and listened to her answers carefully. Charlene was accompanied by a senior social worker and a female solicitor who made it clear she was not in any trouble. Her actions in kicking her assailant into the canal was completely within the laws of self-defence.

They took careful note of all she said only the officer who was making notes glanced at her curiously and raised an eyebrow when she told them about Detective Sergeant Swanson. She was not challenged on her statement, the woman officer only asked questions to clarify a few points.

Charlene felt enormous relief when it was over having feared she would be locked up in some sort of prison.

The Pine Springs childrens' home was in a quiet valley in the North Wales countryside away from almost everywhere. Of the other five kids there, three girls and two boys, all except a boy called Jason seemed preoccupied with their own problems, they talked of little else. Jason said nothing to anyone, his head almost permanently stuck in car magazines. He intrigued her.

The psychologist she saw was a good and understanding woman who listened attentively and asked questions gently and without judgement, getting her to explore her feelings. She seemed keen to help her.

Charlene had been there almost a week before boredom set in. The teacher who came daily was good but had to go at the pace of the slowest, that was Jason. The other kids told her Jason was a weirdo and a serial car thief who loved to race around the streets evading police for as long as possible. It was hard to imagine this plump, pudding-faced kid doing anything as dangerous as that.

After their meal one evening, she picked up one of his magazines. He snatched it back, throwing her a how-dare-you-scowl.

The Brat

'I only wanted a look, Jason. I think your cars are really cool.' She smiled disarmingly even though she felt like punching him 'if you don't want me to look that's OK.' She turned and sauntered across the lounge, picking up the TV remote and settling in an armchair. A minute later he was at her side. He dropped the magazine in her lap without a word, turned, and walked away.

Next day Jason offered her another magazine and spoke to her for the first time 'do you like cars, then?'

'Yeah, I do, but I don't know much about them. These mags are full of good stuff and I like to learn.' Again, he walked away without comment.

She read the magazine cover to cover, it really was interesting. Could she learn to drive like Dawes one day? The prospect thrilled her.

Magazine finished, she went to bed and thought about Dawson, wondering what he was doing. She really missed him, scary looking though he was, he was always kind to her. She remembered him stroking her hair as she cried into his massive chest. His hand felt huge and heavy, almost covering the whole of her head but so gentle and comforting. She thought of the foster carers, social workers and kindly care home staff she had known. They were good people, but nothing like her Dawes. She felt so secure when she was with him, this big, ugly man who had saved her life.

She thought about the car chase again. God, he was so cool. She was certain they were going to die, yet he stayed so calm. How did he do that? And Joanne and Jaineba, too, they were nothing like what the girls at school had said about lesbians. The playground gossip was that they were all big butch women whose clitorises were so large they could rape young girls with them, turning them into lesbians, too. Why on earth had she believed such crap?

Then that bitch Marcia had forced her do that sex stuff to her just to make her feel bad. She shuddered as she recalled it. She threatened to do it to her friend Julie and now Julie was dead, poor innocent little Julie. A tear ran down her face, she wouldn't even be able to go to her funeral.

Brushing sad thoughts of Julie from her mind with difficulty, Charlene focussed on Dawson. She saw his face clearly in her mind's eye, feeling the longing to be protected by him. She imagined her face buried in his chest, his huge hand stroking her head.

Turning over and hugging her pillow, Charlene's thumb found its way into her mouth for comfort. She sucked, baby-like, weeping quietly into the pillow, overwhelmed by a tsunami of misery. God, I miss you, Dawes she thought, I wish you were my daddy.

*

Chief Superintendent Elise Elwin sat, elbows on desk, unconsciously tugging her left earring. The report she was poring over was from the Chief Constable's office causing a worried frown to mar her handsome face. Tears of frustration were threatening to run, but she forced them back. Her carefully compiled dossier had been brushed aside like so much wastepaper. The paragraph that stung the most read: *"Current intelligence suggests that there is insufficient evidence to substantiate the claim that there is an organised child prostitution ring operating throughout North West England. Therefore, considering current demand on resources, further investigation is terminated forthwith. We should, however, be ever mindful of the possibility of such an organised criminal enterprise... "*

She threw the document across her desk, sitting back and clasping her hands behind her head, releasing a long sigh. So, that was it. The word of a dozen abused kids isn't enough she thought, social workers statements are of no value because they were not direct witnesses.

Charlene Keenan had given a cogent statement, especially her account of Swanson. Elise suspected he'd been doctoring reports for a while now, but there was nothing she could take to Internal Inquiries. If only Charlene's record had been clean, but she was a convicted house breaker, shoplifter and an accomplished liar. Even so, Elwin could not countenance that she was a willing prostitute. That Charlene was an abused child was evident to anyone who cared to listen to her.

She pushed aside her now-cold coffee then banged her fist on the table. She'd be damned if she'd give up. Damn the complacent bastards to hell, she thought, I'll not stop trying even if it does mean committing career suicide.

Elise Elwin had gained her present position though intelligent, innovative policing over many years, overcoming male chauvinism and prejudice. Could there be a way to gain this so-called *evidential support* without using their precious resources?

She felt a deep need to protect these vulnerable kids. She loved children, had longed for a child herself but her womb would not cooperate. That, and her ambition had cost her her marriage. No, she could not, would not, give this up.

Elise knew that to use non-police resources without authority, to provide intelligence to a civilian, would cost her the career she loved if it came to light. She considered it a risk worth taking for the sake of abused children. She reached her decision and lifted the desk phone 'Bill, see if you can dig up the number for that Dawson Jukes bloke.'

Chapter 18

Charlene looked at Facebook with mixed feelings. Jezebel Justiz had just announced an extra, surprise gig at the Manchester Arena in two days' time. There was a clip of an interview with her and her manager on the local TV News. She was gushing about the venue had become unexpectantly free and, as she had three days before she flew home, she'd throw an extra "Thank you" gig. Asked if she felt nervous returning to the city where she had narrowly avoided a deadly acid attack, her manager jumped in and answered. 'Now that we have proper security and not the cowards who guarded her last time, we feel confident that the gig will go off smoothly.'

Charlene's face flushed and her chest tightened, how dare this man accuse her Dawes of being a coward? Why didn't Jezebel jump in and tell the truth? 'You lying bastard' she shouted at the screen, 'Dawes would never leave anyone.'

'What's up Charlene?'

She looked up to see Jason, his porridge-coloured face held a concerned look. 'Has someone hurt you?'

Charlene explained the situation, unsure that Jason understood it all, but he nodded sympathetically his eyes never leaving hers.

'Why don't we go and see this bloke and put him right?'

Charlene looked at him nonplussed 'And just how do we get out of here and get to Manchester, Jason?'

'We nick a car, I can drive you, easy. We just gotta get out of here.'

She thought for a moment then asked, 'do they lock the gardening shed at night?'

'No, there's nothing in it worth shit. Just a few spades and gardening stuff.'

'There's a fifteen-centimetre gap at the bottom of the back gate' she told him 'and it's only a dirt path. We could dig it a bit deeper and get underneath, easy, but where do we steal a car?'

Jason gave her a sly smile, his piggy eyes dancing with excitement 'that's my gig' he said.

And so that night just after eleven thirty they found themselves walking down the lane towards a row of houses that were once farm labourers' cottages. The first two appeared to be unoccupied weekend retreats the next one however sported a white BMW five series. Jason crouched and peered through the letter box. 'Bingo' he said, his eyes

The Brat

animated. 'it's all on the hall table.' He took two bamboo support sticks he'd taken from the garden shed and taped them together. Charlene watched in amazement as he took a wire coat hanger from under his coat and fashioned a hook. He pushed his rod through the letterbox and a few seconds later he was dangling the fob in front of her, a smile like a Cheshire cat on his face. 'A piece o' piss.'

They backed off the drive and Jason drove them down the country lanes, Charlene played with the Satnav until she understood it. After five minutes of watching Jason's reckless driving she spoke. 'Jason, you're driving like a twat, we're never going to get there like this.'

He ignored her and pushed his foot further down scraping around a bend and only just making it.

'Jason' she screamed and punched him hard on the shoulder at last getting his attention.

'Wassup?' he shouted, his eyes glowing, 'this is fuckin' sick!'

'I got us out because I need to get to Manchester, you prick. We'll never get there at this rate.' Reluctantly he slowed down and drove sulkily on until they were on the A55 heading North then an Audi Quattro driven by a young Asian man drove alongside and parped his horn, grinning across at them.

Jason let out a wild yell as he took up the challenge. He floored it and shot up to ninety miles per hour, the Quattro jiggling on his tail. Charlene screamed his name but the look in his eyes told her he was past listening.

Horns blared and headlights flashed at them as they raced on. This was only going to end badly unless she stopped him. She had to act.

Charlene called his name once more as they screamed around a roundabout, fishtailing dangerously out of it. She reached over seeing the shock on his face as her hand found his balls. She started to squeeze. He yelled and thrust a hand down as he tried to pull her off, but she squeezed even harder.

'Slow down you crazy bastard or I'll crush 'em.'

Jason hesitated for a second, his need for speed fighting the pain, 'We'll crash if you don't let go Charlene' he yelled. The car weaved dangerously from crash barrier to verge. Charlene didn't answer, just closed her eyes and tightened her grip.

'Please, Charlene' he screeched 'Oh, shit!'

Jason braked hard and the Audi shot past, horn blaring, its driver giving a one finger salute. Charlene eased her grip but kept a firm hold. They were nearing a Little Chef Café and she ordered him to pull in. The place was closed, the carpark empty. She released him and glared into the face 'You lame-brained fuckin' idiot. What the fuck was that all about, Jason, eh?' Eh?

The Brat

He looked down, red faced, unable to meet her furious gaze 'just wanted some fun, that's all. I could have beaten that tosser.'

'Right, mate, I'm out of here. You're driving like a prick, Jason. I know a real bloke who drives ten times better than you and he don't drive like no prick.'

Jason started blubbering, tears pouring down his fat cheeks, his pudgy body racked with sobs. 'Please, don't leave me Charlene' he wailed 'you're my friend. I never had a girlfriend before, not any friend ever as clever as you.'

She took her hand of the door catch; it would be difficult to get to Manchester without him. She had no money for fares and hitch-hiking would be dangerous.

She saw a way to get him to cooperate. 'OK, Jason, I'll stay if you promise you'll stick to the speed limit. I'll also help you meet my friend Dawes, he's a cracking driver. If I ask him, he'll maybe teach you some cool tricks, but you got to drive right, OK?'

As they drove on, she told him of the car chase she and Dawes had been in. Jason was in awe, he kept saying 'wow, that's fuckin' sick' like they were the only words he knew.

As they reached to outskirts of the city, Jason asked her 'what do we do now Charlene? How are we going to get to see this bloke Weitz and your mate Dawes?'

Charlene didn't answer him, she hadn't got a clue but didn't want to admit it. She knew the hotel Jezebel and her manager were staying at, she had imagined herself simply walking in and up to his room, telling him to stop lying about Dawes. She queried the satnav for hotels and found the Lowry easily enough. The place was lit up brightly, there was a small crowd of die-hard fans outside the front entrance even at this late hour and security men blocking the doors to all but guests.

Jason parked the car and they walked around the back of the hotel. There was a large bouncer at the rear door. How the hell was she to get rid of him?

The industrial dumpster they were hidden behind was full of hotel refuse. It gave her an idea. She examined it, wastepaper and cardboard separated into two piles for recycling. Returning to the front of the hotel she moved among the fans asking, 'you got a lighter I can have, mate?' She knew how to smile at lads and, after three askes she got what she needed, winked a cheeky thanks, and returned.

The fire started small, so she lit a couple more places then, grabbing the gawping Jason she retreated into the shadows. A minute later the guard spotted the flames. He spoke into a walkie-talkie and went to examine the skip. Charlene pulled Jason behind her as they crept in the shadows along the hotel wall. Sure enough, the door opened, and two men ran out with fire extinguishers.

The Brat

As the door swung too, Charlene grabbed it and went through, a nervously giggling Jason hard behind her.

She found herself in a service corridor. Turning left into a carpeted area, she tried all the doors. The fourth one was unlocked; it was an office with a phone on the desk. Charlene picked it up and read the faded notice Dial zero for reception.

'Mr Weitz's room, please.'

The receptionist asked 'who are you? Why are you ringing from the lower admin office?'

'I'm one of Jezebel Justiz's backing singers, this is very important, OK? No one must know. Tell him I have information about a Dawson Jukes, he'll want to know, believe me.'

The woman sounded hesitant 'may I ask your name?'

Charlene put on her urgent act 'Look, this is top secret, I'll get fired if anyone finds out. Why do you think I sneaked in here to call? Now, can I ask your name?'

The woman hesitated 'One moment please.'

Charlene sent Jason to the door to keep a lookout through the glass panel. It was a long two minutes before a harsh voice came on the line 'What's this about Jukes? Who are you? Why the hell are you waking me at this goddamned hour?'

'Mr Weitz, my name is Charlene Keenan, I'm fourteen years old and Dawson Jukes' latest screw, I want to tell yer everything I know 'cos of what he done to Jezebel.' She blurted this out in a breathless voice. 'I must see you alone, if he finds out, I'm dead.'

'Jesus Christ! Is this true? How can I trust you?'

'It's true alright Mr Weitz, but if you don't want to know, I'm out of here, it's too dangerous.'

There was a pause 'how did you get into the Hotel?'

Charlene never missed a beat 'My cousin's a chef here, he got me in through the kitchens.'

Another pause 'I can meet you in the lobby in five minutes, OK?'

'Are you for real, mate? There are cameras in there, Jukes is in security, he's got mates everywhere. No way, I'm gone.'

'OK, Ok, I'm in twelve oh two. Can you make your way up here?'

Charlene replaced the phone and searched through the desk drawers looking for anything sharp that might help her if she needed a weapon. She was shaking inside wondering if she dared go through with her plan. Her eye fell on a phone. It was an older model, scratched and dusty. She switched it on. It held a forty percent charge. It gave her a flash of inspiration.

'Jason, go back to the car and wait, we may have to make a quick get-away.'

'What about that big bastard at the door?'

The Brat

'He's there to stop people getting in, not out, tell him your dad's drunk and you're getting away from him for a bit.'

Jason's eyes lit up 'wow, Charlene, you're the coolest fucker I ever met' then he was gone.

Charlene found the service stairs, deserted at this time of night. She slipped the phone into the breast pocket of her jean's jacket and pulled the flap down and spread the buttonhole, poking a finger in to make sure it was aligned. She opened the other pocket, too so the effect was balanced. I just hope I can be as cool and brave as you, Dawes she prayed as she approached the door of twelve oh two.

Weitz came to the door dressed in a bathrobe over pyjamas. He scowled at her then glanced up and down the corridor 'this better be good, girl, or you're in deep shit. Whaddya got?'

'I ain't standing here telling yer, I might be seen.'

Someone coughed down the hall, Weitz's eyes flashed alarm, He didn't want witnesses.

'Fer Chrissakes get in here' he snapped pulling her in.

Charlene opened her eyes wide, looking fearful 'please don't hurt me Mr Weitz, I'm only a kid.'

Weitz shut the door behind her, calming down now that she was out of sight. 'come through here, Charlene, and don't be frightened, OK?' He put on a crocodilian smile and patted her on the shoulder. 'So, my sweet, about Dawson Jukes, you say he's screwing you?'

Charlene looked him in the eye, 'Yeah, he does, and I can tell you where and when, too. I know who it's arranged through.' her insides were fluttering 'what's it worth to you, mister?'

Weitz's smile was cynical 'OK, I thought there'd be a catch. I'll tell you what I'll do, you give me something I can use against that sonofabitch and I'll make it worth your while.' He patted his bathrobe pocket like it contained money then rubbed his fingers together. The gesture was unmistakable. Moola.

Charlene described where Jukes lived, told him how Alexi used to drive her out there and wait until he'd finished with her and that he paid two hundred a time.

He reached for his phone 'do you mind if I video this?'

'Fuckin' right I do. Are you crazy?'

'So, how do I get proof, then?'

He's booked me for tomorrow night at his place. If you go, or send someone, you can film me coming and going. He never draws the curtains anyway because it's out on the moors with no one around for miles.' She watched him fiddling with his phone, thinking, a suspicious scowl on his face.

'Look, mister, I'm risking my life doing this. I'm only doing it because I love Jezebel, she's the

The Brat

coolest, right? Always tells it like it is, yeah? If Jukes or my pimp find out, I'm dead.'

She had told him the time and how to find Dawson Jukes's house. He opened his laptop and checked on Google Earth; he saw it was exactly as she described it. After a long pause he agreed.

At the door she stuck her hand out and he pushed fifty pounds into it and let her out.

'There'll be more once I've nailed that bastard, good, OK?'

Outside again, Charlene felt euphoric, her heart sang with joy, she'd pulled it off. She turned the corner to where they had parked, and her joy evaporated instantly. Jason and the car were gone.

Charlene searched the nearby streets to no avail. What had he done? Surely, he'd not gone joyriding. 'Oh, Jason, where are you, dude?' she muttered.

Walking past the Crown Court on Minshull Street Charlene saw bright lights and smelled food. She realised she was starving. The smell came from a soup kitchen parked at the bottom of the street. Behind it was another van brightly lit. As she approached the food van a woman with a kindly face ask if she was hungry. 'Just get in the queue love' she told her. There was no challenge, no awkward questions about her age and why she was on the street at this late hour. These good people fed a need, and that need was food for the homeless, the drug addicts, the prostitutes, male and female, that frequented the area. They did it for humanitarian reasons, nothing else.

Paper plate loaded with a meaty stew, she stood against the wall wolfing it down with a plastic spoon. Almost finished, Charlene noticed two girls eyeing her up from across the street. A small one about her own age with lank brown hair and an obviously stuffed bra, and a bigger, slightly older girl. They were dressed for night business.

The smaller girl kept nudging the older one and nodding towards Charlene. She would have liked to stay for a cup of coffee but decided to move on. Too late. The girls swiftly crossed the road, the big one first with her mate half a pace behind her.

'Hang on bitch' the small mouthy one said. 'You working our patch, are yer?'

Charlene stopped and shook her head 'No, I'm on me way home.'

The large girl blocked her path where's yer wedge, bitch. We gonna tax yer.' She looked mean and determined.

'I don't have any money and I'm not stealing your punters.' Charlene's face set hard. A month ago, she would have handed over her money and fled but Dawson taught her how to bluff at poker and Joanne had taught her some very nasty tricks. Charlene had been bullied all her life. She decided it stopped here.

The Brat

'It'll be up her quim' said the small girl 'you hold her, I'll stick me hand up.'

Charlene's face turned to stone as she slowly pushed her hand into her jean's jacket pocket and made a fist. The move was not lost on the bigger girl.

'You got a blade, bitch?'

'Only one way to find out, cow.'

'She's bluffin' said the mouth, 'do 'er.'

Charlene leaned slightly forward on the balls of her feet, staring unblinking into the big girl's eyes. She twitched the hand in her pocket.

The bigger girl lost her nerve, whores with knife-scarred faces didn't make much money, dead whores made none. She stepped back and sneered 'If we catch yer around here again yer one dead whore.' She pushed her friend back across the street where they were joined by an older woman. Charlene joined the queue for coffee feeling elated. She'd used her head and come out on top; Dawes was right, violence was a last resort not a first.

Charlene was distracted by a young woman from the van behind the food truck 'Hi, love, if you need condoms or clean needles come and see us.' She pointed out the van and moved on down the queue telling other people.

Charlene now took her coffee black without sugar because that was the way Dawes drank his. She didn't notice the older woman had crossed the street until she was upon her.

The woman spun her around violently. She was a bottle blonde in her late forties with a face like a broken brick.

'You threaten my girls with a blade, bitch?' The woman shoved her backwards against the wall, hot coffee splashed on Charlene's hand so that she almost dropped her polystyrene cup. There were plenty of people watching but no one said or did anything, they just stared. Charlene was trapped. The woman raised her fist to strike. Charlene grabbed the front of the woman's low-cut top and pulled it out, simultaneously pouring her scalding coffee down Brick Face's ample cleavage.

The effect was both immediate and comical. Loud shrieks echoed around the street, as Brick Face spun away trying to rip off her steaming top. Several of the watchers howled with laughter. Across the street two shocked girls looked horrified. Charlene swiftly crossed over, her temples pulsing, her fists clenched. The younger girl ran away screaming. The older one stood transfixed for a moment then followed her friend. Charlene was hot on her heels, tripping her as she crossed a carpark.

The girl rolled on her back and held her hands up 'Don't cut me, please, don't cut me face' she pleaded 'yer can tax me, it's up me fanny.'

Charlene held the girl down by her throat, spread her legs and pushed her fingers up the girl's vagina.

The Brat

She pulled the tightly rolled wad and sniffed it contemptuously.

'You want to wash it more often yer dirty bitch.' she told her. She let the girl up 'follow me and I'll carve yer.'

The petrified girl nodded 'gotcha.' She hurried away without a backward glance.

At Piccadilly Gardens, Charlene jumped into a taxi 'Didsbury please, drop me on the main road, I'll shout when' she told the driver.'

The driver was looking at her in his mirror 'A bit young to be out this late on your own, aren't you?'

She wasn't in the mood for talking, the adrenaline of the night's excitement had worn off. She felt as limp as a dishrag. 'Parents are fighting, going to me aunt's place.'

He started talking again but she cut him off 'Sorry, mate, I'm not in the mood, if you want a tip, just drive, OK?'

The driver shrugged and pulled into traffic. She sat back against the cushions unable to believe what she'd accomplished that night. A couple of months ago some bigger girls at school had bullied her and she'd been fearful of them. After meeting Dawson, Joanne and Jaineba she'd changed. They had taught her so much in such a short time, she marvelled at it. She had no idea people like them even existed. Had she always been capable of these things but hadn't known it?

Charlene took out the stolen phone and ran the footage, without the sound it would edit down just fine she thought and without the sound track it could be interpreted any way she said. Weitz was going to be sorry he ever stitched up her friend Dawes.

She reached Didsbury a short walk from 'her ladies' house.

'Drop me here mate.' She unrolled the money she'd taxed the girl for. Eighty pounds, it was a decent haul. She noticed the metre said thirteen pounds fifty pence.

'That'll be sixteen pounds, love' he said smiling.

She was too tired to argue and gave him the smelly top twenty-pound note. 'Keep the change, mate, you deserve it.' She got to the house in the predawn glow to find no one home. She didn't know that Joanne and Jaineba were six thousand miles away in Guyana.

Creeping into the garden shed, she found a couple of sun loungers. It wasn't ideal but, covered with an old tarpaulin, she got some fitful sleep. Tomorrow she would see if her plan worked or if her bluff would be called. A lot rode on the outcome.

Chapter 19

Dawson's phone rang, he was surprised to see the number. 'Hi, Chief Superintendent, what can I do for you?'

'I'd like another meeting, Mr Jukes, but away from HQ. Have you still got transport?'

He confirmed that he had, and she gave him directions to the village of Bramall a little way south of the city to a gastro pub called the Axe and Cleaver.

'I'll buy you dinner tonight' she told him 'I have something I need to discuss with you, it's a bit sensitive.'

Dawson realised whatever it was it must be off the record or she would have called him in or discussed it on the phone. He was intrigued 'OK, shall we say seven?'

She was perched on a barstool when he arrived, a drink in one hand and a menu in the other. He had to look twice. Gone the austere hair bun and plain face replaced by flowing locks that touched her shoulders before flicking up. Her face was subtly made up. He had a "wow" moment. Here was a handsome woman in her early forties who kept herself fit. The knee length skirt showed a curvy posterior and slender legs, the close-fitting pink blouse enhanced her ample bosom without being showy. Classy, he thought, very classy.

The pub was busy, and they sat at the bar waiting for a table. He knew better than to ask questions in such a public area even though his curiosity was burning. They dawdled over their drinks making small talk which Dawson found difficult. He was about to offer another round when they were called to table.

The food was delicious and the service impeccable, she kept chat to a minimum, steering clear of the subject of work. Meal over, she said 'the canal is just a few dozen yards away, won't you join me for a stroll?' She smiled broadly to disguise the formality of her request.

The towpath was deserted save for an older woman passing with two dogs. The late evening sun was setting through the newly greening trees, casting long shadows on the water. A leisure barge was tied up some three hundred metres away, its chimney smoking blue. A sweet whiff of applewood smoke drifted down to them. They walked in silence for a minute, Elise deep in thought. She stopped abruptly and turned to him, 'what's your interest in Charlene Keenan, Dawson?

The Brat

Why are you so ready to involve yourself?'

Dawson's eyes widened; he drew a sharp breath. 'What the hell sort of question is that?'

'Sorry, but you're not married, you have no partner, no children of your own, no record of working with youngsters, so why should you take so much interest in a runaway kid?'

Dawson now understood the reason for her question. He smiled a little ruefully 'I wanted none of this, Elise, I found her in acute distress as you know, and I sort of got dragged into her affairs.' He sighed as his huge shoulders sagged, a sudden deep sadness overcoming him. 'I've always lived a dangerous, selfish life, Elise. I've no right to inflict my lifestyle on any woman, asking Margaret to wait for months on end while I was on a job I might not come home from.'

He paused, scratching his ear 'and another thing, just because a bloke has no kids doesn't mean he doesn't want any. I'd give my eye teeth for a daughter like Charlene. She's brave, sassy, and highly intelligent. When she told me her life story I wanted to cry. She never once whined, never displayed one iota of self-pity, she just related how things were for her. All she wants is to belong, to have someone in her life who loves her. How could anyone not want to help a kid like that? Also, Elise, when some bugger tries to kill me, I take it personal.'

Elise looked him in the eye seeing nothing but truth. Her instinct told her here was a man with his own problems, but one she could trust.

She nodded her acceptance 'OK, what I'm about to impart is confidential, understood?'

'I've signed the official secrets act, Elise.'

'Yes, but even so…OK, there is some evidence of a large Russian underworld organisation selling drugs throughout the country on an unprecedented scale. They are mainly responsible for this so-called county lines dealing. They are also people traffickers and into organised prostitution. Child prostitution is but one facet of their operation and a small one at that.'

Dawson was up with her 'I see, so closing down the child operation would only alert them to the fact you're after them. You want information on the wider operation, yes?'

'You catch on fast.'

'I was in the Intelligence Corps, Elise.'

'Quite so. We believe the kingpin behind the operation here in the North West is one Dmitry Nikoli Petronovski, a former Colonel in the SVR.' She went on to outline the suspicions of his involvement with organised crime.

'The truth is we police are restricted in the way we gather information whereas you, a civilian, can use methods we can't.'

The Brat

'So, you want me to shake the tree and see what sort of birds fly out.'

They strolled on a few paces 'That's about the size of it, Dawson. Nothing you discover could be used in court, of course, but it would point us in the right direction, tell us where to look.'

'And you can't get an inside source?'

'We've tried. All their top echelon are Russian imports, no one else is allowed into the inner circle. The British talent are just foot soldiers, they are never told anything sensitive.'

'So, what do you want me to do, Elise?'

Her eyes narrowed shrewdly 'We know from the search of your property you own some pretty sophisticated surveillance equipment Dawson.'

'It's not against the law to own it.'

'That's why you've still got it.' She paused, squinting into the setting sun. 'I also suspect it wouldn't bother you to employ interrogation methods we police could never use.' She looked away, embarrassed by her suggestion that he might use force to loosen tongues.

Dawson didn't reply immediately thinking through the implications of his involvement. she was obviously desperate to obtain information. Protecting this underclass of kids had become a personal crusade of hers. He would be deniable, of course, so there'd be no help if things went tits up. On the other hand, these ruthless Russians were using people like Charlene to line their pockets, not giving a damn for their victims. And now another young innocent girl lay in the mortuary, drowned like a rat in a sewer. These people had to be stopped by hook or by crook, but it would involve a hell of a lot of risk to himself. *Well, you're not exactly risk averse, are you?*

Closing out his inner voice he said 'I'm not some petty informant to be used and discarded, Elise. I don't dance to anyone's tune. If I help you, I'll do it in my own time and in my own way.' He looked hard into her eyes making sure there was no misunderstanding. 'I'll not tolerate any interference from you, it that clear?'

She looked shocked at the vehemence of his statement, but she understood his position.

'Very clear. If our arrangement were to be discovered, Dawson, it would not only end my career but probably put me in the dock. So, you see, I've a strong motive for being straight with you.'

'OK, Elise, but understand that by using me you'll be opening a box that can't be closed.'

She gave him a long appraising look and realised he wasn't boasting.

'I'll take another look at his mansion, do some covert surveillance, maybe stir him up some more. Angry people don't think straight.'

Her eyebrows rose an inch 'You've been there already?'

The Brat

'I interrupted his fishing trip yesterday with a few lead pellets and I gave his chauffer a headache. I don't suppose they've made an official complaint, though.'

As they walked back to the car, she gave him an unlisted number. 'Memorise it. Just leave messages, I'll get back to you as soon as I can. As for expenses, I'll pay you personally.'

'No need for that, Elise, I want these bastards out of business as much as you do.'

She looked at him nervously 'Please, be careful, Dawson. I have a bad feeling about these people.'

*

Chapter 20

Petronovski swore volubly, his face crabbed as he allowed a servant to scalpel and tweezer birdshot from under the skin of his left thigh. 'I'm putting a bounty on that bastard Jukes. Fifty grand for putting us on to him, a hundred for bringing him in. I want every criminal in the country to be on his case.' He slapped the servant around the ear 'Be careful you clumsy bastard.'

On a couch opposite Petronovski's chair Ivanov was lying face down while another servant picked the four pieces of shot from his arse.

'He broke Jackson's finger, too. What's with this fucking finger fetish the bastard has?' He glowered at his own broken finger, 'I'll break every bone in his fucking body when I catch up with him. I want to torture that cunt until he screams for mercy.' The man removing the shot from Ivanov was nervous, causing his hand to tremble and he cut too deep. Ivanov roared with rage 'Ow, Jesus Christ, I'll fucking get you Jukes, you son of a fuckin' whore.'

The Brat

It took half an hour before both men were shot free and patched up. Petronovski sat behind his desk. Ivanov found sitting too uncomfortable and stood glowering. Half a dozen phone calls later both men were satisfied. There would be no escape for Jukes now. Every petty criminal in the North of England would be on the look-out. Doormen, security guards, and drug dealers would all be out to make a quick buck.

'We'd better have the cellar prepared for waterboarding, Ivanov, and dig out your thumbscrews.'

*

It wasn't long before the word of the reward filtered to Elise Elwin from her sources and she rang Dawson to warn him.

'Is there anywhere where you can stay away from them, Dawson?'

'Maybe, I'll have to ask around. You said they had Russian Embassy connections, didn't you?'

'Not officially, but they have someone high up the food chain there, for sure, why?'

'I can't say at the moment, but it could be important.'

Dawson rang Major Bell and explained there was some evidence of a political connection with the Russian mafia thing. The Major told him that they couldn't act until he had proof and they couldn't give him the use of any facilities because he was no longer a soldier.

'You can use my holiday cottage in Shropshire, Dawson, it's just outside Telford but if you're later questioned you conned me saying you wanted a holiday, fair enough?'

'Sure, I know the rules, Major. No official involvement at any level, ever, Or else.

The Major's cottage was a small two bedroomed single story one much like his own place only with whitewashed walls and a lower ceiling. The shepherd who had once called it home would not have recognised the place now. The huge hearth held a log-burning stove, the kitchen extension was state of the art and what had been an adjoining sheep barn was now the master bedroom with a large en suite facility. Dawson whistled, he knew Bell was from a banking family, now he knew it was a wealthy one.

He cleared the kitchen table and laid out his equipment and checked it over. The laser eavesdropping microphone and the digital recorder were essential, as were his drone and his adapted speargun. The night binoculars would be useful, too. All were in good order. The police had refused to release his shotgun as they said they were still reviewing his licence, whatever the hell that meant. Maybe he should get a lawyer onto it. He still had the chauffeur's shotgun but figured carrying it could be more trouble than it was worth.

The Brat

His phone rang, Elise sounded worried 'Dawson two things. First, I have just received information from a reliable informer that the Russians have put a reward on your head of £100,000, alive only. What is it you have that they want?'

'Dunno, I'm sure.'

Her voice went hard 'don't give me that, Mr Jukes, you must know.'

'OK, Elise, for your ears only. I was a member of a secret, deniable military intelligence unit that caused some of their dark operations to go badly wrong. Some of their highly trained operators got killed, which really pissed them off. Their replacements are a bunch of jokers. Just look at the mess they made of their recent nerve agent hits.'

'No, not well executed at all, I must admit' she conceded.

'They don't know for sure that our unit ever existed, they want to find out. This is where crime and politics meet.'

'OK,' she said accepting his explanation, 'sounds like the less I know the better. '

*

Weitz was slurping scrambled eggs into his mouth when his phone rang. 'Yeah?' he said impatiently, sending egg spraying forth. He lifted another forkful, waiting to blast the person who'd had the temerity to ring him this early.

'Hi, it's Charlene Mr Weitz with some more information for you.'

'Shoot.'

'Just thought I'd tell you you've been had, mate. You see unless you go on the Internet and tell people you were lying about Dawson Jukes; I'm going to the police about you.'

Weitz laughed 'and just what are you going to tell them, honey? I'm a bad man who lied about your friend?'

'No. I'll say that you got me into your room for sex, that you paid me fifty pounds for it. I still have the money you gave me with your prints and DNA on it, pal. I also have video footage of you taken in your room handing me the money.'

'OK, you got video, right? And where was the camera, up your ass?'

'I've just sent it to you pal, take a look.' She cut the call.

Weitz watched the edited video footage instantly recognising how much damage this could do him. 'Shit!'

He rang her back 'So....so what is this, a shake down? How much?'

'Listen mate, I don't want your money, I want you to go on the Internet and to the papers and say that you stitched Dawson up.' She heard him take a deep breath. 'If you don't, I'll put it all on social media.

The Brat

You'll get a lot worse shit than Dawson got. Think about it, I'll ring back soon.'

'Wait, wait, don't go. Listen, kid, maybe we can do a deal, why don't you come and meet me, bring the money and the video and I'll pay you real good, OK?'

'Fuck off.' Charlene hung up.

*

Weitz, breakfast forgotten, rushed to Jezebel's suite, his heart pounding. Who else had the kid told? If Jezebel got word before he could put his spin on things, it could get very nasty. But just what the hell could he say to make him look clean?

He banged on her door, a tired looking security man let him in 'she was partying last night Mr Weitz and she has a guest. She won't be pleased being woken at his hour,'

Weitz glared at the man 'Get her goddamned maid to wake her now, we need to talk.'

*

Jezebel was coming down off last night's drugs and drink when her maid roused her. Being disturbed early did nothing for her mood. She kicked the young man in her bed 'Git your ass outta here, boy, I got business to tend.' The young man yawned and gathered his clothes over his arm and made for the bathroom.

Despite her frail condition, Jezebel looked appreciatively at the naked man's tight butt. 'For what it's worth you're the best lay I've had in a long while' she called. The young man gave her a thumbs up sign without turning or breaking his stride.

'What the hell is it that's so urgent I gotta kick a damn good fuck outta my bed?' She turned to her maid 'Don't just stand gawpin' girl, go get me some goddamned coffee.' She turned back to Weitz, 'well?'

Weitz coughed nervously, he cleared his throat and began to explain what had happened, telling her it was a stitch-up and he could buy himself out of the situation. 'The kid is ringing back soon, I'm sure we'll hear her price, then I'll lure her to a meeting and get the money and video back.'

*

For once Jezebel Justiz didn't say anything as she assessed the situation. This was serious. Any scandal involving an under-age girl could impact badly on her and her career. On the one hand, Weitz was a good manager, getting her top gigs and publicity. On the other hand, he was greedy, robbing her blind every chance he got. This could be an opportunity to get rid of him without him waving his watertight contract in her face. She was a well-established artiste, now, a dozen top agents would be glad to have her on her own terms.

The Brat

'OK, let me think about this' she told him.

'There's nothing to think about, Jezebel' he said glibly 'I get this kid to come to the hotel and have security nab her. I grab the money and the footage then it's all her word against mine.'

'So, if it's that easy why not just do it without bothering me?'

'I didn't want you hearing second hand, I got enemies.'

Jezebel Justiz was a self-centred whining woman, but she had grown up from the gutter and had an instinct for trouble. She sensed this gig could be big trouble.

'I don't think it's gonna be that easy Marcus. For starters, you say this kid is just fourteen and she comes up with a sting like this all by herself? I don't believe it.'

Weitz saw her line of reasoning. 'So, you think this Jukes guy is behind her?'

'I'd say so, wouldn't you?' Maybe he's screwing her, maybe he just hired her, I dunno, but this could be serious for you.'

'You mean serious for us, don't you Jezebel?'

She riveted him with a cold, hard stare, her silence speaking volumes.

'Oh, I see, so you'd abandon me. Me, the guy who got you to where you are. Well, that won't happen, lady, I got a contract, try dumping me and just see what comes next.'

'Read the clause on criminal activity, shithead, you ain't got a prayer. Anyway, with child sex claims hanging over you no one will touch you with a sterilised stick. You got yourself into this, lying about that Jukes guy was your idea, Weitz.'

'You played your part in it, too, Jez, remember?'

'Sure, I remember, but what artiste doesn't do what her manager says, especially if he's threatening to quit mid-tour if she doesn't toe the line?'

He looked at her, his face pale, 'I never…'

He'd held sway over her for two lucrative years, but it looked like the lady was growing tired of him. He forced an obsequious smile. 'Don't you worry your pretty head 'bout nothing, Jez, I'll fix things good, OK?'

Jezebel looked at him sourly 'You'd better Marcus, you'd better. You've screwed enough of my backing singers to be labelled a sex pest. That don't sit well with the public these days, the "Me too" crowd are damned powerful.'

Weitz heart sank as he realised just how precarious his position was in this age of trial-by-Twitter. 'I'll put it right Jez, there'll be no cost to you.'

'Damned right there won't be, now, see if you can find that young guy and send him back, I ain't through with him yet.'

She waved him away with a dismissive gesture. 'Where the hell's that coffee?' she bawled.

The Brat

Weitz scowled and left, his face creased with tension. The "Me too" movement consumed him with dread. Witch hunts abounded. A mere sniff of underage stuff was a career killer.

Twenty minutes later Charlene rang back 'well, Mr Weitz?'

'OK, kid, Ok, you got me, now, what's it gonna cost, huh?'

'You still don't get it do you, dumbfuck?' She drew a deep breath 'you go on all the social media where you put that shit about Dawson Jukes and you tell the truth, OK?' And you apologise, too.'

'Is Jukes there with you now? Put him on kid, OK?'

Charlene lost patience. 'He's not here, fuckwit. Now, unless you tell the truth yer lying bastard, I'll do what I have to do. I'll even describe your circumcised cock.'

'You never saw my cock, what the hell you talking about?' he screamed.

'You're Jewish, ain't yer? You've been circumcised, people will think how come a non-Jewish kid my age knows about this shit unless it's true?'

Weitz's voice quaked 'Listen, Charlene, I'm a married man' he pleaded, 'this will ruin me and my kids will starve. You don't want that, do you?' He continued wheedling before she could answer 'and you love Jezebel, don't you? This could ruin her career; you want that to happen? Bring the stuff back, I'll give you a thousand for it.'

'Shove yer money up yer arse, mate. I've told you what I want, do it by five o'clock tonight or I go on the Internet and to the cops. Goodbye tosser.' Charlene hung up and switched off the phone, she needed to conserve the battery. She smiled to herself, happy she'd done something to make Dawes proud of her. Now, where to look for that little prick Jason?

Later, she took herself to a McDonalds to eat, already that day there had been a couple of men loitering in Piccadilly Gardens who had looked at her speculatively. She knew what they wanted, and she hated them for it. In McDonalds there were other kids her age, so she didn't look out of place. She sat on the periphery of a large group of noisy teens while she slowly ate keeping a wary eye out for anyone paying her undue attention. After an hour she left.

Charlene was passing an electrical goods shop and glanced inside. Her attention was immediately drawn to a picture of the wrecked BMW on the local news. The text running under the picture read *Unidentified youth in critical condition after police car chase.* Her mood changed immediately. Oh, God, Jason she thought, you bloody stupid git, what have you done? She felt an enormous pang of guilt, if she hadn't put him up to bringing her to

The Brat

Manchester, he'd still be alright.

The taste of impending victory over Weitz turned sour in her mouth. 'Fuck' she muttered as a tear started down her face.

Charlene spent the day wandering, wondering if Jason had parents who would be devastated by this. The guilty feeling haunted her all day.

As the five o'clock deadline approached, Charlene pushed her guilty feelings aside. There was still a job to do otherwise Jason would have been hurt for nothing.

She went into Manchester Central Library and told a sympathetic librarian she'd lost her library card and she needed to email her mother urgently to arrange to be picked up. No, she couldn't remember her mother's phone number. The librarian put away her offered phone and looked at her screen. She pointed 'number six computer, over there. Use pin number 1272.'

Charlene searched for Weitz; he had capitulated. There were his weasel words blame-shifting to a junior staff member who had mis-informed him he claimed. He had stopped short of praising Dawson's bravery in saving Jezebel, but Charlene was satisfied. Next, she searched for Dawson, but he didn't have any social media accounts, at least not under his own name. Not wanting to draw attention by staying too long, she left waving thanks to the librarian.

Charlene stole a new-looking sleeping bag left in a doorway by some homeless person. As evening fell, she ate at a McDonalds again then went back to Didsbury and her ladies' shed. She'd have to go back to Wales soon she knew but whilst there was hope of seeing her friends again, she'd wait another night.

Charlene woke in pitch darkness feeling scared, something had woken her. Had she heard a noise? She couldn't be sure, so she lay still, trembling, listening. Then the shed door opened and a powerful torch shone in her face, blinding her.

'What have we got here, then?' a heavily accented voice asked. She jumped up struggling to free herself from the sleeping bag and started to scream. A fist hit her in the jaw and the lights went out.

Chapter 21

Dawson got a text from Intelligence HQ *some interesting stuff but nothing conclusive. Please stay another day and collect.* Dawson's face tensed, he wanted to close with these bastards, to get his hands on someone's throat and squeeze some truth out of them. What had they said in his military assessment? A tendency to be impetuous when stressed. He'd worked hard over the years to cure himself but every now and again the urge to beat some deserving bastard to a pulp arose in him. It was part of his PTSD problem, he knew.

He centred a finger between his eyebrows on an acupressure point. Pressing gently, he breathed slowly and deeply as he'd been shown by his therapist. Gradually his rage subsided. He took up his position again and resumed his watch.

At ten a.m. a car with diplomatic plates arrived at the house to be met at the front door by Petronovski himself. The man the chauffer let out was tall with a slight stoop and Savile Row dressed. The two men greeted each other like old friends then went into the house and the driver drove around the back. Dawson took video and still shots, his interest was aroused but the two men did not appear in any of the rooms he could eavesdrop on.

After an hour, the weather turned sunny and warm. A door opened onto a patio at the side of the house. A woman laid a table with two place settings and a large wine jug. Dawson aimed his red dot sighting laser on the jug and then the invisible listening beam. The tiny vibrations caused by their speech would be picked up in the liquid. The laser would measure these minute vibrations and translate them back into words.

A few minutes later Petronovski and the diplomat came out in shirtsleeves and sat. A meal was served, and Dawson started recording. The wine jug was not ideal as they occasionally lifted it to pour wine and replaced it in a slightly different place. He had difficulty refocussing when this occurred.

As he watched through his binoculars, Dawson realised they were talking very seriously about something. Their body language was tense, and smiles were non-existent. Dawson hoped that this would be the breakthrough he needed. If there was a serious political facet to this, MI5 or his old unit would deal with everything and he could stand down.

The lunch went on for almost an hour, every time the female servant appeared, they stopped talking

The Brat

until she had performed her service and left. So, whatever they were talking about was secret, clearly the servant was a Russian. He saw why the police had difficulty infiltrating if even the indoor staff were Russians. The men seemed totally absorbed in the subject under discussion. Then the sun went behind clouds and a chill breeze sprang up. Petronovski and his visitor returned inside, whatever they were talking about seemed to have been concluded satisfactorily as they shook hands on leaving the table.

Dawson sent the information to HQ; it would be several hours before they made contact as the translators would need to do their work and make a transcript before the intelligence people could assess the value or otherwise of the recordings. They would then go into conference to decide what action, if any, needed to be taken.

He was tired now but stayed alert, watching. At four o'clock, the diplomatic limousine left. Dawson munched more high energy bars, drank some water and went to sleep. At last light he moved away from his hide to defecate into a plastic bag, which he tied off tightly and buried to avoid giving his presence away by animal interest. Who knew how long they'd keep him here?

He'd been back on watch only a few minutes when the short stocky figure of Petronovski appeared on the portico accompanied by two large men. They stood for a moment under the light and spoke briefly. They were dressed formally in black tie. A RangeRover collected them and they left at a leisurely pace. Clearly, they wouldn't be back for some hours, so it was time to sleep.

Shortly after midnight, Dawson was awakened by the sound of the returning Range Rover. It drove to the front door and Petronovski got out accompanied by the two men. He weaved his way unsteadily indoors. The other two men appeared to be sober. Of course, Dawson realised, they'd be his minders so no booze for them. That Petronovski was drunk was obvious. He'd sleep it off overnight so the likelihood of anything significant occurring before morning was practically zero. Dawson dozed off again.

Around 3 a.m. Dawson was awakened by the arrival of a Landrover Freelander. His night vision binoculars picked out a single occupant. The vehicle drove to the front door, security lights blazed as it approached. A big man got out and rang a bell. It was several minutes before the door was answered, so, the man had not been expected. He spoke briefly to the man who opened the door then they both went to the back of the Freelander. The vehicle's angle now obscured his view, but Dawson could see the two were carrying something between them, but what? A body? Then the front door closed behind them and a light came on in an upstairs room followed by another from a room adjacent to the hall. There was no glass of any size to focus his laser on properly, the voices were muffled and brief.

*

Inside the house Charlene was shaken to full consciousness; Ivanov towered over her. 'So, we meet again, clever little bitch.' He sneered at her 'you'll not be feeling so fucking clever when I've finished with you.' He regarded her for a moment, seeing both fear and defiance in her eyes. 'We're looking for your friend, Jukes, girl. I'll give you a chance, tell us where he is and we'll let you go.'

Charlene was terrified, her head and jaw ached, she managed to mumble 'Dunno, trying to find him myself.'

'What were you doing sleeping in that shed?'

'It was just somewhere to sleep out of the cold. The house seemed empty so I thought no one would mind.'

The slap came hard across her mouth 'Don't take us for fools you little bitch. One of the women who owns that house works with Jukes, that's why we check it out regularly.'

Charlene fought her fear and lost. She started crying, weeping like the terrified child she was as her heart froze. They would surely kill her now.

Ivanov spoke to the man who had brought her 'you have done well, Artem, when we catch Jukes, he'll talk in the hope of saving her skin. Put her in the cellar for now, I'll tell Dmitry first thing tomorrow, he's drunk tonight and won't appreciate being disturbed.'

Charlene looked around the high-ceilinged cellar with fearful eyes, there was an old steel bed in one corner with a grubby mattress but no covers. So, she thought, they've kept people here before. She shuddered and tried to shut out the thought of what those prisoners' fate may have been. Then the light went out leaving her in total darkness. She felt her way over to the bed, heart pounding, her hands trembling.

She didn't know how long she lay in darkness, sniffling with fright, but eventually she fell into an exhausted half sleep filled with dreams. Jason was

The Brat

tearing around in a car, refusing to hear her pleas to slow down. The car was racing down a narrow street towards a high brick wall. They hit the wall and Jason flew off screaming through the windscreen. She woke with a start, there was a faint light coming from somewhere above her.

Charlene rubbed her eyes and looked up. There, next to the ceiling, at what must be ground level, was a tiny window. She dragged the bed over and stood it on end then tipped it against the wall. Climbing up, she found the window unlocked.

She tried to get through the window as the bed wobbled beneath her feet and her clothes snagged on the catch. The opening light scraped her head painfully, still she had to try. Climbing down, she stripped to her underwear, tying her clothes into a tight bundle made from her jeans jacket. She threw the bundle up to the bed end then clambered back up again, the bed rocking dangerously. She reached the window, grabbed the sill and held on, steadying her makeshift ladder. If she fell now the noise would surely alert the people upstairs then her escape attempt would be doomed.

Stuffing her clothes out of the window, she slid her right arm and shoulder out followed by her head. She pushed all the way to one side, where she was stuck for a moment until she used her legs to force enough gap to get her left arm through, praying the bed wouldn't slip. Dragging her left arm behind her she squirmed until her elbow was through minus some skin. Using the arm as a lever on the window frame and grasping some turf with her right arm. Her head and shoulders were at last through. Now there was just the matter of her hips which, since the onset of puberty, were not as narrow as they used to be. She wriggled and writhed pulling hard, tearing her knickers on the window catch and leaving some more skin in the effort. She lay on the path for a couple of minutes panting from her exertions.

Charlene dressed then crept along the wall. She found herself at the side of the house as the first streaks of dawn pierced the clouds. Behind her was a patio with table and chairs. Across the lawn, a hundred metres away, was a high brick wall with a large double gate two hundred metres to her right. So, that was the front of the property. That would be where the road was. If she could climb the wall she could run. Maybe there was a farm or a house where she could get help.

To her left a hundred and fifty metres away a tree grew close to the wall. Would she be seen in the growing light? Could she outrun grown men? Maybe they were all asleep. She had to try; she knew that big bloke she'd set the mob on would kill her the first chance he got. The image of his soulless black eyes staring into hers came before her.

Light flooded from the cellar window, she heard an angry shout. She made her dash for freedom.

*

Five a.m. and Dawson was fully awake, he chewed on some high energy fruit bars and drank a little water then stood up to stretch his legs. He took his binoculars and did a sweep. In the deep shadow at the side of the house he thought he saw a slight movement, then it stopped. He waited, keeping the binoculars trained on the spot. There it was again; someone was creeping along the wall. A small indistinct figure, barely visible in the poor light, was crawling cautiously along the wall. He couldn't make out any detail at first then a light came through a ground level window. The figure started sprinting towards the perimeter wall to be brought into sharp focus as floodlights illuminated the entire garden.

'Charlene' he cried aloud as shock hit him. He brushed away confused thoughts, grabbed his speargun and a few darts and broke cover, running towards the wall. As he descended, he heard a shout go up and suddenly the grounds seemed a mass of activity. Then a dog barked.

*

Halfway to the tree Charlene was bathed in light that seemed to blaze from behind her like several suns casting shadows of her at odd angles on the grass. Hearing the dog her heart leapt. She was almost at the tree now, but the growling animal seemed to be almost upon her. She daren't look back for fear of what she might see. She ran harder than she had ever done before, sheer terror making her legs pump furiously. The growling got even closer, she screamed in anticipation of vicious fangs sinking into her flesh, then, as if a miracle had occurred, Dawson was astride the wall.

'Run, Brat, run' came loud, clear and full of urgency. He was a good twenty metres away from the tree as she grasped a branch and started pulling herself up. The teeth sank into her jeans.

Dawson crouched down and pointed his speargun. To miss and hit her would spell disaster, to allow the dog to pull her down would be equally disastrous. The man in pursuit was still fifty metres away shouting. If he was armed things would be deadly for them both.

Dawson squeezed the trigger, and the bolt flew into the dog's ribs behind its shoulder. The animal yelped and fell back, writhing in its death throes. He shouted to Charlene, 'run up the hill, Brat, run into the woods and wait.' He turned his attention to the man rapidly closing with him. The guy was in tracksuit bottoms and t-shirt and trainers. There was no sign of a weapon, but then, why would he need one to run a little girl to earth with a dog? The man

The Brat

looked trim and athletic. Behind him there was another shout near the house, but Dawson concentrated on the task in hand. The man didn't break stride when he aimed a karate kick at Dawson's head. Dawson sidestepped and pushed his opponent hard in the back, sending him headfirst into the wall. The guy managed to get an arm in front of him partially breaking the impact. He wasn't finished and spun, punching Dawson hard to the side of the head. Dawson grunted as sparks flew before his eyes and his knees sagged. He grabbed the man's swinging arm and pulled him onto a well-timed throat punch that felled him instantly. He stamped down hard on the man's ankle and heard it snap as the guy's scream of pain died in his choking throat, rolling, unable to get a breath. The punch wasn't hard enough to be fatal, Dawson knew, but the guy would be eating soup only for a while.

Dawson looked towards the house to see a man running back inside. He guessed he was going for a weapon. It was time to be gone. He sprinted for the tree and climbed rapidly up. As he was going over the wall, he heard a shot followed immediately by the whoosh of shotgun pellets flying past his head. Then he was down and sprinting after Charlene who was almost at the edge of the wood near to his hide. 'Wait in the woods' he yelled as he powered up the slope.

*

In the house there was near pandemonium, half a dozen minders seemed to be yelling at once. Then Petronovski appeared at the top of the wide staircase, his voice cut through the din. 'Silence, you idiots. We'll apportion blame later; this is a chance to get Jukes. Get to the vehicles, he'll be trying for the motorway. Block all the lanes. Move!'

In the woods Dawson saw Charlene bent over clinging to a sapling breathing heavily from her exertions. She'd missed his hide by over 50 metres. There was no time to divert nor for explanations. 'Quickly girl, the car is this way.' It was a quarter of a mile away down a disused track. He had to slow down as Charlene was still winded, so it took what seemed an age to reach the car. That he'd left all his equipment behind was a problem for another time.

It seemed to take an age to reach the car, Charlene went to say something, but he cut her off 'Get in quick, girl.' He dived behind the wheel, and reversed up the track, bushes scraping the car's sides, knocking the wing mirrors flat in as he gunned the engine.

Then they were out onto the single-track road and speeding towards the main road a mile away. Once there, stopping them would be difficult for any pursuer. Dawson was beginning to feel some relief; there was no sign of anyone following. The lane ran between high hedges hiding them from view across the

The Brat

open countryside but also restricting his view, too. As he reached a T junction, he swung hard left. There, blocking his way was a RangeRover, two men in the front seats looked grim. Before he could take any action a Jeep 4x4 came from behind to slam into him. Ivanov jumped out, an automatic pistol in his hand. He came alongside but kept a safe distance 'Give up Jukes, or I'll shoot the girl.'

Dawson's heart sank. Beside him he saw Charlene's tears running down her cheeks, a defeated look in her eyes. He whispered 'it ain't over yet, Brat, you'll see.' It was bravado and he knew it, but it might just give her a scrap of comfort. He climbed out of the car and raised his hands. That they wanted him alive was obvious or they'd both be dead by now. Into his head came the slogan he'd heard so many times in his training days "It ain't over until it's over." But he was damned if he could see even a glimmer of hope.

They were dragged into the huge hallway of Petronovski's Manor by Ivanov and another thug and thrown on the floor. A sharp kick to his ribs followed. Ivanov regarded him coldly 'so, Mr smart-arse, you're not as clever as you thought you were, eh? You are in for some serious pain you bastard.'

Petronovski appeared, barking orders in Russian, 'take them to the cellar, quickly. Give the servants the day off, send them away, I don't want them unnerved by the screams.' He looked at Dawson with distain 'We'll soon see how hard you really are, Jukes.'

Dawson and Charlene found themselves in the cellar, the bed Charlene had used as an escape ladder now gone. A minute later there came a hammering from outside as the window was nailed shut and boarded over.

Dawson sat on the floor with his arm around Charlene who was quietly sobbing into his chest. He was thinking of what would come next, of the tactics they'd employ. Had they found his hide and his spying equipment? Probably, he thought, and that gave him the germ of an idea.

They hated him but what they wanted most of all was information, so they'd use Charlene as a weapon. It would work, too, there was no way he would see the child suffer. They'd kill her of course, but they wouldn't want to prolong her death, probably a quick bullet to the head. He, on the other hand, would be in for a long and painful death of that he was certain. What was his best course of action? Maybe he could bluff them, but that would take some doing.

Charlene continued sobbing gently. He whispered in her ear, afraid the room might be wired. 'Listen, Charlene, I can't tell you now, but I have a plan, plus friends on the outside. Don't give up hope, OK?'

There was a pause, the sobbing stopped 'OK, Dawes, if you say so.'

The Brat

'I do say so, now, be a brave girl and believe in me.' He said this more to comfort her and reduce the horror of what she must be feeling. To be in the dark at the hands of these merciless thugs was a terrifying prospect for him so what Charlene felt like he couldn't imagine.

Half an hour later the door opened, and light flooded the room dazzling and disorienting the prisoners. The huge figure of Ivanov loomed in and dragged Dawson to his feet. He heard Charlene give a cry of despair as the next person to enter was Marcia Catanova.

Catanova leered at Charlene 'well, well, if it isn't my little lady lover. Not so cocky now are you, you little shit.' She slapped the terrified youngster around the ear and pushed her from the room and up the steps.

In the kitchen Charlene was thrown to the floor and Dawson was tied into a dining chair. Petronovski stood at the breakfast bar swirling a brandy glass in one hand and holding an electric carving knife in the other. He eyed them malevolently. He nodded at Ivanov who moved to Dawson's side and grasped his little finger. Slowly he pushed it back. Dawson bit his inner lip as the sharp pain surged through him, determined not to cry out as he felt the bone snap. Then Catanova moved in and slowly broke the pinkie on his other hand. She moved to his next finger and started to bend it until Petronovski spoke in Russian.

'If you want to dig their grave yourself, Marcia, then carry on.'

Catanova saw the sense in this and stopped, stepping back deferentially as Petronovski put down his brandy and moved forward, holding up the carving knife.

Smiling mirthlessly, he spoke to Dawson, 'Mr Jukes, you have two options the first of which is to answer my questions promptly and truthfully. The second is to watch as Ivanov cuts off her ears followed by her nose then fingers. Marcia here wants to perform female circumcision on her; shall I toss a coin as to which happens first?'

Dawson looked across at Charlene. The poor child was trembling and whimpering, utterly distraught.

'I'll answer your questions' growled Dawson 'though it won't do you any good. I've sent a report to certain people who will ensure your demise should anything happen to us.' He nodded at Charlene, 'let the child go, she knows nothing.'

'Nice bluff, Jukes, am I supposed to tremble now?' Behind him Ivanov sneered and Catanova laughed aloud, a nasty sarcastic sound.

Catanova moved to Charlene and undid her jeans, pulling them down her legs. The girl shrieked and wet herself.

'Leave her alone you bitch. Touch her and I won't say anything, I'll probably die under torture, but you'll learn nothing.' He stared at Petronovski a cold

The Brat

hatred in his eyes. 'Your bastard masters in Moscow will not be pleased.'

*

Petronovski regarded his prisoner. He hadn't made a sound when they broke his fingers though it must have hurt like hell. This guy was trained to resist torture, who knows what he could suffer before he either had a heart attack or talked. The threat to the girl was his best card. He waved Catanova away with an impatient gesture. 'Listen, Jukes, I am a man of my word. Answer my questions and the girl will not be harmed; you will die quickly from a bullet to the heart.'

Dawson nodded 'OK.'

'I shall ask you a mix of questions some we already know the answers to, so, if I catch you in a lie it will be the worse for her.' He nodded at Charlene who was weeping silent tears and looking imploringly at Dawson.

'What is the name of the secret unit to which you belonged?'

This was a bluff, but Dawson couldn't take a chance with Charlene's safety.

'We were simply referred to as The Unit.'

There was a glimmer of satisfaction in Petronovski's eyes.

'And which army base do you use as your HQ'?

This was one of the catch questions. 'We don't, we're based at RAF Chicksands.

Petronovski nodded, his eyes veiled 'So, not from the main HQ? Not York?'

'Not for the last ten years.'

'How long ago did you leave the service?'

'Four years.'

Again, the nod, the cold grey eyes blank 'and what was the last active operation you were involved in?'

'Are you sure you want to know? My people are aware I am watching you, If I go missing, they will assume the worst then it will be all over for you lot.'

Petronovski moved with lightning speed, bringing his fist into the side of Dawson's head. 'Do not try my patience, bastard.'

Dawson felt his consciousness slip for a few seconds, and he shook his head to clear it. He took a deep breath and looked his tormentor in the eye. 'OK, Petronovski' he said with an air of finality, 'so be it, but it'll cost you your life.'

This registered with the Russian. Jukes may not be bluffing he thought as a chill ran down his spine but then Moscow certainly wasn't bluffing either. He'd been tasked and he had to deliver. If he got what they wanted, Moscow could arrange a new ID, a new country to work in, anything was possible. He remained silent watching Dawson closely.

'The last op I was involved with was against a young Israeli intelligence officer who was selling

The Brat

secrets to your bosses. Mossad had no idea until we told them, then they didn't believe us. Their man was the son of a former director and high up for his age. He had recently trodden on our toes. Mossad thought we were out for revenge. He was working in England under the name of Moshe Goldblum, a supposed diamond dealer's assistant. We arranged for him to meet with an accident.'

'How was it done?'

'His was one of the easiest hits ever. The guy was an adrenaline junky; he loved free climbing and often went solo. Arranging for him to slip was child's play.'

Petronovski took a swig of brandy while he considered this. He resumed his questioning about the internal organisation of The Unit.

Now Dawson was on safe ground, the Russians knew nothing about The Unit, so he spun them some plausible lies about the size and strength of the Unit and its capabilities.

After half an hour Petronovski felt he had all the info he could get. 'Put them back in the cellar, I have to make a phone call.'

Catanova moved towards Charlene, pure hatred radiating from her, 'Can I...'

'No, you can't' snapped Petronovski, 'not until I've verified this information.'

Catanova sulked but said nothing.

In the cellar Dawson whispered to Charlene that the place would be bugged and not to say anything.

Charlene stared at him a great sadness in her eyes 'I'm scared, Dawes' she said in a small voice 'and I'm sorry I got you into this shit.'

Then the light went out, leaving them totally blind. Dawson leaned into her ear and whispered 'It ain't over yet, Brat, I can't hear no fat lady singing.' He didn't feel anything like as confident as he sounded, and his broken fingers hurt like hell making it hard to think clearly.

'You got a plan then, Dawes?'

'I'm working on it' he said smiling into the darkness, but Charlene wasn't having it.

'Don't bullshit me Dawes, these bastards are going to kill us both. That crap about letting me go if you gave 'em info was a load of bollocks and you know it.'

She was right, of course, and far too intelligent to fob off with some made-up tale. He sat wracking his brains for something to say that would bring her a crumb of comfort. He could think of nothing so remained silent. He had expected Charlene to scream and bawl at her fate but after a pause she said 'well, that's us fucked then' her voice sad and resigned. He didn't bother to chastise her for her bad language.

*

The Brat

Upstairs Petronovski spoke to Moscow, his information supported what little his Kremlin bosses knew and a lot of what they suspected about this mysterious military unit. The climbing accident story checked out; Goldblum had fallen to his death in what was believed to be a long-overdue accident by people who had little understanding of the freeclimbing sport.

Petronovski sat in his darkened study thinking. Yes, Moscow was pleased and offered him protection but that meant leaving the UK. He loved it here, he could play lord of the manor, a lifestyle he thrived on. He thought of the man in his cellar. Jukes had never showed fear for a moment and hardly blinked when they broke his fingers. That indicated toughness and training at the very highest level. His threat of his ex-unit's reprisals sounded real, too. If they were that secret, they would eliminate him and anyone else they thought might know too much about them. He had no illusions about the British secret services. They were charming, ruthless bastards who would smile apologetically as they politely killed you. He came to his decision quickly and called for Ivanov and Catanova.

'OK, this is what we'll do. Between here and Macclesfield there is a large stretch of moorland. You will find a quiet spot, dig a deep grave, and I mean deep, I don't want foxes or badgers digging them up, understood?'

'What's wrong with the grave in the woods here?' ask Catanova.

Petronovski's eyes narrowed to slits and his lip curled 'Do you really think I'd be stupid enough to bury their bodies in my own back yard? Yours, yes, no one would come looking for you' he sneered. She blanched and look down, her face scarlet.

'I will have the cellar forensically cleaned, there must be absolutely no trace of the prisoners having been here. The equipment we found in the woods will be buried with them. The people we are dealing with could be highly dangerous if they thought their security has been compromised.'

Ivanov spoke, his face grim 'I want to torture that bastard until he screams for mercy.'

Petronovski slapped his hand down on the table, his voice rose 'He's already bested you once you damned fool. We can't afford to take chances. You will dig the grave, leaving them tied. Take a Kalashnikov and stand well clear when you shoot them, don't give Jukes the slightest chance.'

Ivanov's eyes blazed, his mouth turned down at the corners, 'you said to get him to dig the grave, what am I, a fucking peasant?'

'I've changed my mind, that's all, now, do as you're told.'

Ivanov's face was sullen as he muttered 'OK, boss.'

Chapter 22

It was long hours before they came for them. With their hands still cable-tied behind them they had their mouths taped over. Ivanov oversaw this, standing well out of kicking distance, an AK 47 pointing at them. Two men marched Dawson up the cellar steps behind Ivanov, Catanova and Charlene came behind. In the hall Petronovski called Ivanov to one side and murmured briefly, his voice inaudible while Catanova loaded a small pistol, sneering at Charlene. Ivanov nodded at his boss then led the way through the front door, Catanova dragging Charlene like a wayward puppy.

Outside, Dawson looked up at the sky, he guessed it was the early hours of the morning. They were bundled into the back of a Range Rover with blacked out windows.

'The child locks are on; the windows are set to driver control' Ivanov said needlessly.

Catanova climbed in the front passenger seat and turned towards them a small .22 automatic in her hand 'if you give any trouble, I'll shoot you with this. The bullet will stay in your body so there will be no damage to the car and not enough noise to attract attention.' Dawson stared hatred knowing she was right.

They drove off quickly, the big vehicle showing its agility in the narrow lanes. Ivanov was an expert driver. Twenty minutes later they pulled off the road up a rough track. After ten minutes crawling slowly upwards Ivanov pulled over climbed from behind the wheel looked around. Satisfied that the location was suitable for his purpose, he got a spade out of the back. He glowered at Catanova 'keep an eye on them and don't get too close.' She scowled her distaste at him but remained silent.

Dawson watched Ivanov through the windscreen he was having great difficulty digging. The moorland heather and tangled roots of centuries coupled with large rocks soon had him sweating profusely. He returned to the RangeRover dragging first Dawson and then Charlene out. Charlene tried to scream through the tape her eyes wide with terror, but she only managed a muffled squawk. Dawson knew the hole wasn't even started properly so he guessed Ivanov's purpose. He caught Charlene's eye and shook his head, trying to let her know this could be the chance he needed. Ivanov pushed Charlene to the ground then stood three metres from Dawson. He

The Brat

handed Catanova a knife 'free his hands so he can do the digging.'

'But Dimitry said…'

'Fuck what Dimitry said' he barked; his face still puce from his efforts 'he's not the one trying to shift this shit.' He spoke to Dawson 'you're going to dig the hole, Jukes. Try anything and the girl will get kneecapped and buried alive.' He prodded Charlene with the rifle barrel to emphasise his threat.

Catanova cut the cable ties and quickly stood back. Dawson picked up the spade, scowling at his captors. He ripped the tape from his mouth 'It'll get it dug, just leave the child alone you evil bastard and that applies to your bitch here.' He turned and went to the hole. Catanova followed him to within two metres, her pistol pointing.

Dawson had had plenty of experience digging slit trenches during his army basic training. Ivanov had been doing it all wrong. Trying to dig straight down through heather and its roots was the quick way to exhaust yourself. The trick was to slice underneath them and remove the top layer, laying it aside then, once soil had been reached, it was relatively easy. He'd make it look hard, though, and await his chance. He examined the spade, it was a heavy duty one with a thick, sharp blade. If I get a chance, he thought, oh, if only I get a chance. He dug on slowly, methodically, the grave gradually sinking deeper.

*

In his office Major Bell had run over the transcripts of the recordings Dawson had sent him several times looking for any clue that might explain why Dawson Jukes had failed to contact him for the last 24 hours. That he had not heard from him lead to only two viable conclusions: One, that he was dead and, two: that he'd been captured.

'That stuff he recorded is mind-blowing, that the Kremlin is getting their mafia to spy and carry out hits for them explains much, Bernard' said Colonel Nigel Houghton.

Major Bernard Bell stopped his fingers rhythmically drumming his desk. 'It would explain the total balls-up they've made of the recent poisoning jobs, sir. None of their regular agents would have performed so poorly.'

'And now they are going to try and blackmail the security minister's private secretary. At least we'll be able to nip that in the bud. I can't believe the silly bugger was naïve enough to believe that girl was eighteen.'

Bell's mouth hardened into a thin line; his brow creased 'I'm more concerned for Jukes. If he had ended the surveillance, he would have told us, he wouldn't just clear off without reporting to me.'

The Colonel agreed. 'I suspect he's dead. I don't suppose he'd been wearing a locator button?'

'After his time, I'm afraid, they weren't standard issue until 2017.'

The Brat

'Well, Bernard, It's your call. You either forget Jukes and leave this Petronovski free in the hope of gathering more information or you organise a covert op to pick him up. I'll sanction whatever you decide, the Head Shed would soon have him talking.'

The Major nodded, knowing the scientific torture methods they had at their disposal. Sophisticated drugs, waterboarding and sleep deprivation in a combination led to the best of trained agents giving up their secrets. It also left them physically unmarked allowing many options for their elimination.

'Petronovski is the sort of bloke who richly deserves it, sir, he and his cronies, too.'

After the colonel left Major Bell sent an encrypted email.

*

Dawson dug away the thin topsoil until he reached the peat bed beneath. Now it was possible to slice huge spadefuls at a time, but he kept his speed down. But, inevitably, the grave grew deeper.

Finally, the ever-watchful Catanova called to Ivanov 'it's deep enough, now.'

Ivanov was leaning on the vehicle, smoking. The Kalashnikov was on its roof within his easy reach, the now silent Charlene lay near his feet. He threw away his cigarette and glanced over. The trench was almost waist deep on Dawson.

'I want it deeper, another half metre.'

Catanova's scowled and half turned towards him 'I reckon it's plenty deep enough for the two of them, now.

Ivanov bridled at this 'I said I want it deeper, woman, you heard what Petronovski said.'

Realisation flooded Dawson's brain like a searchlight. He remembered Petronovski calling Ivanov aside in the hall.

Dawson positioned himself so Ivanov couldn't see his face. He looked up at Catanova, his eyes narrow and hard 'he wants it deeper because you'll be joining us, lady' he whispered, 'what do you think Petronovski said in the hall when he called him aside?' Her face told him his barb had gone home as her eyes widened and her mouth fell open. She aimed her pistol at his head.'

'If you kill me now, he'll know you've sussed him.' His face was calm as he watched her confusion, her face switching between doubt and fear.

Her pistol was tiny, designed for a woman's handbag, for close personal protection only. The short barrel would be hopelessly inaccurate at the five-metre distance between her and Ivanov. She half turned, Ivanov was lighting another cigarette, his lighter flaring bright in the pre-dawn gloom as he bent into the flame. She took a rapid step towards him intent on shortening the distance.

Dawson leapt out of the trench covering his chest with the spade blade. Hearing him, Catanova

The Brat

whipped around and fired two rapid shots at his heart both bullets slamming harmlessly into the thick spade. He was on her then, grabbing her gun arm and pushing it aside as he rammed the spade blade under her chin in one fluid motion. Catanova let out a strangled gasp and lost her grip on the pistol as Dawson took it from her.

Ivanov was stunned by the speed of events, his night vision partially destroyed by the flare from his lighter. He turned and picked up the Kalashnikov, swinging towards Dawson who was now sprinting towards him. Ivanov pushed the safety catch to the automatic position.

Dawson fired. The Range Rover's side window shattered to the left of Ivanov who had regained his wits now. Focusing his attention, he smirked and swiftly raised the weapon to his shoulder, knowing he couldn't miss from the closing range.

A flash of movement came from his left as Charlene sprang to her feet and hurled herself into Ivanov's arm, knocking his weapon aside as a long burst erupted from it.

Ivanov screamed 'bitch' as Charlene reeled away, tripping over a large rock and falling headlong into the heather some four metres from him. Instinctively, Ivanov sent a short burst after her before hurriedly swinging back to Dawson. He was too late, Dawson fired from two metres.

The tiny bullet entered Ivanov's chest close to his heart. He screamed in pain and rage; the AK47 drooping, but he wasn't finished yet as he brought his weapon to bear again.

Dawson fired again, closing to point blank range, emptying the pistol's magazine into Ivanov's chest. The Russian slumped to his knees, his face contorted with hatred, bloody foam already at his lips. 'Fuck you, Jukes' he spat before pitching face first into the heather.

'Charlene? You OK? Where are you? Where are you, Brat?' Dawson couldn't see her, a feeling of panic rising within him.

From behind a rock, he heard a stifled moan. 'Oh, Christ, no' he groaned as he stumbled towards the sound. She was lying on her back in deep heather, blood was staining her jeans a couple of inches below her belt.

He fell to his knees beside her pulling the tape from her mouth and lifting her head gently. Her eyes met his, staring out of her gaunt face. 'You got them both Dawes, yeah?'

'Yes, Charlene, I got them baby, thanks to you. Now, I must look at your wound, so be a brave girl and let me, OK?' She managed a weak nod.

The wound was a small sickle shaped slit. There wasn't much blood, it was not a direct-hit wound. The bullet had hit a rock and shattered; Charlene had

The Brat

been hit by a fragment. He felt her back, his fingers probing gently, there was no exit wound.

'I'm going to die aren't I, Dawes?'

'No, baby, you're not. I'll get help.' He smiled, trying to look reassuring 'I'll look for one of their phones, OK?'

She smiled weakly 'OK, Dawes.'

He rose and returned to Ivanov's body. He found a flick knife in the thug's jacket pocket but his phone, which was in his shirt pocket had been pierced by a bullet. Cursing, he threw it down and ran to Catanova, finding her barely alive, her eyes were glazed and her breathing shallow and ragged. He retrieved her phone from her jeans, the signal was good and he rang 999 telling the operator he needed an air ambulance, he described the bullet wound, cutting through the operator's advice 'Yes, yes, I'm experienced with bullet wounds, it's more important you get the chopper up and triangulate my phone signal. I'll switch on the vehicle's headlights.'

He returned to Charlene's side still on the open line and cut her bonds. 'It's going to be fine Charlene; help will be here soon.'

She smiled 'thanks Dawes.' There was a pause, when she spoke again there were tears in her eyes, her voice was barely audible 'do you think God will forgive me for being a whore, Dawes? I saved your life, didn't I? Does that make me a good person now?'

The tears ran freely, unashamedly down his craggy face as he clutched her to him, rocking her gently, his heart pierced by her words. 'You've always been a good person Charlene, you have never been a whore, sweetheart; you were raped and abused. You've done nothing to be forgiven for darling girl.'

She was shivering now, going into shock, he realised she must be bleeding internally.

'Call me Brat, daddy Dawes.'

'You'll always be my beautiful Brat, baby, always, now save your strength, help will be here soon, you're gonna be OK.'

Her eyes flickered, her voice barely a whisper 'it's stopped hurting now, Dawes but I can't see any more. I'm glad it was me not you.'

'Help's coming really soon, Brat, you're not going to die, I won't let you.' He pulled her tighter into his chest, willing her to hang on.

After fifteen minutes comforting her and speaking to the emergency operator, she let out a sighing breath, and slipped into unconsciousness as Dawson heard the first beat of the helicopter blades.

Two minutes later the helicopter landed, and paramedics rushed to him. Dawson was brushed aside as they worked on Charlene pushing a drip into her arm. Another voice called 'there's one still alive here the man is dead.'

The Brat

Dawson realised he could help no further and leaned on the vehicle in a daze. After a little while a kindly voice said 'are you alright, sir? I could give you a sedative.'

These words had a galvanising effect on him 'No, no, I'm fine thanks. How is she?'

'Too soon to say, sir. She's lost a lot of blood but we're about to take off with the casualties, so if you wait here for the police, sir.'

Dawson nodded 'there are things I must do.'

'The police will be here any minute now, sir, they'll want a statement.'

Then the man was gone, and Dawson felt the downdraft as the chopper took off, the familiar smell of burnt kerosene filling his nostrils. He watched as the flashing lights faded into the dawn. A long way off he saw blue lights flashing on the main road coming towards him. The daze left him instantly. That bastard Petronovski would get away with this if given time. He'd lie, arrange an alibi, coerce witnesses and use all his influence to wriggle out of charges. Well fuck you Petronovski he thought, you won't wriggle out of this one.

Picking up the Kalashnikov Dawson removed the magazine, there were only two rounds left. He found a full one in Ivanov's coat pocket. Searching the RangeRover, he discovered another full mag in the driver's door. He quickly fitted a fresh magazine and cocked the weapon. Petronovski would be expecting the vehicle back soon. Dawson would not disappoint him.

The RangeRover bumped, jumped and lurched as Dawson pushed it back to the main road. He was slammed repeatedly against his seatbelt as he jolted down the track, but it barely registered with him. His mind was filled with a desire to kill, a lust for vengeance he had never know before, not even in war.

Passing the police cars speeding towards the crime scene, Dawson kept to the speed limit. He wouldn't draw attention to himself unduly. He'd already worked out the first part of his strategy, after that there was no point even trying to guess what would happen. He reckoned there could be ten or even a dozen men at the mansion, two at the gatehouse the rest inside plus Petronovski. Too bad for them.

The road ran alongside the boundary wall of Petronovski's place before turning in a wide loop to face the gate making the approach fifty metres of straight lane. This was done to give the gate guards time to see who was driving any approaching vehicle.

Dawson drove up at a brisk speed and flashed his headlights. When this drew no response, he blasted the horn and flashed again. They were expecting Ivanov to be returning, his mission accomplished, and he was not the sort to be kept waiting. The gates swung open and a man, an AK47 at his side, emerged

The Brat

from the bunker and waved. Dawson stopped and lowered the nearside window. The shock on the guard's face would have been comical in other circumstances but Dawson was in no mood to appreciate it. He pointed his weapon and waited until the man had recovered enough to shout a warning to his companion and start to raise his weapon before he shot him in the face.

The man in bunker pressed an alarm button and dashed out, rifle at the ready. Dawson blew the back of the man's head off with a well-aimed three round burst before he could even raise the weapon to his shoulder.

At the house there was confusion then panic as they realised they were under attack. By this time Dawson was halfway to the house his foot hard on the accelerator. He didn't let up as he approached the front portico. Up the steps and into the double front door he drove barely registering the enormous bang and the splintering of wood as he crashed through into the hall.

A man ran out of the small office on Dawson's left, pistol in hand and took a wild shot which shattered the windscreen and ricocheted into the wall. Dawson, pointed as fired another short burst. The man flopped lifeless, blood pumping from a hole in his forehead.

Diving out of the RangeRover, Dawson rolled to his right towards an ornate Greek-style pillar as a long burst of automatic fire from the top of the broad stairs opposite him riddled the front of his vehicle, starring the windscreen in half a dozen places. Dawson stood up behind a pillar and cautiously peeked out. Stone chips hit him in the face as another long burst slammed into and past his shelter the noise reverberating around the cavernous hall. Dawson switched to single shot. Half a mag was gone already, he couldn't afford to spray ammunition about. Then he heard a sound that brought a grim smile to his face, his opponent's empty magazine hitting the floor as the man ejected it to reload. Dawson swung around the pillar rifle pointing. The man was crouched behind the ornate balustrade at the top of the stairs concentrating on pushing a new mag into his weapon. He was not an easy target, the gaps in the balustrade were narrow. Quickly but carefully, he aimed for the centre of the visible mass, squeezing off a round. The man screamed, dropped his weapon and, clutching his shattered forearm, rolled back out of sight still screaming.

There came the sound of a voice yelling instructions harsh and guttural from further back upstairs then a door slammed, and the screaming was muffled almost to nothing. Someone had dragged the wounded scout away. It all went quiet after that. What people remained were not about to dash into view and get themselves killed. Now they'd be

The Brat

planning a counterattack and they knew his location and they knew the house well.

Dawson took stock of his position. Off to his right and two metres in front was a door. Were there any men in there? How many more were upstairs? He was considering dashing up the wide staircase, kicking in a few doors, taking the fight to the enemy when a movement from behind the balustrade caught his eye. The grenade seemed to float towards him in slow motion. It bounced twice then skittered on the tiled floor before it hit the other side of the pillar and exploded.

Dawson's ears rang, the pressure wave stunned him for a moment, and he stood for precious seconds doing nothing. His training took over. *Move* his inner voice screamed. They'd follow up now he was sure, and he couldn't afford to still be here.

He ran for the door through the dust from the pillar plaster and smoke from the grenade. It partially covered him. Reaching the door, he glanced up to the top of the stairs expecting to see men pointing guns. There was no one there. He pushed the door half open then on a whim he ran back to the RangeRover and climbed in feet first sliding across the front seats. He could see the door he'd opened and part of the staircase from this position. It wasn't ideal but then what was, short of having a four-man SAS team backing him up?

Dawson heard footsteps and the same guttural voice giving orders. He watched through the tiny clear strip at the bottom of the windscreen. Three men crept down the stairs in line abreast, crouching, looking nervously about them, guns to the fore.

The man on the right spoke and pointed to the part-opened door. Two of them ran across but didn't enter. They were at either side of the door. The first man took a grenade from his pocket and pulled the pin. He nodded at his companion who pushed the door wide and fell back against the wall. The first guy threw the grenade inside and flattened himself against the wall. The grenade detonated and the two stood up to follow through. Dawson was out of his hiding place in an instant. Two quick shots left and right and two targets fell. He swung to his left looking for the third man. He was nowhere to be seen. Dawson saw a marble table with a large houseplant on it on the far wall. It was the only place he could be in the wide empty hall. He pushed the safety catch to Auto and fired a short burst then dived for the pillar as a return burst riddled the RangeRover door where he had been a quarter of a second ago. The guy was a good shot, too good to take chances with.

'There's a Police Armed Response Unit on its way, pal. A couple more minutes and you'll be toast. Give up.'

The Brat

The answer was a curse and long burst into the pillar. That had to be his thirty shots Dawson thought. Don't these clowns ever learn? He peeped around the pillar. Nothing. He stepped out aiming low under the plant and sent a five-shot burst. There was a scream of pain 'No shoot, No shoot please. I come out.'

'Throw your weapons out and come out slowly showing your hands.'

An AK 47 without a magazine came sliding out. Dawson said, 'and the pistol?'

'No pistol, No pistol mister.'

The hands appeared, the left visibly shaking then he appeared, a squat man in his forties with light blonde hair and bright blue eyes each side of a broken nose. Blood dripped from his upper left arm where a round had clipped him.

'How many more men here?'

'No more men mister.'

'Where's Petronovski?'

'He fucks off quick when you drive in.'

'Don't try my patience, I didn't hear an engine.' Dawson aimed the AK47 at the man's head. 'Where is that bastard?'

The guy looked terrified 'He use service stairs, go out back.'

'Where's he going?'

'If I tell, you no shoot?'

'OK, tell, I'll not shoot you.'

'He go to his whore across river Greenfield slipway, she has car, he go London, big friend in Embassy.'

'Any more boats?'

'Sure, one more, key under sun visor.'

Dawson felt suspicious. This bloke's voice was the one he'd heard giving orders. He seemed way too keen to spill his guts. Not the sort of muscle a man like Petronovski would employ.

'Turn around.'

'Please, mister...'

'If I shoot you, it'll not be in the back, now, turn around.'

The man turned slowly, and Dawson saw his waistband was clean. A picture of one of the dead men at the door came to his mind. The guy's trouser leg had ridden up revealing an ankle holster. He glanced back at the bodies sure enough the other man had a bulge at his ankle. 'Pull up your trouser legs.'

The man reluctantly complied to reveal an ankle holster, a Glock G 43 automatic pistol nestling against his leg. 'Oh, God, I forget it, I forget it.' his voice rose as panic set in, '*please*, mister, I forget.'

Dawson stepped a pace further back, his finger taking up the first pressure on the trigger. 'Bend down slowly, take it out with your left hand and slide it back to me.'

The guy did as he was told. Dawson dragged the weapon back another metre with his foot without

The Brat

looking down. He bent and lifted the Glock. It was cocked and ready. 'Turn around.'

Dawson's face took on a pitiless blank expression more terrifying than any scowl. The man's knees were now trembling.

'Please, mister... I have family...'

'Lucky old you. Those street kids mostly don't, not that you give a fuck.' Dawson pointed the pistol at the man's lower abdomen.

'Please, mister Jookes, you promise, no shoot.'

Dawson fired 'Like you, I'm a lying bastard.'

The man sank to his knees clutching his guts his eyes pleading. Dawson fired again.

There had to be more men, surely? Dawson tried to figure where they would be. If Petronovski had flown the coup he would have taken some muscle with him. Guys like that look to save their own skins first and foremost. Dawson ignored the room into which the grenade had been thrown and the office where he'd shot the first man was tiny, he'd seen everything in there. He and went cautiously up the stairs. The first room he entered was a bedroom. The man he had shot in the arm was lying dead his blood soaking the carpet where he'd bled out. The next room was an empty bedroom, the third was an office. A woman in her mid-fifties was at a desk shredding papers. She looked up horrified and raised her hands.

'I have no weapons' she said in excellent American English 'Mr Petronovski has left the building.'

'Step away from the desk.'

She obeyed, now looking calm. She was dressed in a close-fitting white blouse and a black mid-calf length skirt. He signalled her with his left hand, all the time keeping his weapon pointing. She did a slow pirouette until facing him again.

'I have no weapons' she repeated. He took all the money if that's what you're after.' She nodded towards a partially open wall safe.

'Who are you?'

'Olga, Mr Petronovski's housekeeper. Can I put my hands down now? I have no weapons.'

Lies make the liar over emphasise he thought 'Ok, you can relax. Where's he gone?'

'I don't know, he has taken all the money. You check the safe, see for yourself.' She pointed across the room.

Dawson turned his back on her and took a step towards the safe. As he suspected he heard a faint rustle of clothing. He spun around; she had her skirts pulled up reaching for the G 43 strapped to her thigh.

He mimicked her accent 'I have no weapons.'

She looked up horrified, just before Dawson put a bullet through her left breast.

There was no more time to waste hunting underlings in the house, if he were to catch

The Brat

Petronovski he had to move fast. He ran for the stairs. He knew there was another RangeRover parked outside. In the security office he stepped over the body and saw what he was looking for. The key fob to the vehicle was hanging on a board along with a boat key with a big cork float attached. Key under the sun visor my arse he thought, glad now he'd shot the man. He took both.

Driving around the back of the house he picked up a track that led out past the stables a quarter mile to the river Mersey.

The boathouse was a mock Tudor building with a short landing stage against which a small speed boat was tied. The boat was sleek and modern, about five metres long with a powerful Mercury 50 HP outboard attached.

Dawson scanned the river; it was in full flood and running fast, the tide just beginning to ebb. The wind was strong here and blowing against the current causing the water to be choppy. Black clouds were gathering downstream and thunder rumbled in the near distance. The only vessel in sight was almost halfway across. It was a weekend cruiser, bobbing uncomfortably in the choppy waters as it nosed slightly upstream to counter the fast flow.

Dawson jumped in the speedboat he'd done a month's training with the Special Boat Service, so pursuit held no fears for him. The engine kicked into life and Dawson opened it to full power, roaring after the cruiser.

He'd gone only a few metres before he had to throttle back. The light boat was hitting waves and jumping dangerously into the air threatening to flip over. Still, even at two thirds speed he was going twice as fast as the cruiser, he just hoped they didn't turn around and see him. He aimed slightly upstream of his quarry. They wouldn't hear his engine in the wind until he was close. On he ploughed bouncing dangerously, using every trick he knew to keep moving fast and to stay afloat.

He was in mid-stream now and two hundred metres behind the cruiser when he saw a man stand up in the stern and raise an AK 47. The hand-clap slap of high velocity bullets passing over his head made Dawson start to jink the boat left and right. Shooting at a moving boat from a moving boat made him almost impossible to hit. The risk increased the closer he got, but closer he must get.

Whoever was driving the cruiser panicked and opened the throttle as the man in the stern stepped over the transom to place one foot on the narrow swimming platform, sending another ineffective burst. The cruiser bounced dangerously, the stern slewing around, sending the man flying overboard. Dawson saw him briefly, his arms flailing wildly as he was swept downstream in the current.

Dawson was now just a hundred metres away and could see the man at the wheel was Petronovski. Getting alongside would be impossible in the

The Brat

conditions whilst the boats were moving. Dawson reached for the rifle and switched to automatic. Shooting at Petronovski would be a fruitless exercise even close to, besides, he wanted him alive.

He steered the speedboat upstream leaping on the waves then he spun around and rode the current downstream crossing close under the cruiser's stern. There was no time for anything fancy, he extended his arm and sent a long burst into the boat just above the propellor wash. He spun away back upstream to come parallel with the cruiser.

At first nothing happened then the cruiser started to lose speed. Black smoke streamed from the engine cowling then disappeared. The automatic fire extinguisher had kicked in flooding the engine compartment with CO_2 the boat would not burn. The stricken cruiser continued to lose way until it stopped and started to drift beam-on downstream rocking alarmingly.

The weather now played its part as the heavens opened and rain speared the water, like grey javelins. Visibility was reduced to fifty metres. Thunder rolled and lightning struck a few metres away from the cruiser

Dawson closed to ten metres and hailed Petronovski 'Give up, man you've got nowhere to go.' He pointed at him and raised his hands, then pointed again, indicating the man should surrender.

Anthony Milligan

The Russian came to the rail a handgun in his fist and opened fire. His shooting stance was professional but the results futile. One round struck the bow but that was the nearest he got. Dawson opened the throttle and circled the boat he could wait until Petronovski ran out of ammo.

Swooping in again Dawson saw his enemy point the gun and fire a single round then the slide stayed back. Petronovski's magazine was empty. He threw the weapon at Dawson in frustration.

Dawson grabbed his boat's bow line. It would be bloody dangerous but to hell with it, Petronovski wouldn't be rescued by anyone. He drove at the bouncing cruiser and, at the last second turned the wheel sharply. The speedboat slid into the side of the cruiser and Dawson threw the rope around a cleat in the cruiser's bow holding on tight as his stern swung in, the current pinned him to the cruisers side. He grabbed the AK47 checked the magazine, two rounds only remained.

A bullet slammed into the console close to Dawson then another plucked his sleeve as he whipped around, hurriedly pointed the AK47 and sent a round at Petronovski who was standing at the rail, leaning forward and down a Glock G 43 in his hand.

Dawson's bullet struck the stainless-steel guard rail close to Petronovski's right and whined off. The startled man leapt back out of sight. He knew the

The Brat

Russian would stay back, out of sight and wait until Dawson's head popped above the side rail. He'd be a sitting duck.

The stern of the speedboat was three metres away from that of the longer cruiser. A plastic twenty-five litre petrol container, half full gave him an idea but it would be dangerous. There was no time to over think. Petronovski had at least four bullets to his one and the man clearly knew weapons. Even if he were panicked now, he would soon calm down.

Diving into the stern, Dawson took the rear mooring warp and tied it to the handle if the fuel drum. He would need all the buoyancy it could give. He slung the AK47 over his shoulder, slipped off his trainers and slid off the stern. The water felt like liquid ice engulfing him and ripped his breath away. Panting rapidly, he hugged the fuel drum tightly under his chin, if he lost his grip, he would be pulled under the cruiser's hull downstream to certain death.

Dawson kicked hard and moved along the cruiser's side towards the stern.

'Come on then Dukes, show yourself. An AK against a popgun? Come on you chicken-shit bastard.'

There was a nervous edge to the disembodied voice. Dawson hoped the guy wouldn't have the courage to approach the rail and see what was happening.

He reached the cruiser's stern and the current thrust him around it. His rope reached its length stopping violently and threatening to snatch the drum from his grasp. He reached up and grabbed the bathing ladder with his left hand then let the drum go and grabbed on with his right. He folded the ladder down into the water. The bobbing of the cruiser lifting him up and down pulled mercilessly on his shoulders and the current dragging at him conspired with the icy cold to sap his strength. It took a superhuman effort but at last he got his right foot on the bottom rung. With three points of contact he managed to heave himself up onto the narrow bathing platform keeping his head below the transom. He lay panting for a moment, but he had no time to waste Petronovski would suspect something and go to the rail at any moment. Dawson slid the rifle off his back and emptied the water from the barrel.

Colonel Kalashnikov had designed a rugged weapon built for the worst conditions on earth. Dawson took a deep breath and stood up, bringing the weapon to his shoulder.

Petronovski was leaning against the port rail, his feet planted, his pistol held in the two-hand stance, his gaze fixed the opposite rail. He believed it was the only place Dawson could appear from. Then he caught a movement in his peripheral vision and whipped round. He fired in haste the bullet narrowly

The Brat

passing Dawson's ear. Dawson took his time and squeezed the trigger. Petronovski's left knee exploded in a gout of blood, gore and bone splinters as he fell shrieking to the deck. His pistol sliding away.

Dawson climbed the transom and walked across to the pistol checking the magazine. It was full.

Ignoring Petronovski's screams he rolled him onto his back. He took hold of the injured leg and wrenched it back removing the shoelace. He examined it briefly. It would do fine.

Holding Petronovski on his back, Dawson said 'I told you if you hurt Charlene Keenan, you'd die screaming.'

Petronovski grimaced 'Look, Jukes, you've won, OK? In that grab bag under the wheel, there's half a million. It's yours, just get me ashore and call a doctor. There's a laptop in the cabin, bring it here, I'll transfer a million into any account you give me.'

Dawson's lip curled with contempt 'Is that what you think this is about? Fuckin' money? Jesus, you make me puke.'

Petronovski was pleading now 'Please, Jukes, I have more money, I can double this, just get me ashore, *please*.'

'Back in your house, when you held all the aces, I told you that knowing about my ex-unit would cost you your life.'

'Please, Jukes…I haven't told anyone yet, The Kremlin… they don't know…'

Dawson placed a kick hard into Petronovski's ribs silencing the man. Rolling him over on his face Dawson made two opposing loops in the shoelace and slipped them over Petronovski's thumb. He pulled with a satisfied grunt as the clove hitch bit tight. He then dragged the man upright thrusting his arm through the steering wheel before tying another clove hitch around his other thumb. He finished the job by tying the loose ends into a neat reef knot.

'The harder you pull, the tighter those hitches will get.'

'Jukes... two million, I can get you another two million, man.'

Ignoring his pleas, Dawson took the boathook from the cabin roof and reached over the stern and retrieved the petrol container.

'Oh, God, what are you doing, Dukes? What the *fuck* are you doing?'

Dawson gave a rictus smile 'the trouble with you nasty bastards, Petronovski, is you believe no other bastards can be as nasty as you.' He gave a harsh laugh, 'you're about to find out different.' He unscrewed the can's top.

Petronovski sagged to the floor as he realised Dawson's intention. He was whimpering now, his arms stretched behind him through the wheel spokes. 'Please, Jukes, no, no, just shoot me, *please*.'

The Brat

Dawson doused the man's trousers with fuel. 'I'm not going to soak you completely Petronovski, because it would be over far too quickly. You're getting just enough to ensure you burn to death and feel every second of it.' He sprinkled more fuel on the deck, running it down to the stern.

Finishing his task, he went into the cabin and found the laptop Petronovski mentioned, it could contain useful information. Returning, Dawson opened a locker beside the wheel and found what he knew would be there. He then took the money and heaved it over the side into the speedboat.

He turned before climbing down into his boat 'the pain you'll feel is only a fraction of what you've caused others you evil bastard.'

Dawson retrieved the stern line and cast off the bow. He took his boat upwind of the cruiser he opened the base of the flare and pointed it. Slowly he pressed the firing tab over until he met resistance then, checking his aim, he pushed it home. The flare soared into the cruiser striking in front Petronovski. He could hear the man's death screams as the flames licked up his body, but it brought him no joy.

He turned for the shore and motored away. A few seconds later the flames reached the petrol container and exploded, sending a gout of flame shooting skywards from the cruiser's stern. The lifeboat would be called out if anyone could see the flames from the shore in the foul conditions rescue or even salvage possible. The boat would go on drifting downstream and blazing until it sank.

Dawson couldn't see the boathouse anymore through the torrential rain, so he steered directly across the current that would place him downstream of it. He would then motor upstream keeping the bank in sight until he found it.

As he tied the boat up his thoughts returned to Charlene. Had she survived? He'd seen people survive much worse wounds, but she was only a skinny kid without many reserves of strength. It's a bloody mess he thought a complete bloody mess.

He was walking up the jetty when he heard an engine. It was still a way off but coming in his direction. He jumped down to the water's edge and found couple of large rocks. Unrolling the grab bag's waterproof fastening he stuffed them inside and refastened it. He ducked under the jetty, waist deep in the muddy stream and sank the money. He had no intention of keeping the cash, nor was he keen on handing it over as proceeds of crime to be swallowed by the government maw. No, he'd find a good use for it.

Back on the Jetty he walked to the RangeRover as a Landrover came into view and stopped abruptly. Two men in black from head to foot got out and Dawson saw the red laser dots appear on his chest. He raised his hands and stood still.

The Brat

The men didn't speak, one stood pointing his weapon while the other one approached from an angle leaving his companion with clear line of sight.

Dawson said 'My name is Dawson Jukes, there's a Glock in my right-hand trouser pocket. He remained still, his hands raised.

'Face down, now.'

Dawson obeyed immediately.

'Hands behind your back.'

He felt the plastic restrains bite into his wrists. The man searched him quickly and expertly, retrieving the pistol.

'On yer feet. Now.'

He felt himself being hauled upright.

The man inclined his head 'Landrover. One wrong move and your gone.'

Dawson was dragged to the men's vehicle and shoved roughly in the back.

'You lads will be from Chicksands then?' he asked.

They didn't answer. Arriving at the mansion, he was dragged out of the vehicle and marched unceremoniously into the Portico. The battered RangeRover he'd driven into the hall was now at the foot of the steps.

'Inside.' The balaclava'd head nodded.

Dawson went up the steps. Inside he saw a familiar figure, his back to him, talking to another man.

'This arsehole claims he's the late Dawson Jukes, boss.'

Major Dinger Bell turned 'My God so it is. Release him please.'

A slightly surprised voice said 'Oh, all right boss.' And Dawson's hands became free a second later. 'Sorry mate.'

'Don't be, you were just doing your job.' Then he spoke to Bell 'What the hell are you doing here, Major?'

Bell ignored the question looking pointedly at the bodies 'this your doing, Dawson?'

'Yes, Major, I was spreading some much needed fuckery.'

'So I see. Where's Petronovski?'

'Bouncing along the bottom of the Mersey, Major, he had an accident.'

'An accident?'

'His boat caught fire.'

'And I suppose you were there?'

'I witnessed it from a distance.'

Bell was silent, considering this remark for a few seconds 'We really could have done with taking him alive, you impetuous bastard. He had all sorts of valuable information we could have used.'

'Sorry Major.'

'You're about as sorry as a fox eating a prize chicken.'

The Brat

Dawson looked puzzled 'Anyway, what are you doing here, Major? I thought you needed a political angle before you became involved?'

'And thanks to those recordings you made we got one. Oh, boy, did we get one.'

Dawson raised a quizzical eyebrow, but the Major didn't elucidate.

'Walk me through the scene, Dawson. Tell me what happened. I can guess most of it, but I want to hear your version.'

'First, I need to know of a young girl called Charlene Keenan she was wounded earlier today. They flew her off the moors in a helicopter.'

'All in good time Dawson, if we are to come up with a scenario that satisfies the media then I'm going to have to know the details fast and I haven't got all bloody day.'

Dawson was tired now and Bell's attitude irked him. He felt his temper rising at this casual disregard of a young girl's fate.

'Neither have I, Major, Dawson snapped 'so you'd better find out what happened to her. You'll get fuck-all from me 'til you do.'

Bell reacted with utter shock; he wasn't used to being defied. 'Are you serious, man?'

'You'd better believe it, Major. Now, can you get on to your comms guy and bloody well find out?'

Bell looked like he'd put his hand in a lucky dip and found a turd. Without another word he went across to a man and mumbled a few words. He returned promptly.

'OK, it's in hand, now, can we proceed?'

Dawson led Bell through the house explaining what happened. The Major nodded but didn't speak until they reached the dead housekeeper.

'And this one?'

'She said her name was Olga, the housekeeper. Look up her skirt.'

Bell lifted the hem 'Ah, I see.' He withdrew a tablet from his pocket and consulted it. 'Olga Eltsina, Petronovski's half-sister and if the latest intel is correct, his one-time lover.'

Dawson's eyebrow twitched 'It takes all sorts, I suppose.'

The Major crossed to the safe and looked in but did not touch it. 'Rumour has it Petronovski kept a large sum in here at all times, anything up to a million pounds. Know anything about it, Dawson?'

Dawson put on his poker face 'The safe was like that when I got here. I didn't see any money in it.'

'So, Petronovski took it with him?'

'That seems reasonable Major. His sort would hedge their bets. He'd grab the cash and run when the shit hit the fan, he's got escape funds. If his men had killed me, then he'd have brought it back.'

Bell grunted, regarding Dawson with a sceptical eye. 'So, any money he had will be at the bottom of the Mersey?'

The Brat

'That's the only place it could be, Major.' Dawson knew that Bell didn't quite believe him, the man had uncanny instincts, that made him a superb intelligence officer.

Back in the hall, Bell went over to the two men who had brought Dawson in and spoke a few words.

'If you're sending them to look for money, Major, they won't find any but there's a laptop on the driver's seat of the RangeRover.'

Bell returned 'right, you shrewd bugger, we'll need a full debriefing but that can wait until tomorrow, I can see need medical attention for those fingers.' He called to a man who brought a medical kit over. 'We'll splint them for now and get you to the MO tomorrow morning. We'll put you up in the mess tonight.'

'That's fine Major, now, about Charlene?'

Bell crossed to his communications man and quickly returned 'She's in the Countess of Chester Hospital. She been operated on and is in the intensive care ward. It's still touch-and-go I'm afraid.'

Dawson's heart sank and his strength drained away as the medic worked on his fingers. 'Can we get to fuck out of here Major?'

*

Chapter 23

Despite his tiredness Dawson slept badly. He kept seeing Charlene's face pale and gaunt against his arm. She had been very brave, and she was a fighter, too, but she had lost a lot of blood. Finally, around five a.m. he drifted off deeply. It was ten thirty when he awoke, sunlight streaming in through the window like yesterday's storm had never happened.

A Mess steward brought him toast and coffee, breakfast being long over. After he had finished, he made his way to Bell's office. The Major looked exhausted, as if he'd been up all night, but greeted him brightly enough.

Dawson went through the whole tale again from first meeting Charlene to the Chicksands men arresting him. He edited the story here and there especially the happenings on the boat and the hidden money. Bell listened without interruption nodding a time or two when something Dawson said tallied with what he already knew.

The Brat

When Dawson had finished there was a long pause before the Major spoke. 'You see, Dawson,' he said at last 'you've created almost as many problems as you've solved.'

Dawson looked quizzical.

'The Russian secret services have out-sourced most of their dirty work to the criminal elements. They thought it a good way to keep a safe distance from the consequences of their nastier plots and ploys. The last of the old guard KGB have either died or retired since 1991. Their successors, all highly intelligent and well-educated people, haven't got the cold war experience of their fathers.' Criminals are not trained to the standard of their spies. MI5 thought it would be much easier to squeeze information out of Petronovski about planned hits of Russian refugees in this country.'

'So, what did I discover, specifically, that led you to become involved, Major?'

'I'll tell you, but it goes no further than this room, OK?'

'I'm still bound by the Official Secrets Act, Bernard.'

'Yes, quite so. Petronovski was about to launch a sting on a very senior politician. The Minister of State for Security's private secretary, one Rupert Wyse-Burton. He's a bit of a playboy. He's forty-five but still thinks he's God's gift to younger women.

The Russians arranged for him the meet an attractive teenager.'

Bell slid a photo across the table. Dawson whistled 'Wow, she's drop-dead gorgeous, though a bit young for a forty-five-year-old, I'd say. What is she, eighteen? Nineteen?'

Bell grimaced 'ah, that's the clever bit, she's only fifteen.'

Dawson picked up the photo again examining it carefully. 'I would never have believed she was under-age.'

'Neither did Wyse-Burton. They had him filmed from every conceivable angle giving her a thorough seeing to. What a blackmail tool that would have been.'

Dawson could imagine Wyse-Burton's dismay when he was approached. A twice-divorced politician roistering was one thing, under-age sex quite another. The man was privy to top secret information as well as attending every Cobra meeting in Downing street. Had they succeeded, the Kremlin would have had a pipeline into every secret of value the government possessed.

'And I suppose our late friend Catanova provided the girl?'

'Correct, except that Catanova isn't dead. Unwell, but still alive.'

'I thought I'd killed the bitch.'

The Brat

'You damn near did. MI5 are glad you didn't, she's talking her head off about the Russian's criminal enterprises and she knows a hell of a lot. Now that Petronovski is dead she feels that doing a deal is her best option.'

'What about those two blokes she killed outside my place?'

'She denies doing it. They don't have enough evidence to charge her and they are anxious to keep her on-side.'

Dawson looked grim 'Jesus, if ever a woman deserved to die…'

Bell looked serious 'I doubt she'll make bail but if she does, I'd strongly advise against going after her.'

Bell picked up another set of papers. 'The killings at the mansion are being explained to the media as a drug-related feud. Petronovski's lot were in serious competition with a mob from Liverpool.' Bell allowed himself a wry smile 'the Liverpool lot are crying foul, of course, but no one believes them.'

'So, will the Russians swallow it?'

'Not a chance, but balls to them. They've been playing us for mugs for years, it's about time they were put in their place.'

The debriefing wound down and Dawson asked 'am I free to go now, Major? I'd like to visit Charlene Keenan.'

Bell scowled 'You're not her kin, Dawson, so it won't be possible. She's still in a bad way, so family only I'm afraid.'

'Family? Her father's dead and her mother's a drug-addled prostitute. She'll be no damned use to her.'

Bell looked embarrassed 'Yes, that maybe so, but the mother was traced as next-of-kin and was most insistent on seeing "my little baby girl" as she put it. From the questions she asked it's clear she's thinking of how much criminal injuries compensation Charlene might be due.'

Dawson was dismayed to hear this but not surprised. He left the HQ. Bell had retrieved his wallet and car but not his phone. He headed for Manchester. He needed to keep John Babcock informed and ask about work. He also needed to speak to Chief Superintendent Elise Elwin, she deserved an update, though he'd have to be careful what he told her. Maybe he could get to see Charlene through her or the social worker Shakina Hussein. He headed for a supermarket and bought a new PAYG phone He sent his new number to his few contacts then texted Elise Elwin.

She texted him back within the hour with a proposed date. *"The Swan With Two Nicks Pub, Little Bollington 7 PM tomorrow. Not Michelin star but nice. Try to make an effort this time."*

The Brat

Make an effort? What did she mean? Last time he'd turned up in clean jeans and a jumper and she'd not complained about his appearance. He scratched his head 'women' he muttered. Dawson owned several suits for work, but they were in his house on the moors. He wasn't ready to go back there just yet. He needed to rest and recuperate his broken fingers still hurt and seemed to get in the way every time he moved his hands. He could relax better in a hotel where he wouldn't have to cook or clean. He knew the police would have left his place in a mess after their search. His compulsive tidiness would force him to get to work immediately.

The thought of meeting Elise Elwin again excited him. She was an intelligent good-looking woman, the sort that made him think of things other than work.

He rang Margaret. 'Hello Margaret, it's me...'

'What the hell have you been up to now, Dawson Jukes?'

It wasn't the response he was hoping for. He affected his hurt voice 'what do you mean, Margaret?'

'Don't give me that innocent act Dawson, you know damn well what I mean. People you were interested in are dead and my sources tell me there's a young girl in hospital with gunshot wounds. I can guess who that is.'

'Dunno what you're talking about Margaret. I just rang to see if you fancied a quiet meal somewhere, maybe tonight?'

'Sorry, Dawson, but you are too bloody dangerous to know and I'm not your go-too screw anymore. Now, if you've got something I can print then maybe we can talk over coffee but that's it, OK?'

He ended the call feeling depressed then he caught his reflection in an office block window. Christ, I look like a tramp he thought. Maybe some new clothes and a haircut will cheer me up. The mess steward had taken his clothes and had done what he could to make them presentable, but the ducking in the river had taken its toll. His idea of a top-class tailor was Marks and Spencers off the peg stuff. Ah, well, he thought, I mustn't disappoint the lady Elise and he headed for the shops.

Chapter 24

The meeting with Babcock was brief. Since the retraction by Weitz and his sacking by Jezebel Justiz, things had eased, and business was slowly building up again.

'I could do with you back Dawson, there's a Chinese businessman due in next week who needs a reliable bloke.'

'I should be ready by then. By the way, where's Joanne Shipley?'

'On her way home, I contacted her the moment you phoned, she's keen to get back to work.'

Dawson left the office feeling more normal than he had in a long time. He made his way back to the Mercure Hotel. His room overlooked Piccadilly Gardens and he sat at the window for a long time just watching the people coming and going, scurrying for buses and trams. His new clothes fit well, and the shoes would lose the tight feeling after a day or so.

He rang Shazmina Hussein, but she was out of office, he texted Elise Elwin enquiring about

Charlene. She hadn't responded yet. Should he go to the hospital and try to bluff his way in to see her? If her mother was hanging around, he couldn't claim to be a relative. He was at a lose end and went down to the bar. It was quiet. He ordered a double scotch, splashed a little water in it and found a seat near the window.

The woman seemed to materialise out of nowhere. She was tall, expensively dressed with blue eyes and black hair. She had the deportment of a model.

'Excuse me sir, but are you being joined later?' Her accent was East European.

Dawson eyed her cautiously was she just a high-class hooker or part of something more sinister? 'No, I'm here on business, why do you ask?'

The woman's eyes narrowed almost imperceptibly; he saw she was shocked by his blunt response, but she hid it well.

She smiled disarmingly 'Oh, sorry, I didn't mean to be nosey, it's just that I'm alone tonight and a woman dining alone feels uncomfortable, you know? One can feel the eyes, almost hear the questions in peoples' minds.'

Dawson went along with the charade giving her a broad smile. 'I'd be delighted if you'd join me, I also hate dining alone.' He let his gaze travel the length of her elegant body.

'That would be nice, what's your name?'

'Dawson, Dawson Jukes.'

The Brat

'Elena Smith, I'm in room 1472, and you…?'

'I'll meet you down here at eight Elena. Do you like champagne by the way?'

He played the cautious sucker as well as he could and hoped she was convinced. He'd had hookers try to pick him up before in hotels maybe this one was a genuine hooker, maybe not.

After she left, Dawson went to reception and enquired about a suite. They had one available on the top floor and were delighted to move him.

She was a fashionable ten minutes late and he was waiting at the bar, Champagne bucket to the fore. He poured her a flute and toasted her health. So far, so good.

It was halfway through the first course that they came into the dining room. Their clothes said they were two middle range executives, their long, slicked-back hairstyles said otherwise. They took a table by the door where people would be constantly passing them. Better placed tables were available. Dawson paid them no heed. He danced attention on Elena, but she drank sparingly, saying she had no head for alcohol and that the champagne was affecting her. She giggled a lot as she told him where she was from, and why she was in England. She batted her eyelids and touched is hand lightly. In other circumstances he would have been aroused, but not tonight. He smiled into her eyes wearing what he hoped was the look of a smitten punter who was going for an expense account shag.

Meal over, she made it plain that more was on offer and invited him to her room for coffee.

He demurred. 'I don't like hotel rooms Elena, I have a suite on the top floor, much more comfortable don't you think?'

Her eyes lit up 'a suite? Wow, yes which one is it?'

'1500, it's quite comfortable.'

'Lovely, I just have to use the bathroom, my lipstick is ruined, I'll be right back.'

Without waiting for an answer, she left. Dawson looked around. The two men were gone.

In the suite Dawson watched as she came to him her hips swinging, lips pouting.

'Don't we need to talk about the financial arrangements first?'

'That can come later darling.'

He looked around the bedroom she had left her evening bag on the nightstand next to the bed, her earrings and bracelet next to it. She closed with him and kissed him passionately. Dawson felt himself responding, growing hard.

'Wait,' he said breathing hard 'I, too, need the bathroom.'

He disengaged and went in. She went to follow but he gave her a smile and thrust the door shut. 'There

The Brat

are somethings a man likes to do in private' he told her.

Once inside, Dawson quickly removed his shirt and ripped the arm off. Next, he took the bathrobe from the shelf and removed the belt stuffing it in the pocket. Grabbing a facecloth, he shoved it into the other pocket. Donning the house robe, he flushed the toilet and emerged smiling. She was already on the bed lying in an elegant pose in her underwear. She stroked the top of her lacy panties.

Dawson beamed widely then knelt on the bed next to her, he snatched her arm and spun her over. She gave a little yelp of surprise as he knelt on her back pushing her face into the pillows. He quickly tied her wrists behind her back. Next, he stuffed the facecloth into her mouth and secured it with the shirt sleeve. He turned her over. Her eyes were blazing not fearful.

'Right, let's have a look in your purse.' The hypodermic syringe was in an eyebrow pencil case. 'what's in this?'

She glared at him defiantly. He made a show of holding up the hypodermic and pushing the plunger until the liquid started to squirt, He inserted the needle in her neck and for the first time he saw fear in her eyes. He removed the gag 'If you scream, I'll push the plunger. I'll count five if you don't tell me what's in it, I'll push the plunger.'

One…two… three…'

'Sodium pentothal' she said' just a truth drug. It would make you quiet and answer questions. I just have to question you that's all.'

'Bullshit! Who are the two guys downstairs?'

'What guys?'

He started to push the plunger 'They are friends of a friend I owe them money. Please, Jukes, I'm just doing them a favour I wish you no harm.'

Either this was the truth, or she was a damned good actor. 'So, what's the plan? When are they due up here?'

She sneered 'If I'm not downstairs unharmed they'll come up soon and they have guns.'

'What room are they staying in?'

'They aren't staying.'

'One more lie and I push the plunger.'

The Mercure hotel values its customers' safety. Anyone can go up to the bar and restaurant on the second floor but there the lift stops. Guests have to change lifts and use their room swipe card to operate the separate residents' lift.

Dawson took out his phone and rang Bell.

'Jesus, Dawson, what the hell time do you call this?'

'Listen, Major, I've a team of amateurs straight out of central casting on my case.' He went on to explain the situation whilst Bell listened intently.

'Do you think you can extricate yourself with the girl without leaving a trail of bodies?'

The Brat

There was a soft knock on the door 'They're here, I'll see what I can do but no guarantees.'

Dawson looked through the spyhole. A short stocky man stood facing the door, behind him was the other, bigger man nervously glancing up and down the corridor. Dawson wrenched the door open and grabbed the startled man, pulling him onto a punch in the guts. The man grunted; his guts as hard as the iron he pumped. Dawson saw his hand come up with the needle. The punch had slowed the guy and the big man behind tried to push through knocked his partner off balance.

Dawson grabbed the needle and wrenched it from his grasp turning it and thrusting it into his chest. The man's eyes lit with horror and he screamed. Dawson pushed him into his more powerful colleague. He was shocked as the second man pushed both of them into the room.

Dawson spun away noticing the woman was no longer on the bed, then there was no more time. The bigger man pulled a wicked looking knife and cautiously advanced his eyes filled with deadly intent.

In training his Scottish CQC instructor had told him the best defence of an unarmed man against a knifeman is, as he put it, 'run like fook.' In the suite there was nowhere to run or was there? The bathroom door was closed, she was in there. Dawson backed off towards a small armchair. The man read his intention and moved fast slashing at Dawson's head. He swung away but managed to tumble the chair into his assailant's path. It bought him half a second. The guy expected him to back off, instead, Dawson stepped forward and kicked out, striking the man just below the knee.

The guy grunted and stepped back. The blow had hurt him but not enough to stop his attack. He lunged at Dawson who now thudded against the bathroom door, trapped. The knife came up thrusting to strike under his ribcage and into his heart. He sidestepped and twisted, the blade went into the bathroom door. Dawson chopped down hard on the man's wrist, but the guy snatched the weapon into his other hand and renewed the attack.

Then the door gave behind Dawson and he was pushed violently back towards the would-be assassin. Her arms close around his neck. The woman had wriggled free and now she was strangling him. The man grinned and moved in for the kill. Desperately Dawson spun around. The knife intended for him embedded itself in her back. She screamed and fell away. Dawson dived for the bathroom and slammed and locked the door behind him.

A muffled laugh of derision came through the door 'That won't save you arsehole.' The accent was Russian. Then the man crashed into the door. The wood splintered but held. Dawson wrapped a hand

The Brat

towel around his fist and smashed the mirror. He selected a slim shard about a foot long and wrapped the broad end in his towel. The door crashed again this time the lock all but gave. The next time the man would be through.

Standing at arm's length from the door Dawson reach for the handle praying his timing would be right. He snatched it open just as the Russian's shoulder would have collided with it. The man shot through; a look of horror crossed his face as he saw the deadly shard flash into his guts. He screamed and sank to his knees grabbing the lavatory seat with both hands his knife clattering on the tiled floor.

Dawson took a deep breath of sheer relief, that was the closest of calls. He picked up the knife and held it to the man's throat 'who sent you?'

The guy just grunted 'fuck off,' his breath was coming in gasps.

Dawson sliced the guys left ear off. He screamed again, his left hand going to the wound.

'Your spleen's punctured, mate. If I get help you can live. Who sent you?'

The man didn't answer, he slid to the floor, his body shivering with shock.

The damage was greater than Dawson thought. The man passed out and a few minutes later he died. Dawson cursed his luck, all of them dead. The knife blow intended to kill him had driven into the woman's heart, she'd died in seconds. He didn't feel any guilt at her death, he knew she wasn't some hapless whore who owed money. An escort always asks for the money up front. No pay, no play is the golden rule.

He crossed to the bed, picked up her bag and emptied it, examining it closely. There was nothing other than lipstick and a small purse with a few banknotes. The lining was silk, but it looked poorly sewn in, yet the bag was clearly a designer one. He tore the lining out and found an ID card with the woman's photo. Tossing it on the bed, he crossed to the mini bar and poured himself a scotch, sinking it in one go. Taking out his phone he photographed the corpses and the ID card. He sent them direct to Major Bell's phone with the caption A bit more fuckery.

Two minutes later a furious Bell rang him back. 'What the *fuck* have you done now you crazy bastard?'

'And a good evening to you, too, Major.' Dawson set the small armchair upright and sank into it. 'I was attacked in my room just now, I thought it was all over with the death of Petronovski, but these clowns set a honey trap. It was like something out of the eighties.'

'Christ, man, when you knew it was a trap why the hell did you not just walk?'

'They'd have caught up with me sooner or later, Major and later they might have sent competent people.'

The Brat

'How the hell did they catch up with you so soon?'

'I booked my hotel on-line in my own name, like I said, I thought it was over.'

Bell went into a rant about how hard it would be getting a cleaning team up North at short notice.

He went on until he annoyed Dawson who cut him off abruptly. 'Major, it's obvious they'll send someone to check when these clowns don't report in. I can't be here when it happens. Is there a safe house anywhere near?'

'In Manchester? No. The nearest one is in Birmingham.'

'Christ almighty, you Southern buggers think the universe begins and ends in fuckin' London and the South East.' He checked himself, taking a deep breath. Falling out with Bell wouldn't be helpful. 'Anyway Major, I believe these guys had a room here, a search of it might bear fruit.'

'Could you do that for me, Dawson? It would save an awful lot of time.'

Dawson's hackles rose. He was tired, he was stressed, he was pissed off and Bell was thinking only of himself, using 'me' and not 'us' in an attempt at emotional blackmail.

'No, I couldn't Major, they could be here at any minute. I'm out of here.' He hung up and switched off his phone.

Dawson quickly packed his small suitcase and went to reception 'I've been invited to stay with a friend tonight, but I would like to retain the suite for tomorrow is that's possible?'

The smiling receptionist checked her computer 'Yes, sir, that will be OK, I'll update your key card.'

Dawson went to Didsbury using three taxi's and a roundabout route, all the time checking for anyone who might be following.

He knew there was a spare key in a tin under the compost heap. Joanne was not stupid enough to leave keys under plant pots or stones. He let himself in and the alarm beeped. Punching in the code he made his way to the kitchen and washed his hands of the compost slime. He helped himself to a drink and carried it upstairs. Tomorrow was another day, right now he needed sleep.

The hand that shook him awake was gentle, even so he was startled and shot up to the sitting position 'Good morning Dawson, did you sleep well?'

'Joanne! When did you get back?'

'About five minutes ago, found the alarm not set, no break-in, whiskey glass missing, and the bottle moved. You are the only one who knows where to key is hidden.'

'Are you and Jaineba back to stay?'

'Yes, we heard about the supposed gang warfare wiping out a rival Russian gang on the Wirral and put two and two together. Besides, both Jaineba and I need to get back to work. How's Charlene?'

The Brat

'Dunno, she's in hospital, they won't let me see her, me not being her kin.'

Joanne's eyes opened to their fullest extent, 'hospital? What the hell has happened to her?' she snapped. 'Get your sorry arse downstairs now, Dawson Jukes.' She ripped the covers off him, said 'huh' when she saw he was naked, then turned and left without another word.

He sat in the lounge opposite the two anxious women. Dawson held nothing back from his friends as he related what had happened although he only outlined his killings in vague terms. Their expressions grew more and more grim. Jaineba began to weep quietly when she heard of Charlene's wound. Joanne put a comforting arm around her.

When he'd finished speaking, Jaineba blew her nose and wiped her eyes. She said 'we were not going to mention this just yet Dawson, but Joanne and I have talked about adopting Charlene. We have applied to foster her as soon as possible.' The process is still in its early stages.'

Dawson wasn't surprised but said 'she can be a bit of a handful, you know.'

Joanne said 'I have never met a girl of her age who is more mature, gutsy and intelligent as Charlene. Jaineba agrees with me, we could home educate her if I work part-time.'

Dawson smiled 'I can't think of anyone better to bring this kid up properly than you two.'

'We've got to get approval yet Dawson.'

Dawson took in the look of longing on Jaineba's face, kindness and concern radiated from her. 'You two tick a lot of politically correct boxes girls. Gay married professional women, one black one white. The diversity brigade will be falling over their tits to take you on.'

'I wish I could share your confidence, Dawson, and of course Charlene has to be consulted yet.'

They left the matter there. Jaineba had a brief to attend to and Joanne went to see John Babcock to discuss working part time should they be successful in their bid to become Charlene's guardians. Dawson rested for the remainder of the day, reading and listening to Jazz FM until it was time to get ready for his dinner date with Elise Elwin.

She was ten minutes late. Do they do it on purpose he wondered? The sun had set over the Cheshire countryside, but the spring sky was still glowing and there was a definite spring-like quality to the evening. She was wearing a mid-length summer flower print dress that pinched in at her waist. Around her neck was a gold chain with a gold ankh resting above her ample cleavage. He was impressed.

Elise leaned in and gave him a light peck on the cheek, she seemed genuinely pleased to see him. She took his arm as they moved through the crowded pub

The Brat

to their table. 'Ok, Dawson, so what really happened? All we poor cops are getting is the MI5 sanitised version.'

Dawson smiled into her questioning eyes and gave her his carefully edited version of events. She sat in silence listening without interruption. After he'd finished speaking, she asked a few questions but seemed satisfied with his story.

'OK, your turn, what are the police doing about this gang's infrastructure?'

'It's all highly secret Dawson, I can't tell you much.'

His nostrils flared as his knife clattered onto his plate as he released it to point a forefinger. 'Listen Elise, I've given you information known to very few outside MI5. I don't need to hear any of your police press-release bullshit. What the *fuck* are you doing about the Couscu brothers, that bastard Swanson and those poor bloody kids they're using?'

She held up a placatory hand 'Whoa, Dawson, it's not as simple as arresting a couple of arseholes and a bent cop. These Russians are into people trafficking, county lines drugs and extortion as well as blackmail and the brothels. It all needs to be traced, Dawson. We want to cut out this cancer once and for all. That takes careful planning.'

'So, when is that going to happen?'

'Soon Dawson, really soon, I promise.'

'

'Good, because every day those kids are being abused is a day too long. If I have to move amongst those bastards the body count will be high.'

She looked at him with opened mouthed shock. Dawson Jukes didn't make empty threats. 'I would strongly advise against any vigilante action Dawson. It could land you in serious trouble and mess up a lot of careful planning on our part.' Her hand came across the table and covered his, her eyes held a warm sympathetic light that immediately calmed him.

'Sorry, Elise, it's just that this stuff really grabs my shit if you'll pardon the expression.'

'I understand' she said without removing her hand.

Meal over and the evening still warm she suggested a walk to settle their food. They turned left out of the pub and crossed a footbridge by an old mill. For a while neither spoke then she asked, 'Are you seeing anyone at the moment, Dawson?'

The question took him by surprise 'er… no, not now. I, er… got the boot a while back, why?'

Her laughter came light and warm 'I can image most women wouldn't be able to put up with your lifestyle for very long.'

He felt his face flush with embarrassment, a regret for the years he'd spent hurting decent women who only wanted love and stability. 'Yeah, well, I've been

The Brat

thinking about that lately. I'm forty-four Elise and I'm getting too bloody old for this rough stuff.'

'But you're very good at what you do.'

He stopped and turned to face her 'I've been a soldier since I was fifteen, Elise. I joined as a boy soldier, transferred to men's service at eighteen and I've been at it ever since in one form or another. Meeting Charlene kinda brought it home to me that I'm damn near old enough to be her grandfather. She's shown me what I've missed and I've only myself to blame.'

'Surely you are not too old if you found the right woman?'

He stared in silence across the fields for a long while. 'It's getting dark Elise, we'd better go.'

In the carpark she suddenly said, 'what are you doing on Sunday?'

'Nothing planned, why?'

'I've bought a bloody great leg of lamb I could use some help eating it. Care to join me?'

His eyebrows arched in surprise but then he beamed a huge smile 'sure, that sounds nice.'

She frowned 'don't be getting any ideas young man, it's Sunday lunch, that's it.'

He grinned and gave a mock bow 'I shall be the epitome of decorum madam.'

She gave him her address and another peck on the cheek and climbed into her car 'See you Sunday.'

When Dawson got back to Didsbury, he found Jaineba curled up on the couch weeping. Joanne was doing her best to comfort her. Clearly something bad had happened. 'What's the matter, Joanne?'

'We have been onto Charlene's social worker to enquire after her.' She paused, reluctant to go further.

'And?'

'There's good news and bad. The good news is she is out of intensive care and out of danger. The bad news is that that fragment travelled downwards into her womb. They had to give her a hysterectomy.'

'Jaineba broke in, sniffling and dabbing her eyes 'That poor child, that dear little girl will never have children. Oh, Dawson, how can life be so cruel?'

A sense of guilt swept through him. He placed a hand on Jaineba's shoulder 'I'm sorry Jaineba, I did my best, it wasn't good enough.'

'You did fine' Joanne said sharply 'don't beat yourself up Dawson, if it wasn't for you, she'd be lying in a shallow grave on the moors.'

Joanne was right of course but even so the feeling of guilt and anger wouldn't leave him. Never had his desire to kill been so strong. The police had better move and quick, he thought, these bastards need stopping.

The next day he got his answer. Up early, he switched on the TV. The morning news reported that police had carried out raids across the whole of the North of England. Many people had been arrested

The Brat

and dozens of women and girls, believed to be victims of modern slavery, had been freed and were being cared for.

There were no pictures which told Dawson the police were serious and had not informed the media beforehand. He gave a cry of joy 'yes, you evil bastards' he muttered. Upstairs the two women gave a loud whoop, so they had seen it, too. They came downstairs in housecoats and threw their arms around him in a hug of pure joy, their smiles dazzling.

'This calls for a celebration' said Joanne we have some champagne and some orange juice if you want Bucks Fizz?'

Dawson was ecstatic 'I'll make us eggs benedict, a celebratory breakfast.'

The women both looked at him in astonishment 'You can cook?' said Jaineba, unable to hide her surprise.

He feigned indignation 'of course I can cook, you cheeky sod, just you wait and see.'

True to his word, Dawson produced excellent eggs Benedict and they chatted animatedly as they ate. At ten a Joanne got a return call from social services, Charlene was sitting up, taking food and asking for them. That put the icing on their cake of joy. By eleven they were sitting around her bed in a small side ward. Charlene was pale and her pinched face looked like she'd been crying.

'They say I'll never have kids' she blurted, that bullet hit my womb, they had to give me a hyster... hyster... something...'

'Hysterectomy' said Jaineba 'you poor darling.' As she reached out and hugged her, there were tears in her eyes.

Charlene, tough kid that she was, tried to put a brave face on it 'don't you go blubbing, Jaineba you'll set me off again.' Then she forced a smile 'this shit world is no place to bring kids into anyway. And no more messing about with tampons, I'll save a fortune and....' She broke off and looked at Dawson choking back a sob 'I thought I was a gonner Dawes, it was your voice kept me going I had to live to say thanks.'

The lump in his throat made talking difficult. 'Listen, Brat, if you hadn't thrown yourself at that Russian bloke, we'd both be history now. You're a very brave girl.' He leaned over and ruffled her hair. 'It's me who needs to thank you.'

Charlene's face darkened 'They tell me my mother's here, wanting to see me. She's got some bloke with her. I don't want to see her.'

'Every mother, no matter how far she's sunk, retains some affection for her children, Charlene' Jaineba said. 'Maybe you should see what she wants?'

The Brat

Charlene looked dubious, 'it'll be about her and her feelings. It always is. Me first, me next, me always, that's my mum.'

'Even so...' Jaineba persisted.

'Well, alright then, but only for ten minutes and her bloke don't come near me. I know the sort of creeps she hangs around with.'

Dawson added a note of caution 'listen, darlin' Brat, you can't go telling your mum what happened to you, OK? Not all the details. For reasons of national security, that Ivanov bloke I shot was a gangland killing, you'll see a lot of rubbish on the TV but don't tell anyone the truth. Those Russians were not just criminals they were spies, too. A lot of stuff is still going on.'

'Yeah, if you say so Dawes.'

'Tell your mum you were in the wrong place at wrong time and caught a splinter, you don't remember anything about it, OK? The less you tell anyone the better.'

'What about the doctors and nurses here?'

'They've been briefed, they won't ask you questions about it.'

'Cool, Dawes, I'll keep me gob shut.'

Joanne dug in her pocket 'I've brought you a phone Charlene our numbers are in it so you can keep in touch.' She didn't mention the application to foster or adopt her as things were far from cut and dried.

Charlene didn't need her hopes raising only to be dashed.

They left her a teddy bear, some flowers, some chocolate and more magazines that she could read in a week then they took it in turns to kiss her goodbye. She flung her arms around Dawson's neck and hugged him tightly. 'Thank you, Dawes, you're the best bloke in the world.' She was smiling brightly as they left the ward. Twenty minutes later she rang Joanne in hysterics.

'That bitch, that fuckin' *bitch*' she screamed 'all she wanted was to sell my story to the papers. I told her to fuck off and if she goes near the papers or TV, I'll fuckin' knife her.'

'Whoa, baby, slow down. You're a minor. They couldn't use your name or your mother's name 'cos it's the same as yours. She's got no chance. I don't think child X would do in this case.'

'The other thing she told me to do was to ask for compensation from Criminal Injuries or some bugger. All she wants is to make money for her fuckin' drugs. She don't give a shit about me.'

Joanne let her get it off her chest then calmly asked 'have you talked to the doctors about it?'

'I spoke to the ward lady, ward sister, is it? I told her not to let her near me again. She said was I sure? Damned right I'm sure. I hate that bitch.'

'The thing is she's gonna ask Social Service if she can take me back. She'll swear on a stack of bibles

The Brat

she's clean if it means getting her hands on some money. I dunno what to do Joanne. I hate being in care, I hate the streets and I dunno what to do.'

Charlene sounded utterly distraught. Joanne could feel the depth of her despair. She made her decision. 'Look, Charlene, Jaineba and I didn't mention this because it's far from certain we'd be accepted but, if you would like it, we have applied to foster you. If that goes well, and I know it will, we could apply to adopt you.'

There was a long silence then, in a small voice Charlene said 'you'd do that for me? You do know I've got a record at long as yer arm, dontcha? I've been done for burglary n' shop lifting an' stuff? They call me a problem child.'

Joanne was close to tears 'Charlene, dear girl, you're not a bad person. Jaineba and me think you'll grow into a wonderful human being if you're given a chance.'

'You really think that?'

'Yes, we do, and Dawson thinks you're pretty special, too.'

'Oh, Joanne, that's so bleedin' cool. Yeah, I'd love that., Can I come straight away when they let me out of here?'

'Slow down Charlene, nothing's settled yet but we're working on it, OK?'

'Yeah, OK, Joanne. You an' Jaineba are the best women I ever met.'

Anthony Milligan

Joanne ended the conversation with butterflies in her stomach, praying all would go well with the process. To get Charlene's hopes up and them have them dashed would devastate her.

Chapter 25

Sunday came and Dawson made his way to Elise Elwin's house. It was a smart three bed detached on an exclusive development. His car looked shabby and out of place among the BMW's and Mercs. It reminded him he still had to deal with the insurance claim on his own car.

He repaid her the compliment of being ten minutes late. She must have been waiting and watching because the front door opened the second he turned into her drive. She was dressed in a flowing ankle length dress that hung loosely from her shoulders. She kissed him lightly on the cheek as soon as he stepped into the hall. 'Come in Dawson, do' she said and led him into her lounge. It was well but plainly furnished, feminine but nothing flash or fluffy. He liked that, it showed she was a practical person and neat, too. The room felt like it was always tidy and not spruced up just for his visit.

She poured him a glass of wine 'lunch will be about twenty minutes if that's OK?'

Her cooking skills were excellent, the medium rare lamb was just right and the sweet that followed a delightful treacle sponge with thick home-made custard.

'He smiled at her, replete 'Wow, Elise, you know how to cook, that was delicious.'

She accepted his compliment with a slight bow and a wide smile. Her face went serious, 'I've never met anyone quite like you Dawson, On the one hand you are capable of great violence, and yet you're not a thug, quite the opposite in fact, a caring soul. Tell me about yourself.'

Dawson felt uncomfortable now, he hated talking about himself. 'There's not a lot to tell Elise. My father was a Regimental Sergeant-Major. Mother died when I was six and dad left the Army to bring me up. I suppose I was a bit of a handful, so he packed me off to the Army's Junior Leaders Regiment when I was fifteen. I joined the main Army at eighteen and served in the Intelligence Corps for twenty-two years, eventually taking a commission. I ended up a captain'.

'So, how did you end up in Iraq?'

'Money. I'd seen what the ex-special forces lads were earning, and I wanted some. I'd done courses in specialist weapons, close quarter combat, boat handling and advanced escape driving too so they overlooked the fact I wasn't ex-Hereford because a lot of my training was with SAS instructors. I did two

The Brat

one-year tours as a bodyguard then I came home, money isn't everything and some of the crap I saw turned my guts.'

'So, why do intelligence officers require those fighting and driving skills.'

'Collecting intelligence is not all cyber eavesdropping, sometimes we have to get our hands dirty. Now, Elise, what about you?' He was anxious to turn the conversation away from himself.

She gave him her background. Oxford University, a first-class degree in criminology. She had joined the Met, then after ten years, transferred North to be nearer to her ailing, now deceased parents. Ambitious, she had quickly climbed the ranks. The man in her life had hated being outshone and this eventually led to a split. 'A lot of blokes resent a capable woman, Dawson, especially other coppers. You're different. You treat women as equals, you say what you mean, and you mean what you say. I like that.'

He drew nearer to her on the settee 'So, if I said you're a dammed attractive woman and I fancy you like mad, you wouldn't slap my chops?'

She smiled and leaned in and kissed him on the lips. 'No, I wouldn't Dawson.'

He didn't try anything on, remembering her Sunday lunch only warning. No point in pushing it, although his loins said they wanted to.

She showed him the rest of her house. Every room was as neat and tastefully furnished as the lounge. When they got to the master bedroom, she said 'and this is the most comfortable room in the house.'

'It certainly looks it' he said pointedly staring at the King-sized bed.

'Play your cards right and you might find out one day,' she laughed.'

Dawson feigned terror. He leapt back covering his crotch with both hands 'If you touch me, I'll scream' he said in a comic voice.

Elise was caught off guard by his sudden humour and laughed loudly, girlishly.

'Oh, Dawson, you daft bugger' she said, wiping her eyes. She came to him then and kissed him passionately. 'You know, you crazy man, I think I'll make an exception in your case.'

'That would be nice' he said and moved to fondle her breast; she was delightfully braless. Her hand slipped around to stroke his buttocks and she moaned softly. As they broke apart her breath was rasping and her face flushed 'Oh god, Dawson, it's been so *bloody* long.'

'Me, too' was all her could manage as they moved to the bed.

She had no first-time-with-a-new-man shyness. She slipped off her dress in one flowing motion then scooped her knickers off. She found his belt as he freed himself from his shirt. Kneeling before him she

The Brat

made lustful little grunts before she took him into her mouth. He marvelled at the depth she achieved. Knowing he couldn't take much of this for before exploding, he gently lifted her and lowered her onto the bed.

Foreplay was minimal. Her legs spread wide as she pulled him on then wrapped them around his back clamping tightly around his waist. He penetrated her slowly, her whimpers of pleasure adding to his urgency. She used her pelvic floor muscles expertly to tease and please him until he could stand it no longer and drove hard into her. She pushed her hips upwards rhythmically in perfect sync with his powerful thrusting 'yes, yes, oh, Jesus, yes' she cried as they climaxed together.

Afterwards, she lay on his chest her eyes smoky with satisfied lust, sighing happily. Eventually she got up and brought them each a large glass of Rioja, 'here, have a decent drink.'

'I won't be able to drive if I drink that.'

She gave him a sly wink 'of course you won't, you silly man, I still have need of you.'

Dawson didn't get a lot of sleep that night, Elise was as hungry as himself. Now he lay propped up by pillows, his hands behind his head in the growing dawn light thinking of his life. Elise had awakened a desire in him he had long been denying. He thought about the house on the moors and knew it had served its purpose. The healing solitude he had sought had been elusive, yet it had been a period of relative quiet he had needed after the stresses of Iraq.

He thought about Charlene and his heart ached. She, too, had awakened desires of a different kind. She was vulnerable and in need of protection, yes, but she was also streetwise, tough and intelligent. She'd had a hellish life, yet she never whined. Charlene accepted things as they were and dealt with them as best she could on her own terms. He felt a deep need to protect her, to care for her, to shelter her from harm. If only I'd had a kid like her he thought wistfully. *Shut up you damned fool and get real* his inner voice shouted.

Elise stirred next to him and sleepily looked at the bedside clock. 'Oh, God, I'll be late' she said and shot out of bed 'Chief Constable's conference this morning.' With that she leapt into the en suite bathroom, five minutes later she was out and dressing. 'No time to make you breakfast, Dawson, help yourself and let yourself out when you're ready.'

He was impressed by the speed and efficiency of her movements as she applied minimal make-up. She transformed herself from the eager lover to the professional police officer in minutes.

'I'll ring you later, Dawson' she said, kissed him and was gone.

He got up, showered, then made himself coffee and toast. He sat at the breakfast bar thinking of the

The Brat

days ahead. The Russian gang was smashed, the police and MI5 would deal with things now. There would be another debriefing, of course, as everyone would need to be singing from the same hymn sheet when it came to the media. He, of course, would be no part of that, sinking back into quiet obscurity. But what about Charlene? The thought of her made him feel sad. She wouldn't need him anymore now that she was out of danger. The people who controlled her life would see him as an unwanted influence. It would be better for her if he made a quiet exit. One shred of hope was if Joanne and Jaineba managed to foster her, maybe he'd get to see her occasionally. *Or should you just butt to fuck out of her life for her sake?*

Chapter 26

He was halfway back to Didsbury when he got the call that wiped all other thoughts from his mind.

'Hi Dawson, You OK?'

'Fine, Major, what can I do for you?'

There was a long pause, Dawson could hear him sighing. 'This is bloody embarrassing Dawson and potentially extremely dangerous. Catanova has escaped.'

Dawson was silent for long seconds taking this in. He pulled over and parked. How the hell could this be possible? MI5 had her in custody, no one had ever escaped from them as far as he knew. 'Jesus, Major, how the hell could that have happened?'

Again, a long pause 'According to 5, Her mental health was showing signs of rapid deterioration, she started by raving against you and particularly against Charlene Keenan. The bloody woman is obsessed by her. Then she descended into a form of passive hysteria brought about by acute stress, they told me.'

The Brat

'So? They got someone in to see to her, surely?'

'Yes, a recently qualified doctor was the stand-by medic. She recommended an urgent psychiatric assessment. The ambulance service said it would have been at least a two hour wait. For that read four bloody hours.'

'So, what did they do?'

'Catanova was still mobile with assistance so they used one of their own cars, one driver, one female escort, she was handcuffed and, as she was in a catatonic state, she was not considered a risk.'

Dawson groaned 'Suffering God, I can't believe what I'm hearing.'

'The thing is Dawson that before she entered this so-called passive state, she made it clear that she wants revenge.'

'So, what happened, Major?'

'She attacked the escort, bashing her in the head with her handcuffs. The driver had his windpipe smashed, he's dead. It looks like as he stopped the car, she's thrown her arms over his head and yanked back hard with the chain of the cuffs. Him and the escort were found at the side on the road. She took the cuff keys off the escort and buggered off with the car.' She took the driver's wallet with about thirty quid and his cards.'

'I thought modern cuffs had a bar that made self-release impossible?'

'The Police do, MI5 are still behind the times.'

'The car will be fitted with a tracker, of course?'

'Yes, it was traced to a supermarket carpark half a mile away, they're analysing the CCTV footage now.'

'So, what are you doing about it Major?'

'I'm informing you; MI5 have informed the police. Beyond that I can do nothing. Her photo is already on all the media outlets with a warning to the public not to approach her, someone will spot her sooner or later.'

'Christ, what a fuck-up.' He slammed the wheel in frustration then rang Elise. She was still in conference, so he left a message to ring him urgently.

Dawson drove to the hospital it would take a good forty minutes at the best of times, but the Monday morning traffic conspired against him. He rang Joanne and told her.

'Oh, God, Dawson, I'm working in Preston, Babcock rang me last night with a last-minute job. You stay with her Dawson if the police don't turn up, I'll relieve you as soon as I can.' She sounded scared.

He rang Elise again, but her phone went straight to voicemail. He was crawling through roadworks, his fear and frustration growing.

Dawson rang Bell, for an update. 'According to 5, she was seen on the store's CCTV taking stuff from the make-up section then she went to the kitchen section and took a large knife. She was looking about her and acting suspiciously. Their security man was

The Brat

waiting by the entrance to detain her if she attempted to leave without paying for the items.'

'But she didn't leave by the front, did she?'

'No, the security man was distracted by a customer asking questions so he can't be sure. He thinks she may have gone through a door marked staff only. It leads to the changing rooms and the staff carpark.'

'What did she take, Major, apart from the knife?'

'We don't know, the video is not clear. But she was at the hairdressing section.'

'She's changing her appearance, Major. Probably cutting her hair and dying it.'

'I thought of that. She would need facilities. She can hardly do it in the street and she has no transport now she's dumped the car.'

Dawson was stumped for the time being 'Please keep me up-dated Major I'm on my way to Charlene Keenan now.'

'You should stay out of it, Dawson, let the police handle it.'

'By the time they get their bloody finger out it'll be time to arrange her funeral. No, Major, I'm going there if the police are there already Ok, I'll piss off.'

'Dawson, I said stay out of it.'

'Major, I'm telling you what I'm going to do, not asking your permission. Now, please keep me informed.' He hung up with a grunt, his knuckles white as they crushed the phone. What was it with officialdom these days? They moved at their own sweet speed, ticking the bloody boxes as they went. Stay out of it my arse he thought and blasted his horn at the motorist in front who was slow to move off from the traffic lights. 'Tosser' he mumbled.

Chapter 27

Marcia Catanova walked slowly, calmly like a person with every right to be there. There could be some clothes in the changing room she might be able to use, a coat maybe.

As she approached the room a young woman came in through the rear door, car keys in hand, and keyed a number into a timeclock. As she turned, she bumped into Catanova who put a knife to her throat. The terrified girl froze.

'You live near here, don't you?'

The girl nodded, wide eyed 'about a mile away, please, don't hurt me, I'll do what you want.'

'You'd better, I'm in no mood to be pissed about. Who is at your house right now?'

'No...no one, my boyfriend's at work, please, what do you want?'

'OK, if you want to live, you'll do as I say, when I say, without question, understood?'

The girl nodded vigorously and Catanova took her car keys and pushed her outside. 'Walk at normal pace back to your car. If anyone asks where you're going tell them you're giving me a quick lift and will be back shortly. One wrong move and I'll slice your face off, now move.'

In the car Catanova handed over the keys 'What's your name, girl?'

'Becky, Becky Anderson… please …'

'Drive to your house at normal speed, Becky Anderson.' Catanova's voice was gravelly due to her neck injuries, which added menace to her cold command. 'Don't fuck me about and you'll live.'

They arrived at Becky's house and Catanova ordered her prisoner out of the car. 'Try to run and I'll catch you' she flashed the knife and the girl, now totally intimidated, walked the few feet to her front door and opened it.

Catanova took the girl upstairs 'Where do you keep your tights?'

Becky pointed to a chest of drawers 'top left.'

Taking a pair of tights Catanova ordered 'take your clothes off, all of them.'

Becky looked horrified 'what for?'

Catanova moved like lightening, grabbing the girl's hair she threw her on the bed, putting the knife to her throat. 'What did I say about fucking me about?' her blues eyes were as hard as steel. 'One more failure to obey and you're dead.' She let the girl

The Brat

up and she undressed herself as quickly as her trembling hands allowed. Catanova ran her eye admiringly over Becky's slim body. 'Stretch marks, so you have kids'?

'One. My little girl, Julia, she's at nursery, my mum picks her up at three and takes her to her house.' She looked at Catanova with pleading eyes. 'Please, there's three hundred pounds in the sideboard downstairs. Please, just take it and go. Please don't kill me. My little girl….'

The slap to Becky's face came hard and fast 'shut up and get on the bed face down.' She used Becky's tights to secure wrists behind her back. She took the other pair and gagged her. 'You lie there like a good girl and this will all be over soon.'

Catanova went to the bathroom and cut her hair into a crude bob then she used the hydrogen peroxide to bleach it blonde. She left the shorn locks where they had fallen. It was too late for caution now, too late for anything except for killing Charlene Keenan.

Her task at last completed, Catanova preened in the mirror pleased with the transformation. She laughed long and loud the sound freezing Becky's soul as she lay petrified, unable even to think.

Catanova glanced into the bedroom and saw Becky still lying face down on the bed sobbing softly, her face turned away. She looked at the bedside clock. Her hair had taken a lot longer than she had expected. She turned her gaze to the girl on the bed admiring her firm buttocks, her long, slender legs, the flair from her tiny waist to her shoulders. She would have loved to stop and explore that beautiful body before tying a pair of tights around her neck and watching her slowly choke to death. But there wasn't time, this woman was nothing to her and time was of the essence. Becky would have been missed by now and someone might come to check up on her. Catanova needed every minute she could get. Charlene Keenan and Dawson Jukes were all that mattered. Without a word she turned, descended the stairs and left.

Driving Becky's manual gearbox Ford was a difficult drive for Catanova, and she stalled at traffic lights a couple of times before remembering the technique. She switched on the radio for news bulletins. The drive up from London to Cheshire would take at least three hours maybe more. The four PM news mentioned her, describing her as a six-foot-tall woman with long black hair. The public were advised not to approach her. This woman is believed to be armed with a knife and has severe mental health issues. No mention of the car was made.

'Mental health issues, she screamed 'I'm cleverer, more intelligent, more fuckin' stable than all of you bastards put together.' She switched the radio off and drove on mumbling to herself.

She believed the focus of the search for her would be in London. Catanova thought the police would be

The Brat

watching the Russian Embassy also the transport systems. They'd watch the airports, too, even though they knew she had no passport and, they thought, only £30. MI5 and the police would be watching all her known contacts in London.

She cackled to herself now, 'I got a car, I got cash, I got a plan and away I dash.' The simple rhyme seemed to please her, and she repeated it several times then laughed manically so that the car swerved and almost collided with the vehicle alongside her. The driver blared his horn and shook his fist. This had the effect of calming her down. If she crashed the car her chance at vengeance would be gone. She *must* have vengeance; she *would* have vengeance.

*

When Dawson arrived at the hospital all was normal. The ward sister was the same one who had been on duty the last time he called. She told him no one had made enquiries about her that day. Charlene was making good progress and would be discharged in the next day or so as an outpatient.

When he looked in on her Charlene was asleep breathing softly into her pillow. He watched her for a full minute, closely examining her young face in repose. Yes, she was young and pretty, but her face also held the marks of strength of character in the strong brow and the determined angle of her jawline. His heart swelled. She didn't stir as he bent and lightly kissed her forehead. 'I'll look after you darling Brat, never fear' he whispered.

Dawson sat in the chair beside the bed thinking. Catanova would find it difficult to walk into a hospital, kill Charlene and get away. Maybe she didn't want to get away? Suicide bomber mentality, he'd seen it before. Nothing else mattered other than achieving the goal. How would she go about it? How would he go about it? They were on the second floor about ten metres from the stairs and lifts so only one possible line of approach up the stairs or the lift, she'd have to turn left and walk to the door. Ten metres in which to pass or be stopped. She'd need to be invisible, he thought, now, how does one become invisible in a place like this? Disguised as a doctor or nurse was his guess but that was not easy to achieve.

Elise rang. 'Hi, Dawson, I've just got out of the conference, what's the matter?' He explained the situation quickly and concisely. 'I'm not in my office yet, I'll look at the computer and see what the latest news is.' She kept her phone on as she hurried downstairs.

'Hi, Dawson, I have it here. Current thinking is that's she's still in London somewhere. That her mental health has collapsed. She stole a knife, they believe, in order to resist arrest. She has friends in the capital and the thinking is she'll use them to escape the country.'

The Brat

'What about the other stuff she stole, have they identified it yet?'

'There is a lot of stuff on that shelf tightly packed together. Their cameras are not state of the art, but they believe hair colouring. Changing her appearance would be what she'd want to do. For the moment she's gone to ground.'

'I believe she's heading up here, Elise. Can you put a protection team on Charlene?'

'Sorry, Dawson, not on the evidence on the system. I couldn't justify it.'

Frustration surged through Dawson; his free hand brushing through his hair. He took a deep breath and told himself to stay calm. 'OK, OK, Elise, I'll stay with her. Me and Joanne will take it in turns until we know she's safe. Catanova might be crazy but she's clever and inventive. I *know* she's on her way here, I just bloody know it.' He ended the conversation.

Forcing himself to sit in his seat, Dawson began to think. Catanova wouldn't use the main entrance. There must be at least a dozen ways to gain access in a building this big. He couldn't possibly cover them but then, he reasoned, he didn't have to. To accomplish her deadly mission Catanova would have to come to this room.

An hour later Elise rang 'They've finished analysing the footage from the Supermarket Dawson. It's not good news I'm afraid. The manager reported one of his staff missing. The girl had clocked in but failed to appear in the store. When they checked the car park cameras, they saw Catanova leading the woman to her car. Fearing a hostage situation, they had to wait to gather the right team. The good news is they found the girl naked but unharmed tied up in her bedroom.'

'God, what took them so long to get around to checking those bloody cameras?'

'The parking is farmed out; those cameras are not on the store's system.'

'So, she could be more than halfway here by now. Jesus!'

'They'll be looking for her on the Automatic Number Plate Recognition System. Don't worry, Dawson, they'll track her down. ANPR is damn good.'

'I do worry Elise because you are all underestimating the bloody woman.'

'Listen, if I get the merest hint that she's heading up here, I'll authorise protection.'

She told him she'd keep him up-dated and rang off.

*

Catanova drove on thinking of her strategy. They'd probably have found the girl by now, so they would be able to trace the car. Maybe she'd make it in this car, maybe not. She wasn't prepared to take the chance. A service station was coming up with a

The Brat

junction just before it. She turned off the motorway and found what she was looking for. It had been a farm track, but the farm was long gone. Now it was full of lorries, their drivers sleeping. These guys needed to use the Service station facilities but didn't want to pay parking charges. It was quiet, overhung by trees and there was a path beaten across the field to the service station. She smiled; things could not have worked out better for her. She parked deep beneath the trees.

Eighty-one-year-old Mrs Mary Drew sat drinking her coffee and nibbling her way through a blueberry muffin, her car keys beside her plate. She was alone at her table. Catanova watched her for five minutes whilst slowly sipping her coffee and pretending to read a magazine. She took in every detail before deciding. Yes, she'd do nicely. The old lady started gathering her things preparing to leave. Catanova made her move.

She beamed a wide smile then let it fall away to a look of concern 'excuse me for asking, please, but I'm in a bit of trouble. I've broken down and I'm not in a recovery service. I must get up to Chester to collect my little girl from the child minder. Could you possibly give me a lift?'

The old lady looked discomforted 'I'm sorry, I never give lifts to strangers, it's so dangerous these days.'

Catanova let a tear fall, 'I understand, I'm so sorry for asking, it's just that when I saw that cross around your neck, I mistook you for a fellow Christian and I'm desperate, my daughter, she's only three…'

The old lady's face twitched through several emotions, guilt being the prime one. She looked down, embarrassed, her hands clasping and unclasping her handbag 'Oh, dear, I'm not following Christ's teaching very well, am I? I can take you to the Chester turn-off, I'm going on you see, to my granddaughters.'

The car was a Nissan Micra which Mary Drew drove at a steady fifty miles per hour in the inside lane. Catanova sat and seethed.

'Mary, I must get on, at this speed I'll never get there. Take the next exit.'

'But what about your daughter?'

'I haven't got a fucking daughter you silly old cow.'

Mary glanced across horrified as she heard the irritation in that rasping voice. Her face paled as she saw the knife. 'I can take you anywhere you want to go, please don't harm me.'

Catanova smiled 'that's better Mary. Now, take the next exit and pull up on the hard shoulder at the top of the slip road.'

When they drew to a halt Mary was ordered out of the car. They stood for a moment until another car

The Brat

passed then Catanova ordered her into the boot. The pensioner was terrified. 'Please, please…'

Catanova flashed the knife 'shut up and get in.' She pushed Mary's arthritic limbs in, ignoring her agonised cries.

Driving at just over seventy miles per hour, Catanova arrived at the hospital just over an hour later. She drove a tour of the car park looking expertly at the parking cameras before choosing a position in a blind spot. She couldn't leave her hostage in the car while she went about her grim business and she had nothing to gag her with. Looking around Catanova made sure she was not being observed. Opening the boot, she looked down at her victim. The old lady was wide eyed and whimpering in terror but unable to move her cramped limbs.

Catanova leaned in smiling mirthlessly. She gripped the old woman by the throat and squeezed, 'say hello to Jesus for me.'

*

Dawson sat in his chair and took out his phone. If Joanne was working, he couldn't ring so he texted her giving her an update and requesting she ring asap.

Charlene had turned over muttering in her sleep. She seemed to be deeply under. He was pleased. Sleep was good for the healing process. Then Elise rang.

'Hi Dawson, ANPR picked up the car travelling north on the M6. A police intercept was sent after her, but she seems to have disappeared around Junction 3 at Coventry.'

'Do you think she gone into the city centre to steal another car?'

'It's a possibility but it's also quite close to Corley service station, she could have gone there to maybe get a lift or hijack another vehicle.'

'So, the bottom line is she could be anywhere in any vehicle.'

'I'm afraid so, Dawson but it means I can justify sending police protection. You can go home when they arrive.'

'That is good news, how many are you sending?'
'Two. One plain clothes in the entrance foyer and one uniform outside her room.'

'For a place this size? Are you kidding?'

Else snorted 'look, Dawson, she may not even be headed to the hospital. She must have trusted allies on the Wirral or in the Greater Manchester area. Maybe she feels safer in the North. And there's Liverpool and Anglesey with fast ferry connections to Northern Ireland, no passport required she could then slip into Eire with ease and from there anywhere in mainland Europe. She's not wanted there.'

'You may be right, Elise, but my gut tells me she's headed here.'

The Brat

'She'd be mad to do that, Dawson she would be bound to get caught.'

'His nostrils flared as he crushed the phone tightly 'when are you people going to realise she doesn't care about getting away? The bloody woman's as mad as barking snake'

'He heard the hurt in her voice as she blamed the cuts for a lack of manpower, and he apologised for his outburst. There was nothing to be gained by arguing so he said goodbye and hung up. An hour later a young police constable appeared looking serious and business-like. The ward sister gave him a chair and he took up station in the corridor. He looked young, fit and keen but Dawson decided he'd stay too.

*

Surveying the rear of the hospital Catanova saw a smoker's shelter near a door. There were two nurses and a man in street clothes all puffing away at cigarettes. Eventually one nurse stubbed her smoke out and used a swipe card to enter the building. Catanova watched for an hour as various people came and went casually holding the door open to allow others in. Eventually there was a flurry of activity as a change of shift had people scurrying to and froe with cars coming and going. This was her chance, there were always stragglers. She left the car and went to sit in the smokers' shelter. After a couple of minutes, a young nurse came hurrying to the door. Catanova got up and followed her. The girl smiled and obligingly held the door open for her before hurrying down a corridor. She was in.

The second door along the corridor was marked Cleaners. She went in. A corpulent woman, her back to her, was struggling out of an over-all at the far end of the room. A door marked toilets was on her right and Catanova went in and entered a cubical. She sat listening until the woman left then she walked out and into the changing area. A line of pegs held over-all's. She went along feeling in the pockets and looking for one her size. She struck lucky; someone had left their ID card in their pocket. She gave a satisfied smile. No one looks at ID cards once a person has passed through the security process assuming the wearer is entitled to be there. Someone as lowly as a cleaner attracted little interest anyway.

She put on the over-all and cap and threw the ID card around her neck. Off to the left was a cleaners' store there she found a wheeled cart with buckets and mops and a host of bottles of various cleaning liquids.

Catanova allowed herself a little cackle 'Mrs Mop will give 'em the chop' she said, then pushed her trolley through the door. Now to locate Charlene Keenan.

Pushing the trolley slowly down the corridor Catanova looked through each door. She entered he

The Brat

first unoccupied office. There was a computer on the desk but it was switched off so a password would be needed. She cleaned the floor for a few minutes then left. In the next office a lone woman sat behind a desk working on a computer. She went in. 'All right I clean in here?' she laid her accent on thickly. The woman looked up and nodded then went back to work.

Catanova worked steadily, always keeping an eye on the woman. She could force her to find the room number she required then kill her but in the sparse office there was nowhere to hide a body, and someone could come in at any time.

She was still pondering this when the woman asked her 'will you be long? I have to go to the loo.'

She smiled 'You go, I finish here, I wait for you, it's OK.'

'I'm not supposed to…'

Catanova held out her ID card towards the woman who was too far away to see it in detail. 'It's OK I'm vetted; I need another five minutes, I'm already behind time.'

'The woman gathered her handbag 'OK, I'll only be a minute or so.' And hurried through the door.

Catanova wasted no time in going to the computer and hitting the enter button. She typed in Charlene Keenan and a second later Charlene's record appeared. Ward 12A. She closed the screen and the screen saver once more appeared.

When the woman re-entered the office a couple of minutes later Catanova had was steadily mopping her way towards the door. She was about to exit when the woman said, 'thank you, it's about time the cleaning staff did in here and you've done a good job.'

Catanova smiled and gave a little bow then left. Pushing the cleaning trolley slowly along the corridor she was passed by a lot of people including doctors and nurses. No one paid her any heed. She read the signs carefully until she spotted the one that she needed. Wards one to fifteen it read with an arrow pointing up the stairs. She pressed the button for the lift.

As she was pushing her trolley against the lift's back wall a voice called 'hold the doors' a young male doctor jammed himself into the lift before she could press the doors open button. 'Sorry for that' he said then turned to face the door, ignoring her. Catanova smiled behind his back. Nobody looks closely at a cleaner.

The doctor got out at her floor and turned right, she turned left and started to mop the corridor. Ten metres away on her right sat a policeman looking bored. She nodded at him and he nodded back. She affected a stoop then started to mop the corridor slowly, carefully, a bored expression on her face.

She was passed by visitors and staff alike who all crossed to the other side of the corridor as they

The Brat

hurried about their business. She mopped her way to the ward door, the knife to hand under a duster on the trolley.

As she went to enter the ward, she saw the side ward with 12A over the door immediately to her right.

'Hold it there, please.' The young policeman was on his feet.

'I have to clean' she said

'Fine, but I have to check your ID first.'

Catanova feigned confusion and reached for the ID card with her left hand covering the picture as she slid her hand under the duster. 'This one, sir?' She thrust it forward.

The young man reached for it looking down. She struck then, stabbing him in the side. He fell away with a cry of pain and she dashed through the door into Charlene's ward.

The cry aroused a tired Dawson from his chair, his senses instantly on full alert. Charlene woke up. Seeing Catanova with a knife. She gave a terrified scream.

Dawson blocked the way. Catanova was holding her knife low, arm withdrawn tensed to strike. He realised instantly she was experienced with a blade as she closed with him, a snarl of hate on her face.

She made a lightening lunge, aiming at Dawson's guts. He leapt aside as the blade sliced along his side painfully. She started making short prodding motions any of which could be turned into a strike.

Dawson stood square between her and Charlene. There was no time for fear, no time for thought, now it was all about not getting killed. He crouched; hands spread loosely at waist level, his concentration total.

Behind him he heard Charlene moving. Catanova struck again this time he managed to deflect her arm, but she spun away before he could close with her and return a blow. Then Charlene was there, water jug in hand. As Catanova spun away Charlene hit her in the side of the face. The jug shattered and Catanova's face exploded in a spray of red droplets. She shrieked in pain and rage; this was not going to plan. She turned towards Charlene. Dawson rushed at her and took a swing only to feel the knife go into his left forearm until it hit the bone. Charlene used the glass handle of the jug like a knuckle duster and managed to punch Catanova in the arm, but it was a light blow.

The murderess backed off slightly. She now faced two people both of whom she was desperate to kill.

'I've got reinforcement coming lady, give up now.' The young policeman was propped in the door holding on with one hand as his knees wobbled under him. He pressed the red button on his radio. 'Give it up.'

Charlene screamed her hatred and lunged for Catanova as Dawson moved in. She panicked, turned

The Brat

and ran for the policeman. He was too weak to defend himself and she grabbed him around the head, put the knife to his throat and dragged him backwards out of the ward her eyes blazing her madness.

'Wait here Charlene.' Dawson followed Catanova at two metres distant watching. She said nothing, her breath coming in rasps as she headed for the stairs keeping her knife tight to her hostage's throat. She didn't see the big athletic woman coming up the stairs behind her until a hand gripped her wrist pushing the knife away from the policeman's throat.

Catanova whirled around, snatching her arm free, lashing out at this new attacker. Only Joanne's swift reaction saved her from the blade. Blocked from going down, Catanova pushed the policeman towards Joanne and dashed up the stairs. Joanne caught the policeman and lowered him gently. Dawson pushed past her and dived in pursuit of Catanova..

The door at the top was a fire door. Catanova crashed through it onto the flat roof, setting the alarm screaming. She looked around for the fire escape and saw it opposite her at fifteen metres distant. She was almost there when Dawson spun her around his wounded left arm deflecting her blade, his right gripping her collar. He pushed her violently back and the knife soared into space.

Catanova's back was pressed hard into the safety rail as she arched over. She looked at him with cold contempt 'So, we're here again, Jukes. You couldn't do it last time; you won't do it now.'

Dawson felt himself barged aside. Joanne had crouched, thrown herself into his legs and grabbed Catanova's ankles. She stood up rapidly and thrust Catanova's legs into the air 'He might not, bitch, but I will.'

Catanova's eyes bulged in terror as her arms thrashed wildly. She seemed to hang for a brief second before plunging out of sight. There was a brief scream and a thud. Dawson and Joanne looked over the rail. She lay sixty feet below, a pool of blood already spreading behind her head.

'I would have done it, Joanne.'

'Yeah, I know, but I needed to do it, Dawson. The misery she caused Charlene and all those other kids. I…' She broke off then shrugged 'just the thought of her surviving, you know? Serving some half-arsed sentence in a soft psychiatric hospital then getting early release. No way!'

They went back to the ward and a scene of intense activity. Two doctors and a nurse were working feverishly on the constable who was lying on the corridor floor. He seemed only semi-conscious. In the ward Charlene was being calmed by a nurse whilst a doctor was examining her bloodied feet. When she saw Dawson and Joanne, Charlene's face

The Brat

was a picture of relief. She thrust her arms out. 'Hold me Joanne, hold me, please.'

Dawson looked down and saw that the cause of Charlene's injured feet was the broken jug pieces she'd unflinchingly trodden on in her bid to save him. He felt very humbled. The girl had the guts of a terrier.

The police would be here soon enough, and they'd want statements, he sat down in the quietest corner. He was beyond tired now, but he still had a couple of calls to make.

'Hi, Elise, it's over, Catanova is dead, Charlene is safe. I've a couple of wounds but they're just scratches.'

He heard the concern in her voice 'Dawson, get your wounds seen to, OK?' Statements can come later.'

'Yeah, will do, thanks Elise.'

He rang Bell and before he could gather his thoughts Bell jumped in. 'Oh, hi, Dawson I have an update, apparently she's a blonde now and…'

'She's dead, Major, it's over, we'll need a media release.' Dawson couldn't understand why he felt dizzy, why his thought processes were slow. He looked up, there was a man standing over him.

'Excuse me, sir, you are bleeding quite badly, I'll have to see to you right now.'

Anthony Milligan

Dawson looked down at his side and arm which was soaked in dark red blood. His last conscious thought was ah, dark red, a vein, not an artery.

When he awoke Joanne was leaning over him full of concern 'How are you feeling Dawson?'

'I'm feeling a bit confused Joanne. What the hell's happened to me?'

'You fainted from blood loss, crazy man. You were lucky Catanova's knife missed vital organs though you have a pretty serious slash wound and your arm is a mess, too.'

Dawson tried to sit up but couldn't, intense pain knifed through his side as he tried.

'Whoa, Dawson, take it easy or you'll rip your stitches. There's nothing for you to do it's all been taken care of, OK? Any statements will wait, you have to get better first.' She smiles at him 'There's a policewoman who wants to see you, she says it's a personal visit. Do you want to see her?'

'If her name's Elise, damned right I do.' Joanne went away and two minutes later Elise walked in a worried look playing about her face.

Elise sat down and took his hand 'How are you feeling Dawson?'

'I feel as weak as a kitten, Elise, but I'll get better. How's the case going?'

'I'm not here to talk about the case Dawson. It's going OK, we're going to win big on this one, and that's all I'm saying for now. I've had your surgeon

The Brat

issued an instruction that you are unfit to interview. That's an order young man.' She smiled and squeezed his hand 'I want you better as soon as possible for personal reasons.' She winked and his heart soared.

'Now that's what I call motivation, Elise.'

*

A week later, interviews over and statements made Dawson sank back into the obscurity he loved. Catanova had been painted as a mentally disturbed woman who had entered hospital and attacked a policeman and then jumped to her death from the roof after a member of the public gave chase. The woman wished to remain anonymous.

On his release, Dawson visited the jetty and retrieved the grab bag. He took it to his house on the moors and counted it, then he counted it again to make sure. Five hundred and twelve thousand four hundred pounds all in used notes. He had an idea what to do with the money and worked on how he could achieve it. He pushed it under his bed then went for a walk.

The moors were bathed in spring sunshine and a warm breeze brought the fragrance of wildflowers and herbs to him. He breathed it in deeply, pausing on a hillock to admire the view stretching from horizon to horizon. He loved the desolate beauty of the place. The solitude he had so craved in this lonely place had worked its magic; a young girl had done the rest. Now, he knew it was time to move on; to re-join society. His lease was up at the end of the month and he wouldn't renew it.

Returning home, he switched on his new TV set in time for the news. The pending trial of one hundred thirty-seven people charged with child sexual exploitation, people trafficking, drug dealing, and

The Brat

brothel keeping was still front-page news. This was the biggest case of this type ever.

The Couscu's, arrested at Manchester airport with a large amount of cash, were facing charges of attempted murder and rape. Detective Sergeant Swanson charged with malfeasance in public office and child sex abuse hung himself whilst on bail.

It looked like the trial would drag on and on, but the gang were off the streets for good. One hundred and forty-three trafficked women had been freed. Most had returned home after making statements. One woman and a witness had returned now the threat had diminished, determined to see justice done. The anonymous woman had been raped and her prayer book, rosary beads and gold crucifix had been taken. She seemed more outraged by the theft than the rape itself. She would make a very credible witness both here and in her home country.

Dawson sighed and poured himself a large whiskey, his problem now was how to get half a million pounds into the system legitimately. He believed he had a solution. A Delaware offshore company. The Americans were more secretive than the Swiss. If the company didn't operate in the USA everything went tax-free and unaudited. Donations from such a company would be untraceable. Charlene would get a first-class education and a charity would be set up to help abused children like her. It was much better than seeing the cash swallowed into the proceeds of crime maw.

Anthony Milligan

In Didsbury he discussed his plans with his three favourite women who were all in favour. Charlene was now fostered by Jaineba and Joanne, they would home school her and give her the stable home environment she needed.

'Her counselling and therapy sessions are helping her enormously' Jaineba said 'she's even stopped swearing, well, almost' she grinned.

'And I've named my ladies the Jay birds' said Charlene cheekily. She became serious, 'will I still see you Dawes, or will you be off abroad somewhere trying to get yourself killed?'

'Those days are over, Charlene, I'm not going back to that life, ever.'

Joanne asked, 'what are you going to do now Dawson?'

'I've been talking to John Babcock. He needs a cash injection and I need to step back from the front line, so we're forming a new company. It'll be Babcock and Jukes Personal Security Services from now on. John will look after the business side; I'll do the recruiting and training.'

On the first of September that year, Charlene's fifthteenth birthday, the Charity Waifs and Strays Support was launched to great fanfare. Jaineba and Joanne were the patrons. Charlene, Dawson, Elise Elwin, the Chief Constable, were among the invited guests. Jason, his right leg in plaster leaned on a crutch beaming at Charlene who kissed his

The Brat

cheek and ruffled his hair like a big sister. He'd lost weight in hospital and his once pudgy face was now quite handsome.

Margaret Jennings reported for the Manchester Evening News. Joanne and Jaineba were the stars of the show. Dawson avoided the TV cameras like the plague, posing as a friend of the couple just there to lend support.

When the hullabaloo had settled and the guests departed, Charlene came up to him her eyes shining. 'I love you Dawes for what you did for me.'

I love you, too Charlene and I'd like to ask you a favour. Could you, just for once call me Dawson?'

She looked at him her face serious then she threw her arms around his waist and buried her head into his ribs 'No, I bloody well won't. You'll always be my darling Dawes and I'll always be your Brat.'

The End

About the author

Anthony Milligan started writing at the age of nine. He's been at it ever since. A British Army veteran, he's served in a few trouble spots around the globe giving him wide experience.

He has been a sales manager, business owner and private landlord. A world traveller he's married to Jean. He now writes full time.

Contact: ppap.writeme@gmail.com

Other books include:

When Terror Strikes
https://www.amazon.co.uk/dp/B0787MNBJ3
The Pendulum Swings
https://www.amazon.co.uk/dp/B0855KY7MF
A Sting in the Tale
https://www.amazon.co.uk/dp/B07FTVYMWQ

Printed in Great Britain
by Amazon